THE LITTLE BROTHER

THE
LITTLE
BROTHER

A NOVEL

VICTORIA PATTERSON

COUNTERPOINT

BERKELEY

Library of Congress Cataloging-in-Publication Data

Patterson, Victoria.
  The little brother : a novel / Victoria Patterson.
    pages ; cm
  ISBN 978-1-61902-538-7
  I. Title.

PS3616.A886L58 2015
813'.6--dc23

2014044892

Cover Design by Michael Fusco
Interior Design by Megan Jones

COUNTERPOINT
2560 Ninth Street, Suite 318
Berkeley, CA 94710
www.counterpointpress.com

Printed in the United States of America
Distributed by Publishers Group West

10 9 8 7 6 5 4 3 2 1

C.P.

*In the majority of instances human beings,
even the evil-doers among them, are far more
naïve and straightforward than we suppose.
And that includes ourselves.*

—FYODOR DOSTOYEVSKY, *THE BROTHERS KARAMAZOV*

PART ONE

1.

THE NAME ON my birth certificate is Daniel Robert Hyde but everyone calls me Even. I'm named after my father, Daniel Hyde Sr., even though I'm the second-born son. My brother, Gabriel, was born fifteen months before me, but our mother, Gina, and our father decided to name him after her father.

Grandpop was on his deathbed, riddled with bone cancer, when Gabe was born, and they hoped to give him one final legacy-like gift. Despite a falling-out years before, they also hoped to be included in his will. Grandpop went on to live seven more miserable, miraculous years, and when he died he left us a large sum of money, a silver Buick LeSabre, and a Boston Whaler named *Cool Breeze*.

Gabe should have been named after our father, and Gabe always thought it one of many injustices that I got the name. We grew up in Rancho Cucamonga, a city nestled in the foothills of the San Bernardino Mountains, about an hour northeast of Los Angeles. Nothing much has happened in Cucamonga, and no one of note has come from here. It's white-populated with a sprinkling of minorities, and with families whose main recreation is consumption, mostly at the massive shopping center, Victoria Gardens, a metropolis of stores and restaurants. In some ways, Cucamonga is synonymous with wandering through the consumer wasteland: a blur of palm trees and parking lots, escalators and promenades, mezzanines and restaurants, Muzak and lights.

When you drive along the 210 freeway, you can see the beige tract houses blended together in one giant swath, camouflaged like a sand field, all the way to the base of the mountains.

As a child I was quiet, on the tall side, gawky, and I didn't have many friends. Of the friends I did have, most were girls. I preferred their company, though by middle school this changed.

Once, I overheard my dad telling my first grade teacher that I was more like a girl than a boy. This was in 1994. I sat in the corner with the books, pretending to read, during their parent-teacher conference. Usually my mom attended these, but for some reason this time my dad was there. He was expressing concern, but my teacher told him that this was usually the case with exceptional boys, and that they grew into exceptional men. "It's a matter of sensitivity," she said. I'm convinced that she raised her voice just enough to ensure that I would hear. I looked at my dad. By his expression, I could tell that he believed her, and I still feel gratitude. I had enough trouble later on proving my masculinity, and I can't imagine what it might have been like had she not fed us this morsel of relief.

Gabe was jealous of me, which leads to how I got my name. According to family legend, when we were toddlers, Gabe pointed at me and said, "Even." The story has been repeated so many times that I can give a reenactment, as I imagine it:

Having bravely endured my pediatrician appointment, which included a series of immunization shots, I was granted a red lollipop from a bowl in the lobby by a cranky old woman who answered the phone and took down appointments. Gabe, on the other hand, had thrown a fit during his shots and was still red-faced. "Even," he said, pointing at me, his index finger and arm trembling.

Our mom, a stalwart of discipline and stoic in life, especially when witnesses are involved, knelt to look at Gabe and said: "No lollies. No lollies for bad, bad boys."

Gabe stared at her and then at me, and I stared back at him, a frantic acknowledgment of the injustice vibrating between us, my lollipop clutched in my fist at my side. I'd already unwrapped it from its plastic sheath.

"Even," he said again.

I also wanted to make it right, fair, equal, just, even, and my hand reached for the bowl to take another. I didn't want to give him mine. But the mean old woman pushed the bowl away.

Tears and red faces, now from both Gabe and me. We often spiraled each other into frenzies, appreciating the force in a coupled phobia, emotion, or tantrum.

Judgment from the old, cranky woman, from the other mothers in the waiting room, from the pediatrician, who poked his head into the lobby, and then Mom yanked us by our arms and shuttled us to the parking lot.

According to our mom, as we sat side by side in our car seats, I handed my lolly to Gabe, and his tears turned to a shuddering of breath. A smack and suck of lips, and then he passed the lolly back. On and on, our mom watching in her rearview mirror as we shared.

By the time we arrived home—our mouths sticky and red and the leftover fuzzy-stick on the car floor mat—we were holding hands and sleeping.

Gabe continued to say "Even" in his childhood quest for equality, when he received a larger portion of dessert than I did, or when there were more presents under the Christmas tree for me, or when he had better crayons—even, even, even—until he'd named me, and then my parents called me Even, too.

Even though Gabe is older, he's usually mistaken for the younger brother. He's the one who looks more like our dad, who inherited his nerdy features, including his nasal breathing and bad eyesight, though Gabe rarely wears his glasses or contacts and has a record of minor car accidents to prove it.

Small as a child, Gabe didn't reach his full height and weight until well into his senior year of high school. My maturation was steady—no sudden growth spurts—and so for most of our lives, I've always been a full head taller.

Our physical features are similar—downturned mouths, stooped shoulders, cowlicks at the backs of our heads, greenish-hazel eyes.

Our mom would often tell us, "The whole reason your dad and I decided to have two children is so that you'll always be there for each other. You'll look out for each other." We took her words to heart.

OUR PARENTS DIVORCED in 2001, when I was beginning the eighth grade and Gabe the ninth. Dad's drywall business had boomed, and he bought a house in Newport Beach. After a bitter custody battle, when the judge pulled me into his chambers for a private conference and asked which of my parents I wanted to live with— my mom, in Rancho Cucamonga, or my dad, in Newport Beach—I said one word: "Dad."

I COULDN'T UNDERSTAND what was happening to our parents and to Gabe and me during those formative years, and I would have been surprised had someone pointed out that my personality was similar to our dad's, with my determination to separate, my stubbornness, a will toward self-creation, a sense of self-preservation, and an insensitivity to others if my own well-being was in the crosshairs. A ruthless work ethic pointed not toward the making of money, like Dad, but toward something intangible, something as formless as I felt during those years.

I worshipped him then, even though he wasn't around much: He worked all the time. But I believed that his success proved his superiority, and as his fortunes increased, most everyone seemed to grant him deference, which only reinforced my belief. Besides, he understood me in a way that our mom never had.

Mom believed anything art-related encouraged homosexuality and weakness. Dad encouraged my artistic sensibilities, telling me, "Making money's easy. You're going to do something with your life, something greater than making money, something creative, something that I could never do."

One time he brought home a bunch of leather-bound books for me—mostly classics, *Remembrance of Things Past* and everything by Thomas Hardy. He said he got them from a dead man's library —and though I was still too young to read them (I must've been about seven or eight), just having them made me feel enriched and different, a shifting of consciousness—they were for me, just me.

Mom never forgave me for choosing to live with him. She accused me of having a heart made of stone, and of being a materialistic and selfish child.

I learned later that Gabe felt that my leaving him was a double abandonment—first his dad, then his brother left. At the time, I didn't care, or rather I didn't let myself care. I couldn't afford to, so I didn't think about him.

I also learned later that our dad didn't fight for Gabe. "I had to let Gina have one of you," he explained. "It wouldn't have been right to take you both, and I felt that you and I were better suited for each other."

Mom's depression accelerated, culminating in a diagnosis of chronic fatigue syndrome, which seemed to make her happy. She has a talent for being happy with ever-increasing amounts of unhappiness, and a diagnosis of an elusive and incurable ailment pleased her.

"Your dad doesn't think I'm good enough," she would say. "Now that he's a big shot, he's embarrassed by me. That's why he divorced me." Her wardrobe consisted of a revolving array of nightgowns, robes, sweatpants, and T-shirts.

I'm embarrassed by you, too, I wanted to tell her.

Those first days before the school year began I spent wandering Newport Beach, celebrating my good fortune, stunned by and happy with the significant upgrade in my living environment.

Dad's new home was walking distance from the beach; the sky and ocean big and blustery, palm trees shushing in the wind, waves glittering and crashing on the rocks and shore. Moistness in the air that I didn't know I was missing until I breathed it in. A heavy, satisfying smell of ocean and seaweed mingled at night with the aroma of smoke from the fire pits on the beach.

His new house was a four-bedroom, three-bathroom colonial built in 1973, with a pool and an attached garage. Address: 111

Opal Cove. From the balcony off my room, over the rooftops of the other homes, there was a strip of an ocean view. Each morning at around eleven, the high school girls' cross-country team jogged past my window like a welcoming crew—lovely and lean in matching shorts and sports bras, with midriffs exposed—and I watched their ponytails swinging behind them, until they disappeared down the street.

I'd never seen beauty like this before, except sometimes on television, and now even the TV was better: Dad, though he didn't have much furniture yet, had a giant flat-screen with hundreds of channels.

Dad and I stared at it for hours after he came home from work (I was alone to do what I wanted during the day), numb, the super-bright colors vibrating: real cop shows and fake cop shows, movies on cable, CNN, Fox News, *Law & Order*, *Survivor*, and *The Sopranos*. Even the commercials were mesmerizing. Surround sound, so that the noise came from above and behind and below us.

We ate our meals—he specialized in omelets and grilled cheese sandwiches; I made pasta and meatloaf or else microwaved frozen dinners—in front of the TV, something that Mom would have prohibited.

Otherwise, we dined out. He preferred dark restaurants, themed toward royalty, with blazing fireplaces and thick slabs of steak and mashed potatoes on plates so hot the server would warn: "Don't touch, please don't touch, careful."

At the restaurants, he conversed easily with our servers, the bartenders, and the valets, his voice distinct and gravelly from years of smoking, though I believe he also practiced to make it intimidating: a low, grumbling, serious tone. (People noticed and commented on his voice more than anything.)

One night, we were passing through the bar on the way to our table at Banditos Steakhouse, following the swaying backside of the hostess, when a uniformed arm reached out and stopped my dad. The bar was bustling, men and women lined up behind those sitting on the barstools.

"Mr. Daniel Hyde," the man said in an exaggerated, friendly drawl, "my man."

"Sheriff Matthew Krone," Dad said. "America's favorite sheriff." They came toward each other, patted each other's backs in a loose-armed masculine hug, and then backstepped. "Wearing his uniform at a bar," Dad said, assessing him.

"Good Lord," the sheriff said, as if noticing how he was dressed for the first time. He took a long drink from his glass, wiped the foam from his upper lip with the back of his hand, and then said, "Ladies love a man in a uniform." He was balding, with wispy, pale hair. His head was big, full-cheeked, pinkish, and animated. Hooking a blond in a low-cut dress by the waist, he swung her toward us.

"Isn't that right?" he asked.

"What?" she said. "What?" It was loud and she had no idea what was going on.

"Say yes," he said.

She put her hands in front of her. She had a clownish downturned mouth, and she said in a baby voice, "You gonna arress me, mist-er shewiff? Pwetty pwease."

The sheriff pretended to handcuff her in a rather detailed mime, and when he was done, he slapped her ass.

To my surprise, my dad laughed. His head was tilted, and one of the lights from the ceiling streamed down on his receding hair-line, a reddish-gray tangle like a tumbleweed. The glass from his spectacles glinted in the lighting, and his hands dug into his pockets in an aw-shucks manner. I felt both protective and embarrassed, as if the woman and the sheriff were the cool kids, making fun of him without his knowledge.

The sheriff made a big deal about Dad, telling the woman: "Hyde Drywall. This man who you're looking at right here, this amazing man, he invented it: porous, easy to use. Great noise control. Made a killing, first with the government. State of California said, 'Please let us use your product.'"

"That's not what the government said," said Dad, his cheeks flushed.

"What do they know," the sheriff said, flinging out his hand. "Fuckers didn't have enough evidence to sue. Case dismissed!"

"Oh, my," the woman said, putting her hand to her cheek. Then she turned back to the bar, seeming to understand—with a glance at the sheriff—that her time as the entertainment had ended.

Dad introduced us: the sheriff's handshake was firm and clammy, his breath beery. "Evan," he said, "nice to meet you."

"Even," I corrected.

He smiled, as if he didn't understand or didn't care.

In the blaze of his attention, I became hyperconscious of the acne on my chin and forehead. I've always been aware of how I must look to others, and during my teenage years even more so, painfully so.

"Handsome boy," he said. "Takes after his dad." He continued to stare, homing in on my insecurities and making me more aware of my dad's nerdy appearance. (He certainly wasn't handsome!)

Shy, awkward, embarrassed, and getting a bad vibe, I looked away.

He said, "Your old man's a helluva guy," as if my dad wasn't listening.

My dad beamed.

When we got to our table, I wanted to ask about the government trying to sue him (the first I'd heard about it), but instead I asked, "How do you know him?"

Dad pulled a leather wallet-like case from his back pocket and handed it to me.

I opened the fold. Inside was a badge. "Is it real?" I asked. The other side had a weapons permit, and I knew then that somewhere in Dad's house was a gun.

"Does it matter?" he said, adding, "I paid a lot for that." He took it from me before I got a better look and slipped it back into his pocket.

"I'm the reason," he continued, settling into his chair, "that man is a sheriff, and we both know it. It's real if and when I want it to be."

He was using his roughest Clint Eastwood voice, and for a second, I envisioned him as a small boy, trying to make himself threatening.

I must've looked at him strangely because he grimaced.

"Don't worry about him, Even," he said.

"Why'd you call him 'America's favorite sheriff'?"

He lifted a roll from the basket, split it with his thumbs, and inserted a knifed hunk of butter. "That's what Limbaugh calls him since he caught that scumbag," he said. "Look it up." (I did: America's hero, not America's favorite sheriff. National attention for the quick capture of the kidnapper of a six-year-old blond girl from Tustin.) He stared at the bread for a second and then took a bite. Chewed, swallowed, added, "A good man. My friend. A family-values guy. He's going far, just you watch."

Dad claimed to be "a family-values Christian," but he avoided church. He didn't really want to think about religion, God and spirituality, death and the afterlife. But he did believe in the sacrifice story line of Jesus Christ, and that Christ not only approved of his wealth, but also considered Dad's striving and possession of riches in this world evidence that he deserved a good place in the next.

Dad offered his own story as proof that radical transformation was possible. A high school dropout, he rose above poverty, neglect, and an abusive father and by his early teens was already working menial jobs and saving money to build his first business. What was your excuse?

Sometimes he would look at me for a moment, after a particular indulgence purchased with cash from his thick-wadded money clip—he kept the hundreds visible on the outside, the smaller denominations moving inward to the dollar bills—and then ask, "Happy, Even?"

I knew it was a rhetorical question.

When we were at home watching television together, his cocktail glass clinked with ice. He held the glass by the rim with his fingertips, let it dangle, a cigarette in his other hand and an ashtray nearby.

I'd get a warm sensation under my sternum, watching him get choked up during some movie or documentary, or even something I read to him, a Raymond Carver poem or a passage from a book that I liked.

"Isn't that something?" he might mutter, turning his head until he redirected his emotions.

He'd signal that he was going to bed by taking off his glasses, folding them, putting them in their case, and setting them on the table next to the remote.

"Good night, Even," he'd say, stretching, scratching his scalp, squinting at me—he could barely see me without his glasses—the corners of his mouth downturned. "Sweet dreams."

The rim of his glasses left a soft pink imprint in the flesh where they sat on his nose. Sometimes he pinched and rubbed this area with his forefinger and thumb.

He'd put his hand on the top of my head and smooth my hair.

"Night, Dad."

No rules. I could stay up and watch TV until morning if I wanted, another reason that I preferred my dad's. Many nights I did, making microwave popcorn, letting the kernels drop to the floor as I watched mindless TV—the cleaning lady came twice a week, no need to worry—pulling a blanket over myself, and then waking on the couch the next morning to a muted TV and the bubbling sound of Dad brewing coffee in the kitchen.

No espresso machine for him. No lattes or cappuccinos or frothed milk. Those were for wimps, fags, and the French, he once told me straight-faced, and when I laughed, he looked confused, and then more serious. But then we both laughed. We had no idea what was to come.

2.

AN OLD-SCHOOL, HEAVY-BREATHING, stethoscope-wearing dermatologist liberated me from the worst of my acne with a tetracycline prescription, so that through eighth grade and high school, I was able to blend into my environment. As in Cucamonga, I found peers who were prone to conformity, swayed by popular culture, and entitled. But they were also higher-income families and were apt to begin trends rather than just follow them. They manifested a confidence mixed with boredom and a willingness to wear blinders in order to create and maintain their insularity, knowing that their pasts, presents, and futures were anchored in the security of money. Every other family in Newport Beach seemed to own a golden retriever named Delilah or Charles, along with a second home in either Mammoth or Palm Desert.

Despite my camouflage abilities, I remained, in some aspects, alienated, heightened by hormones and a deep understanding that my exterior was a deception. But the way I looked allowed me to remain in the background like a chameleon: invisible, observant, protective. Teachers liked me. I made some friends in the eighth grade, and we ate our lunches together under an awning by the commons, rode our skateboards after school, surfed, and played Xbox and PlayStation.

Fortunately, a popular kid named Mike, an athlete who didn't like the company of jocks, took a shine to me, saving me from much social misery. Big, good-natured, kind, and funny, Mike went on to play and star in varsity football and basketball in high school, and we remained best friends.

Gabe visited Dad and me on the weekends. According to the custody agreement, our mom was supposed to have visitation rights with me. But she banished me from my childhood home since I had chosen to live with Dad. Not that I wanted to visit her or Cucamonga anyway. Every other Tuesday, we had strained phone conversations, and one month she sent me three rambling letters, hoping to induce guilt for my "ultimate betrayal."

During Gabe's visits, we pretended that nothing had changed. We went to the movies, ate, watched TV, slept, and acted like everything was all right.

Dad didn't normally spend time with us. But now he took us miniature golfing and go-kart racing, making an effort to be with us—to be with Gabe. These short bursts of entertainment-fueled activities were meant to be for our benefit but also appeased Dad's conscience.

Gabe, still a head shorter than me and twenty pounds lighter, wore his jeans low with untucked, baggy T-shirts, and he often smelled of marijuana.

He's always been funny, good at imitating people, and those days he liked to call me his "genetic replicate by one half."

Mom used to say that I came out of the womb glum and pondering—"Sort of like you are now"—and that she'd put me in my high chair and tried all sorts of things to get me to laugh: jumping into view with a banana in her ear, pretending to answer her shoe like a phone, acting like a monkey. I'd just stare at her— "That same stare you always have, like you're just putting up with me." Then when Gabe would simply toddle into the room, my face would light up. He didn't have to do anything. Just seeing him made me happy. No one could make me laugh like Gabe did.

His diminutive stature helped his skateboarding, and he'd gained a reputation by this time. He was good, really good, far better than me. He specialized in a move called the boneless, where he grabbed the board near the wheels, took his front foot off the board, then planted the board on the ground and jumped. While in the air, his front foot would drop back onto the board and he'd land with his knees bent. He could do the boneless anywhere, with variations and exaggerations, and people would gather to watch. Skateboarding, he was in his element. But he couldn't skateboard all the time.

I didn't realize how angry he'd become—about the divorce, my leaving—but I got my first hint on a Saturday night when we spent the weekend together at Dad's house.

There'd been a strain between Dad and Gabe, but things seemed to be going better, especially without our mom's presence to stoke Gabe's animosity. We had dinner at Banditos Steakhouse that night and everyone seemed to be in good enough moods, though no one talked much. We chewed and drank and half smiled at each other for most of the meal. Dad thumbed his wad of cash and then decided to slap his credit card on the table before the check came. Our server picked it up, brought it back, he signed, and we were done.

At Dad's house, we positioned ourselves in front of the TV screen, and after some discussion settled on an old James Bond movie (*Live and Let Die*). Despite the noisy, violent, plot-laden film, my eyelids kept shutting, so I excused myself and went to bed. A cumulative three-night battle with insomnia (a recurring problem, to this day) had left me excited about what I forecasted— from my nodding head, full stomach, and heavy eyelids—as certain sleep. I turned one last time, and the light from the screen shone on their similarly engrossed profiles, our dad's chin and nose weightier with age.

In bed, a current of unconsciousness was just about to pull me deeper in when I heard a thudding noise. I allowed the thud to come from my sleep world, but soon—after another thud—I had to acknowledge its reality. I sat up in bed and listened for more.

At first nothing, but then a crash sounded, and Dad yelled, "Listen: Calm down!"

I switched on the light. Then I heard Gabe scream. This was followed by another crash.

"Don't touch me," Gabe said. "Get away"—a scraping noise. A sound like furniture being turned over, scuffed against the floor.

"I'm not trying to hurt you"—Dad.

"Don't, I swear to god, you fucking faggot."

"Gabe, c'mon," said Dad. More shuffling.

"I'll do it!"

"Gabe, no."

"I hate you!"

"Gabe"—a scuffling, a shriek, and then a whistling pause, and it was as if I knew what was going to happen before I heard the unmistakable sound of shattering glass as the big TV screen exploded.

I came down the hallway, and in the half light, the house had an eerie feel. My bare feet made soft pats on the wood flooring. After the screaming, the lack of noise sounded hollow, like how it might be to fall into a void.

Pausing before the living room, I saw Dad and Gabe standing over a heap of broken glass. Both were breathing heavily. Two recliners lay overturned on their sides, the coffee table was perched at an angle, the base and frame of the TV had shards of glass at their perimeter, and the couch had shifted a few feet. A thick metal ashtray leaned sideways against a wall among a scattering of butts and ashes.

I made an involuntary cough noise, and their faces lifted in unison, turning to me with a stunned blankness, as if they expected me to tell them how to feel about what had just happened.

A wave of nausea and fatigue came over me. "Put on your shoes," I said, "so you don't step on glass."

They both nodded.

I went to my room and slipped on my Vans, and then I went to the closet in the kitchen, gathered a broom, a dustpan, and a Dustbuster, and closed the door behind me. Before going back into the living room, I put the items down and filled a glass with water from the sink. By the miniclock on the oven, I saw that it was 10:13 PM. I drank two glasses of water, standing at the sink.

I took my time, and I thought about how a door from the kitchen led to the backyard, and beyond that there was a gate. I had a powerful urge to leave. I could walk away, or take our dad's Porsche. He kept the keys in the ignition. How hard would it be to learn how to drive? Who were these people? Where could I go? But the water steadied me, and by the last glassful, which I drank slowly, I knew that I had to stay.

I went back to the living room to help them clean. We did so mechanically and quietly, exhausted and cooperative, a somber repentance to our actions, avoiding eye contact.

When we were done—after filling two large kitchen bags with debris and setting them outside by the trash cans, along with the TV frame and its base, and returning the furniture to its place—we went to our separate bedrooms without saying good night.

Back in my bedroom, I lay down, prepared for another night of restlessness, of contemplation and anxiety. But within minutes, I fell asleep.

I would have continued sleeping had someone not awakened me.

I rubbed my eyes and lifted myself to sitting. Half-asleep and disoriented, I must have looked scared, because Gabe said, "It's okay. It's just me."

He sat on the bed next to me. His shoulders bent down so I couldn't see his face and I wondered if he was crying. He used to cry a lot when we were kids—only in private.

"I couldn't sleep," he said. "Took one of Dad's sleeping pills but it's not working for shit. Should've taken more."

It hadn't occurred to me to go fishing in Dad's medicine cabinet. Immediately, I wanted some. Even, I thought.

After a long pause, he said, "I don't know what happened"—he shook his head. Then he looked at me, and I saw that he hadn't been crying, and he said, "It was the weirdest thing, Even. We were watching the movie, it was such a cool scene, in New Orleans, one of those funeral bands going down the street, and a man comes up and he asks this guy, 'Whose funeral?' and the man says to him, 'Yours,' and stabs him, and he goes down, and then the people put him in a casket, lift him up and take him, and it's his funeral, and Dad says, 'That's bullshit,' and I say, 'Shut up,' and he says, 'You shut up,' and I couldn't take it, you know. He'd been grumbling the whole movie; you know the way that he does. Like he knows everything. Fuck, I hate that. You know what I'm talking about. I saw a blast of red, and the next thing I know"—his eyes went big.

We looked at each other for a long time, letting his telling of what happened diffuse some. His cowlick bloomed, making it look like a squirrel was crawling up his head. Instinctively, I ran my hand over my hair in the same spot to smooth it, as if looking in a mirror.

"I didn't mean for that to happen."

"I know," I said. We sat quietly for a moment, and then I said, "Why don't you apologize to Dad?"

"No way."

"Okay."

"I don't know what happened," he repeated.

I said nothing.

"I don't want to be that person."

"I know," I said, which visibly appeased him.

"It's weird," he said.

"What is?"

"How is it that I can feel so bad just looking at him?"

I didn't know what to say.

"Sometimes when I lose my temper like that," he said, looking right at me, "I mean like I did tonight, I feel like I'm most like him."

"That makes no sense," I said. Our dad got mad sometimes, but he wasn't a brute.

"Okay, maybe not like him, but that's when I feel most connected to him." He continued to stare at me. It seemed important to him that I understand. After a long pause, he added, "It's like how I can get through to him or something."

I shook my head. "He's not that bad," I said.

"Tell that to Uncle Frank," he said. Uncle Frank was Dad's former business partner, not really our uncle, but we just called him that. After a bitter feud over the formula for their drywall—and who had invented it—Uncle Frank threatened to sue Dad. But Dad had the patent: He bought Uncle Frank out and changed the name to Hyde Drywall.

"He's not a bad guy," I repeated. "You don't know what happened with Uncle Frank. We were just kids. He's probably doing fine, with all that money that Dad gave to him."

"He's probably living in a trailer park."

I didn't say anything. I could barely remember Uncle Frank.

"You're the one that's just like him," he said.

"No," I said. "I'm not. I'm like you."

"If you're not careful," he said, "you're going to end up like him."

This didn't strike me as an awful thing, but I didn't tell him that. Instead I said, "He's your dad, too."

"You two are soul mates," he said. "Your lives run parallel."

"Shut up," I said, and I shoved him a little in the shoulder.

He smiled.

We got up after that, and we ate toasted strawberry Pop-Tarts, staring at the space where the television used to be.

3.

T HE WEEKEND PASSED, and no one mentioned the fight. Like it had never happened. Gabe and Dad seemed more careful, considerate, and at ease, as if they'd released the pressure on a valve. The following Monday, as I left for school, I watched three men unloading a large box from their truck. By the time I got home that afternoon, we had a TV again, with an even more sophisticated remote and sound system.

THE FOLLOWING SUNDAY afternoon, Dad took Gabe and me to Rose Hills cemetery in Whittier to visit our relatives' graves. "They're all buried at Rose Hills," he told us, as we crammed into his red Porsche 911 Carrera. "We got a discount on family burial sites a long time ago, before it got so expensive. You'll be buried there, me, all of us together. It's about time we go visit." I wondered what could have prompted this from him, possibly the show that we'd watched on the History Channel a few nights before about the genealogy of the Vikings. He'd been really into it.

Once we were in the car, he lit a cigarette. He smoked Newports, which I found funny, about a pack a day, and he claimed the menthol didn't give him as bad breath as regular cigarettes. He told us that our ancestors were German, Irish, and English, hard workers and devout churchgoers. That was where he'd gotten his work ethic, he said. "Your great-great-granddaddy," he said, in a matter-of-fact tone, "the patriarch of our clan, he might've owned a few slaves. We're not sure."

We drove all the way there with the top down, the three of us crammed into only two seats, me in the middle with my ass lodged uncomfortably between the two seats, his golf clubs taking up the space in the back where I might've otherwise sat.

Dad stopped at a little hut selling flowers and bought a dozen white carnations with a rainbow-colored pinwheel stuck in the middle. We drove around Sunshine Terrace looking for gravesites for close to an hour. The cemetery is huge, with nothing but tiny numbered placement markings on the curbs, and all Dad remembered was that ours were somewhere on Sunshine Terrace.

We found a tiny shack at the base of the hill, thinking that it might be an information booth. An old man inside created a makeshift map on the back of a McDonald's cheeseburger wrapper. He coughed, and then said that he was about to close up.

"Good luck," he said.

The sun, low in the sky, cast an amber glow over the grass and trees. The map didn't help much, and Dad put it on the floorboard. We drove one last time to the top of Sunshine Terrace and slowly down, scoping the curbs for their tiny numbers, L.A. glimmering in the distance, swathed in a smoggy sunset.

"We're close," Dad said. "I know it."

Dad pulled the car to the curb, and we got out to look. We walked for a long time, not speaking, splitting up to check the gravesites but keeping within eyesight of each other. There were hundreds of gravestones on Sunshine Terrace—most of them simple and bare, with a few lonely pinwheels turning amid bunches of flowers—and every now and then I saw a maintenance worker raking or trimming the grass. My head hurt, my ass ached, I was cold, and I felt a bit nauseated.

I was still thinking about our great-great-grandfather possibly owning slaves, and how Dad had mentioned the fact so breezily. It bothered me, and I experienced a shifting in my feeling about our family and its history from a sense of pride to ambiguity. I wasn't so sure that I wanted to be buried with them.

We'd given up and had crammed into the Porsche again, this time with the top up, and turned back toward Dad's home, when he said, "It doesn't matter. It's the thought that counts, anyway. We'll come back another time." In the purple-gold sky, the fat moon looked like a glob of cream. I knew that we wouldn't be back, and I didn't care.

4.

ONE WEEKEND NOT long after our trip to Rose Hills, Gabe got me stoned for the first time. Dad left us on a Saturday morning to play golf with Sheriff Matt Krone and some of his buddies. He said it was for business. He'd been spending less time with us, returning to his predivorce pattern of neglect.

"Easy, dude," Gabe said, watching me suck on the joint. He sat in Dad's recliner, legs widespread, taking up space like a king. "That's right. Hold it, hold it, hooold it. Hoooold . . . Okay, release."

Sitting tense and hunched on the couch, I let the smoke out. Coughed, choked, gasped, laughed.

Back and forth we passed the joint, until Gabe pinched the butt dead.

We raided the refrigerator, eating turkey slices, pickles, cheese, apples, and greasy duck liver pâté, which Gabe had not tried before. Forking it from its case, spreading it on Ritz crackers. Then we siphoned brandy from Dad's bar, drinking from wide-bottomed crystal glasses, swilling the dark-copper liquid, and sniffing at it like sophisticated connoisseurs. Drunk and stoned, the living room whirling, we decided to go outside for a Jacuzzi.

Stripped naked, we sat in the bubbling lukewarm water, feeling it gradually heat up. It reminded me of when we used to take baths together as kids.

Gabe dipped his head under and came back with dripping bangs. I followed, hearing the rush of jets, and then I came back up for air. We were both pleased with our camaraderie—whether chemically induced or not—since we hadn't experienced it as much since I'd moved out.

On the horizon, beyond the homes and trees and streets, a vague light blue strip of ocean shimmered.

Gabe nodded toward it, saying, "Nice view." He kept staring with a wistful, preoccupied look on his face.

"Uh-huh," I agreed dumbly. Along with giving me cotton-mouth, pot stunted my vocabulary.

"So," he said, shifting his attention and leaning back against a jet, "dude. The girls are prettier here than in Cucamonga, right?"

I started laughing so hard I thought something must be wrong with me.

"You've got your pick," he said.

"Uh-huh," I said, trying not to laugh so much.

He leaned across the Jacuzzi toward me, and began to tell me about a girl he was having sex with, Chrystal Lemmings. "You remember her," he said. "Long brown hair, blue eyes, nice ass, long legs."

"Sure," I said, ducking my chin into the bubbles. I didn't remember Chrystal, and I wasn't sure I believed Gabe was having sex with her.

"She knows what she's doing," he said. He traced a finger along the water that had collected in the gap between two tiles. "Know what I mean?"

"Uh-huh," I lied.

He closed his eyes and tilted his head back, saying, "She's good."

I started laughing again, slapping at the water with my hands like a toddler would. I couldn't seem to help myself.

"What's so funny?" he said, pushing at my chest. "You think I'm joking?"

"Nah," I said.

"You like anyone?" he asked.

"There's this girl," I said, making my voice confidential. "I've never told anyone."

"Oh, yeah," he said. "Tell me."

"She gives me hand jobs," I said.

"Bullshit," he said.

"I'm serious." My cheeks burned with shame.

"She hot?"

I sat back against a jet. "Not bad," I said.

"She blow you?"

"Sure."

"You feel her pussy?"

"Yeah."

"Nice," he said. "Your face's all red. Do I know her?"

"Nah," I said.

"Wanna call her?"

"Nah."

"What's her name?"

I don't know how I came up with the name Tammy.

"Hmm," he said. "What's her last name?"

I don't know how I came up with the last name Simon.

"Simon," he said. "Tammy Simon." He closed his eyes and started talking about Chrystal Lemmings blowing him, describing the way her mouth felt on his cock, speaking in detail. He was on a roll, and it was like reading pornography online, juicy and explicit. I wasn't laughing anymore. The only noise besides his talking came from the bubbling water.

He paused, opened his eyes, shifted, squinted at me. His face soured, as if he'd tasted something unpleasant. But it came from whatever he saw on my face.

"You look fucked up," he said. "You okay? You feel sick?"

"Nah," I said. But I felt sick, thinking about this girl Tammy Simon that I'd made up, and Gabe and Chrystal, and the pornos and the things that I'd seen on the computer, in relation to me and to Gabe: all that slapping and thrusting and licking and coming. It wasn't that I didn't want to have sex, or that sex didn't excite me, but it also seemed like a physical ordeal. I barely had hair on my armpits and groin. Somewhere between wanting to throw up and needing to cry, I felt a horrible, panicky thumping in my chest. I burped, a slippery gurgle of food and bourbon rising and falling.

"Drink too much?" Gabe said.

"Maybe."

Gabe hoisted himself onto the partition between the Jacuzzi and pool, his half-erect penis swaying. Then he stood for a moment and slapped at his chest like Tarzan. He was small and muscular, his butt cheeks paler than the rest of him, and he turned his head to look at me from over his shoulder. "Get up here," he said. "This'll help."

I lumbered onto the partition, stood beside him. He gripped my wrist and took me with him in a dive-jump-belly-flop into the cold pool. We smacked the surface, and he released me, our bodies sinking. I opened my eyes for a second and saw his hair drifting upward.

It did help.

LATER THAT NIGHT, I couldn't sleep. Gabe, as far as I knew, was sleeping, and Dad had gone to bed early with a migraine.

The alcohol and pot had faded, leaving me uneasy. I tried reading Hemingway's *The Old Man and the Sea* for my advanced English class. My teacher had gushed so much about "Papa's economy of words" that I felt disgruntled, like I'd been promised a steak but what was delivered instead was a plate with a few peas on it.

Finally, I decided to get a drink of water. I drank a glass in the kitchen and then poured another to take with me. Walking down the hallway from the kitchen in my pajama bottoms and T-shirt, holding my glass, I heard music coming from the living room.

The TV screen showed one of those pseudo-pornos with simulated sex but no actual copulation. An oil-slicked, hairless man slammed, with a repetitive slapping noise, against an equally oil-slicked woman, both making exaggerated facial expressions, moaning mechanically.

At first I thought the room was empty, but then I saw the top of Gabe's head in Dad's tilted-back recliner, his feet stretched before him.

I walked over and sat near him, emboldened by our earlier bonding.

He looked over at me and in the weak light from the lamp, I saw his glazed and bloodshot eyes. He was shirtless with his boxers and socks on; one of his hands lay idle on his stomach, the other flopped on the recliner's arm. On the table beside him next to the remote was a bottle of Michelob. It took him a few seconds to speak. "Hey," he said, thick-tongued. "Hey there." He set the chair more upright and muted the TV.

"What are you doing?" I asked stupidly.

"It's the only one you don't have to pay for," he said, slurring his words a bit. He swallowed noticeably and added, "Tongue feels weird." With his thumb and forefinger, he pinched his tongue and pulled it from his mouth.

"Like how?"

"Icanthfeelith," he said, and then he released his tongue and gave me a smile.

I shifted closer to him. We watched the muted TV without speaking for a few minutes. He lifted the Michelob to his lips, made a point to smack its bottom to get the final drops, and then set the empty back. It wobbled on the table and before it tipped I leaned forward and steadied it with my hand.

Another oil-slicked woman joined the couple on-screen, her legs crossed so that you couldn't fully see her pubis. She watched the couple while rubbing her breasts, and then the man pulled her down onto the floor, and she began to fondle his chest and watch over his shoulder, kneeling behind him. I realized that they were in an office space, with filing cabinets and a desk.

"So much for getting any work done," I said.

Gabe looked at me with a blank expression, his mouth slightly open.

"It's a joke," I offered.

His eyes widened; he said, "Ahh," looking at the screen, and he laughed with comprehension.

"Gabe?" I said.

"What?" he said, without looking away from the screen.

"Are you mad at me for leaving you with Mom?"

"Huh?"

"Are you mad," I repeated, "that I left you with Mom?"

He didn't answer. The TV light shone on his face, and he looked empty and emotionless. It bothered me so much that I glanced back at the screen.

"I had to leave," I said. "I had to." I paused, stared back at him. "I know she blames me but I hope that you don't."

He turned to me, glassy-eyed, and I thought for a second he was going to tell me to shut the fuck up, but instead he said, "Can I have that"—gesturing at my glass of water.

"Sure," I said, handing it to him.

He drank it down in one pull, his Adam's apple bobbing. Wiping the back of his hand across his mouth, he said, "Ahhh, good," and set the glass next to his Michelob.

He stretched, turned toward me, fetus-like in the recliner. Serious, he said, "You don't know what it's like, Even. She makes me rub her feet, her back. You should see the meds she's on." A pause, then, "She says she's dying. I hear her crying at night, sometimes all night. I cook, clean, pick up after her. It's like I'm her caretaker."

"God, sorry," I said. "I had no idea it was that bad. Can't you tell her no? Tell her to leave you alone."

He turned back to the TV. "Dad's a shit," he said. Petulant, irritated, his eyes shining. "I hate him."

"Mom's a shit, too," I said after a long pause. But he didn't seem to hear me or acknowledge Mom's fault.

"I mean," he said, his voice rising, "he's a fucking shit."

"He's not perfect," I said, uncertain. "I know that."

"You're naïve, Even," he said in monotone. He kept staring at the TV. "Open your eyes. He thinks he can buy your love. Looks like he's bought it. He's got that sheriff. Thinks he can buy everything. One day you're going to figure it out."

"You sound like Mom."

"Yeah, well," he said. "Since you left, all Mom does is talk about you. They're both obsessed with you. It's like I don't exist."

We were quiet, and I felt sorry for Gabe.

"Why do you play the game, Son?" I said, adopting Dad's voice.

Gabe snorted. "Because," he said, with a better gravelly sounding Dad-voice than mine, "you play to win."

"Son," I said, mimicking Gabe's Dad-voice, making mine deeper, heartier, and hoarser, "you play to win."

He smiled at me and we both laughed.

Our inside joke. Dad had sponsored Gabe's fourth grade Little League team, the Eagles. That meant that embroidered near their numbers on the backs of their uniforms was HYDE DRYWALL.

One afternoon, Dad told us: "You don't play to have a good time. You play to win." Over the years, Gabe and I had repeated this refrain in various forms, keeping the essential core of his philosophy.

"Listen," Gabe said, serious again, "promise me one thing."

"What?"

"Forget it," he said, looking down.

"Gabe. I hate it when you do that."

He shook his head. "Nah, dude," he said. "Forget it."

"I don't want to."

"I'm sleepy," he said. He stared at me, his mouth open. "I'm fucked up. Took some pills. Demerol, I think. Not sure. I don't know what I'm saying. I can't even see you that good."

"Where're your glasses?"

He shrugged. After a moment or so, he shook his head. "I don't know," he said, "sometimes I worry about what's going to happen to us."

"Like what?" I said.

We were quiet for a long while. He had closed his eyes.

"Now I remember"—he said, opening them—"what I was going to say." He looked at me. "Remember how Mom would always tell us that they had more than one kid so that we'd be there for each other, always look out for each other?"

"Yeah," I said. "Of course."

"Promise me you won't let anything fuck us up."

"Like what?"

"I don't know," he said. "Like Mom and Dad."

"They can't do that to us," I said, my voice fierce. "I promise. Nothing will. Nothing can."

He looked at me with relief and affection.

To this day, it pains me more than anything to think about this conversation, and the way that Gabe looked at me.

He trusted me.

5.

B Y MY FRESHMAN year of high school in Newport and Gabe's sophomore year in Cucamonga, I was visiting Mom every now and then (we had called a truce). She had joined a local Presbyterian church, and her ailments had improved. She volunteered on Sundays to sell coffee for a quarter from Styrofoam cups after the services, and she started to care more about her appearance. A four-month Weight Watchers membership helped her lose thirteen pounds, and she and a group of her friends started a walking club: Each morning they walked to Starbucks and treated themselves to lattes. As long as we didn't discuss my decision to live with my dad, we did okay.

Gabe came to Dad's on the weekends, sometimes bringing his friends. They liked it at Dad's for the same reason I did: not much adult supervision. They could drink, smoke pot, have sex, it didn't matter.

Dad had his "lady friend" by then, Nancy, a petite blond in her late thirties: quiet, smart, polite, pretty in a well-maintained way. Nancy worked in his office. On the weekends, she sometimes spent the night with Dad, but she wanted nothing to do with Gabe and me. We didn't see her much and talked to her very little. The biggest indicator of her presence in our lives was the sharp, lingering scent of her flowery perfume in Dad's house.

Once in a while Dad alluded with reverence to Nancy's impoverished upbringing in a small Alabama town (she had a trace of a Southern accent), which included, as I recall, a mother who had a wooden leg, missing teeth, and an appetite for beating her children. Dad appreciated a rags-to-riches story, and Nancy's was a doozy.

Nancy didn't want kids. All she wanted, it seemed, was to make sure she maintained her beloved lifestyle. She was a myopic, rigid, religious Republican, which complimented our dad's more fiscally based politics. Her small-town Southern roots also gave rise to a vocal xenophobia and an irrational obsession with Armageddon.

She had no idea what she was getting involved with when she took up with our dad. But later she stuck by him like a dog, giving comments to reporters that sounded like those of a PR representative. ("Daniel Hyde's greatest sins are being a devoted and generous family man, a successful, self-made businessman, and a selfless contributor to his community. Those that speak ill of him are obviously just jealous of his wealth and success.")

Unlike Dad, I didn't have a girlfriend. Not because I didn't want one. I didn't know how to get one. There were few couples at my high school. Mostly people hooked up at parties, and it was better when it was someone who you didn't know, someone from a different high school, because then you didn't have to see them on a daily basis. By my freshman year, I'd lost my virginity to a more experienced girl from Irvine, in a clumsy, limb-shuffling, spastic two-minutes: It was nothing to brag about.

I had a crush on Maria, a sweet, even-keeled Latina, a senior, older than me by four years, with sharp brown eyes and curly dark hair. She lived in Costa Mesa but went to school in the Newport district because her mother worked for the city. We shared a love of foreign films, and we went to a few art galleries together, but then she got a boyfriend who was in college, and she stopped hanging out with me. She graduated with honors and went on to Stanford, and then to Yale Law School. I keep track of her. I sometimes entertain the notion that she keeps track of me, too, and that my future accomplishments will impress her. But I try not to fantasize too much.

Those days, when I felt down, I sometimes wished that I still lived in Cucamonga. I missed my mom and brother. I couldn't really tell them this, since it had been my choice to live in Newport. But when I went back and visited, it was strange. I felt tangled up, like I didn't belong in Newport with my dad, and I certainly didn't belong back in Cucamonga with them anymore, either.

If all this seems confusing, it was, so much so that I tried counseling through my high school. I had four mortifying sessions with a well-intentioned counselor named Steve, who wore socks with sandals and believed strongly in the advantages of money to gold conversion. It didn't help that on our first session, I tried to be honest, describing the TV-shattering fight between Dad and Gabe. Steve put a hand to his cheek, gasped, and said, "No way! Really?"

In his small, windowless office decorated with cheerful and inane posters, such as one on the ceiling of a kitten hanging on a tree branch captioned *Hang in there! It gets better!*, Steve encouraged me to nurture and parent my inner child.

One afternoon, I canceled my appointment, leaving a message on Steve's answering machine saying that I'd call back to reschedule, and then I never returned.

Gabe struggled as well, but he converted Dad's three-car garage into his personal party headquarters and found his solace in drugs and alcohol and friends. Inside the garage was a tan-felt pool table and Dad's Porsche, and Gabe added a white wicker couch and a minifridge that he got from a garage sale. Dad bought an old white BMW for us to share, and we kept it parked at the curb, and then Dad bought Gabe a truck, which he also parked at the curb.

I didn't like Gabe's friends and avoided them when possible. At the center of his group were Kevin Stewart and another Crystal—not Chrystal Lemmings, she was long gone, but Crystal Douglas.

She claimed to be his girlfriend, but he said that she was "just a girl I see sometimes." She wore distressed jeans, the expensive kind made to look old with expertly placed holes, and she spoke with a practiced, high-pitched, doll-like voice.

I've always been self-conscious about my SoCal suburban accent—hollow and flat—making it a point to enunciate, careful not to overuse the word "like," and to avoid common slang.

Crystal Douglas was the opposite. She took pride in her hyper-regional speech: "Like, ya-know, I rilly think that's rad."

Kevin Stewart was big and brutish and popular, handsome, good at sports, and he always had drugs.

I'll never forget how I met him. Lying on the couch reading *The Stranger* by Camus, no one at Dad's house but me, I heard a loud banging on the front door. We didn't keep it locked and I waited for the solicitor or whoever it was to go away. But then I heard the door squeaking open, and in walked Kevin Stewart, wearing mirrored aviator sunglasses and a baseball cap, Bermuda shorts, and no shirt or shoes, reminding me of Hunter S. Thompson (I'd recently read *Fear and Loathing in Las Vegas*).

He seemed annoyed to see me. "*Hola*," he said. He spoke Anglo-accented Spanish, obviously thinking it clever. "*Dónde está mi amigo* Gabriel?"

"Not here," I said.

I had the impression that he was peering at me through his mirrored sunglasses. Almost a full year older than Gabe, thick-muscled, with a shit-eating grin. To my irritation, he walked right past me, through the living room, to get to the kitchen.

"Smells good," he said. "Is that coffee?"

Dad made coffee every morning, and then let whatever he didn't drink stew all day in its glass pot until he dumped it out at night.

Kevin smacked around in the cupboards until he found a mug, and then he poured himself a cup.

"What are you doing?" I asked.

He sat at the table. "Lighten up, *amigo*," he said, spreading his legs. Tan, with a diamond of hair at the center of his chest, on his left shoulder he sported a large, rudimentary tattoo of a four-leaf clover with a leprechaun peeking from behind it.

"Gabe isn't here," I said. "He's at some skateboarding thing. You can try his cell."

"Is there anything to eat?" he said.

I didn't answer, but he stood and moved toward the refrigerator. He pulled out a carton of eggs, a package of shredded cheese, butter, and a few tomatoes and started making himself something to eat.

I couldn't stand being in the house alone with him and left for Mike's. Mike and his family are Christians, but not in the preaching, let-me-convert-you-or-you're-going-to-hell way. More like they're good people and want to bring something to life rather than just take. They sought meaning and found it through their faith. Both his parents taught elementary school in Newport. Mike wanted and needed a scholarship to USC, thus his involvement in sports. He had three younger sisters, and his home was a bustling, happy environment.

Popular in high school without trying, he could have his pick of a best friend but nevertheless chose me. We enjoyed each other because of our differences, not in spite of them. He liked hearing my stories; his reactions were sincere—astonishment, compassion, pity, disappointment—and he didn't play games with people. It was nearly impossible for me to be cynical around him.

For about a month after I canceled my counseling appointment with Steve, I became a stoner, much to Mike's consternation. I got high at school every morning, before classes, during lunches, and after school every afternoon. My grades dropped. I gave up on college plans. I gave up on myself. I don't even like pot that much. It makes me paranoid and sweaty and dumb. I hear things, imagine things. It's like having the flu on purpose. But I was a pothead, maybe from some misguided sense of self-punishment. I carried a bottle of Visine with me in my back pocket at all times.

Late one afternoon, after I'd gotten high with a group of stoners in the high school parking lot, I sat in the bleachers and watched Mike's baseball game. Mike saw me and waved.

The crowd cheered during the game, but I just stared at the cracks and chipping red paint on the planks of the bleachers, my mouth and head cottony.

When the game ended, Mike trotted over to me.

"Who won?" I asked.

He gave me a disapproving look.

I stared back at him, knowing that my eyes were bloodshot and watery. He held his baseball cap. It had left a sweaty dent in the hair around his head.

"Listen," he said. "I don't like you like this." He started to speak but seemed to think better of it and shook his head. Then he said, "I mean, I know you're hurting, it's obvious. Your family's messed up. There's no doubt. But at least they love you. You love them."

He put his hat back on and wiped his hands on his baseball pants. "I can't deal with you like this," he said. "This is not you."

His frankness alarmed me, as usual. My head went down.

"Get help, man," he said quietly.

I looked at him and said nothing.

"I gotta go," he said. He put his hand on my shoulder for a few seconds. After he left, it felt like his hand was still there.

The following afternoon I ditched school with two other stoners: the son of a man who owned a well-known clothing line, and the son of the Bank of Newport's vice-president. Huge partiers, back-slappers, and high-fivers with fake IDs, they took pride in their bad reputations and spoke a few decibels too loud, calling

themselves "playahs." They got in trouble for things like forgetting to take the empty kegs they purchased for a party back to the
liquor store, cheating with answers to tests inked on their calves
and forearms, and trying to pass off fake prescriptions by using
names like Taco Bella and Colonel Sanders.

We got drunk and stoned at the beach.

Huddled near the rocks, alternately passing a joint and a
Corona, we heard a noise—a cop on his regular patrol coming
toward us. Tired-looking with a bushy mustache, probably in his
forties, the cop walked toward us slowly, watching us shuffle to
hide the blunt and bottle, burying them in the sand.

When he reached us, he said, "What do we have here?"

"Nothing, officer, sir," said Ace. (They called themselves Ace
and Ice. Don't ask—not worth explaining.)

The cop knelt, dug in the sand, and within a few seconds found
our paraphernalia. "Let's go, boys," he said, standing. His black
belt bolstered a baton and a gun, and his name tag read B. LESTER.
"Let's take a little walk to my car."

After a few uncomfortable minutes or so of being searched, we
were lined up in a row and sitting on the sidewalk in front of B.
Lester's cruiser in the sparkling daylight, our heads hung in shame,
when it occurred to me to mention my connection to Daniel Hyde,
and Dad's to Sheriff Krone.

So I did, waiting until my co-conspirators were engaged in a fer-
vent whispered conversation so that they wouldn't notice. Looked
B. Lester right in the eyes. Told him about my dad and Krone. The
only thing I didn't tell him was that I shared my dad's name, but I
imagined saying it: "I, too, am Dan Hyde."

After I spoke he regarded me for a moment, and then he said, "Is that right?"

I gave him a confirming nod.

He coughed into his fist. "Excuse me," he said, looking at me, and he lodged himself inside the police cruiser with the door cracked. We heard static and intermittent voices on his police radio, and then his mouthpiece chirped and he spoke into it with his head turned for privacy, his tone serious, making sure we couldn't hear. He hung the hand piece back on his dashboard.

For five minutes or more, he didn't speak or move. He sat and stared off toward the horizon, letting out a few lackluster sighs.

His police radio lit up and shot out noises and he answered it. I could barely see his profile; his mouth was set in a firm line. This time he let us hear him say "Yes, sir," nodding, "Yes, sir," and one final "Yes, sir," and then he hung up the hand piece again.

Without a word, he stood before us, the sun silhouetting him, his shadow crossing my legs. He seemed to be contemplating us. He ran a hand through his hair, sighed.

"Well, boys," he said, "today is your lucky day, because I've decided to cut you a break and let this go with a verbal warning."

To my embarrassment, Ace and Ice slammed their hands together in a high five, saying "Yes!" as if at a football game.

But B. Lester didn't look at them, and he didn't seem to care, his gaze firmly on me. A direct, pitiless stare, and along with relief, something like shame wrenched deep in my chest.

6.

THE FOLLOWING SATURDAY at Mom's in Cucamonga, I stayed up late with her watching *Caddyshack*, one of her favorite movies. She wore a nightgown and a robe. I sat back on the couch and looked at her pink feet propped on the coffee table next to her mug of white wine, the calluses on her heels and toes from her walking group and the faint veins beneath the skin on her ankles. "We used to be a team, your dad and me," she said, apropos of nothing. "We shared this small apartment in Fullerton for three hundred a month. I worked, he worked. I cooked spaghetti on Tuesdays, his favorite. Forget about portfolios and investments and lawyers: We didn't even have a credit card!"

"Mom," I said, "I can't hear the movie."

"Sorry," she said. But she kept right on talking. "He used to tell me," she said, reaching for the remote, "that I couldn't shake my middle-class practicality. What does that mean? If I'd been able to get a personal trainer, some plastic surgery, a bunch of clothes, some fancy car that I didn't need, that would've been better?"

"Mom," I said. "Please."

She paused the movie and repositioned herself on the couch so that she faced me. After she took a deep breath, she said, "I want to apologize," and then added, "I need to apologize." Her pastor, she explained, had begun a program to help church members inventory their lives. She hadn't been the best mother, she said, in ways fundamental to the development of children. "You need to build up your kids," she said, "not tear them down," and I could hear her pastor saying those exact words to her.

The pit of my stomach whirled, remembering how she used to call me Dr. Strangelove. One night she reprimanded me for taking the skin off my chicken at dinner—"That's the best part!"—alerting me to its existence. I must've been around six. After that I couldn't eat anything that had once had skin. So I became Dr. Strangelove.

"Not a big deal, Mom," I said. I didn't really want to think about it, much less talk about it.

Her quizzical gaze sought atonement.

"Okay," I said. "It's okay. I forgive you."

"Good," she said. She reached for the remote and unpaused the movie.

After a few minutes, she went to her bedroom and returned with a hairy-looking afghan. She sat next to me on the couch and spread the afghan over our legs. Her hand reached for mine. I held her hand until our palms got sweaty, and then I broke free. Something in the way she kept glancing from the TV screen to me made me feel like a kid again.

Gabe wasn't home yet from hanging out with Kevin and some others, and so she began to worry. Every fifteen minutes or so, she'd try his cell phone again. Her leg kept jiggling under the afghan. She looked old. Up close, I saw that her eyelids sagged.

"Well," she said, "this has been so hard. All of it. It's been hard on everyone, but especially Gabe."

After the movie ended, I went to bed, kissing her good night on the cheek. "Get some sleep," I said. "Don't worry."

In those days, despite my occasional bouts of insomnia, I could sleep fourteen hours easy, and I liked sleeping in my childhood bed—the shadows, smells, everything known and familiar in a deep sense.

I woke at around two in the morning to Mom shaking me lightly by the shoulders, whispering, "Even. Even, wake up."

Gabe wasn't back yet, and she was upset.

I made her turn around—I wore only boxers because she kept it so hot in the house, and yet still I sweated—and I put on my jeans and shirt.

"Wait here," I told her. "I'll find him."

Earlier I'd heard Gabe talking on his cell phone about meeting at the playground, and I planned to look there first. He kept his cell in his front pocket, and I tried to call him a few times before I left, imagining the phone vibrating and ringing in his jeans, but it just went to his voice mail.

I took my ten-speed bicycle from the garage and started pedaling around my old neighborhood. It felt good to be outside in the cool air.

I circled the playground—in the dark it had a menacing feel, the deserted swings and merry-go-round creaking slightly in the breeze—and then I stopped near the swings, kickstanding my bike. Gabe and I used to play here. Gabe claimed to have saved my life on this playground, and I suppose he had.

One afternoon when we were kids, I had climbed to the peak of the jungle gym and fell. Gabe, on the partition below, grabbed my arm and slowed my fall, perhaps preventing a snapped neck or concussion. He went down with me because he didn't let go.

While I have no memory of the incident, we both have visible scars, mine on my hairline from where I hit my head, his on his arm from where he scraped against a protruding rivet on his way down. Because of the fall, the city installed a rubber cushion as flooring and sanded the rivets.

I listened to the breeze shaking the tree leaves. A car drove past, its headlights lighting up the jungle gym, creating elongated shadows, and then shrinking back to dark.

Before leaving, I pulled my cell phone from my pocket and speed-dialed Gabe.

To my surprise, I heard his ringtone in the distance, the thumping, tinny-sounding beginnings of "Area Codes" by Ludacris. "I've got hoes. I've got hoes, in different area codes, area, area codes. Hoes, hoes, in different area codes, area, area codes, codes." The song had been popular the year before, but Gabe still loved it.

He didn't answer and the phone went to voice mail. I called once more, following the music to the base of the jungle gym, to a cave-like opening for the largest of the slides, which was in the shape of a huge green snake—as kids it had frightened us, the opening of its mouth. The ringtone echoed inside, and when I looked, I saw the ridged soles of Gabe's Nikes.

I crawled through, leaning forward and pulling him by his calves, sliding him out. He snored and his breath reeked of pot and tequila.

"Gabe," I said, smacking him on the cheek. "Gabe, wake up."

He twisted, woke with a start, and sat up. "Faaack," he said.

I gave him room to regain his composure. It took him a few head-shaking and throat-clearing minutes. Then he squinted at me and said, "Even, what're you doing here?"

"Finding you," I said. "Mom's worried."

He shook his head, a hand on his forehead.

"They left you?" I asked.

He shrugged.

"Not cool," I said. With a rush of gratitude, I thought about Mike. "What kind of friends do that?"

"Do what?" he said, holding his head.

"Leave you passed out in a playground, shoved inside a slide?"

He didn't answer.

We rode double on my ten-speed, Gabe sitting on the bike seat, me standing and pedaling. He put his hands on my waist to steady himself. We took a long detour to a gas station, buying mint gum to camouflage Gabe's breath.

But by the time we got home, Mom had taken a couple of Xanax—the bottle was on the coffee table—and she was sleeping on the couch, her hands folded on her stomach, the afghan slipped to the floor.

7.

THE NEXT WEEK, Gabe called. "Is Dad there?" he asked. "He's not answering at his office." His tone alarmed me. But more than that, we've always had a shorthand receptivity, whereby we both can tell when the other is in trouble.

I sat in one of the dining room chairs near the kitchen. I had just woken to the phone ringing, wearing my boxers and an undershirt, at about eleven thirty on a Tuesday morning.

The night before, I had pretended to be sick—coughing, complaining about a stomachache, spending noticeable extended amounts of time in the bathroom, where I both masturbated and read books—and Dad, a school fanatic, probably because he'd been a high school dropout, let me sleep late and stay home.

"Not sure," I said.

"Find out!"

"He's not," I said, fingering the note he'd left on the dining room table: *Golf with K. Home later.* "He's golfing with Krone and his buddies. I just found his note."

Gabe groaned and then breathed into the phone. We both knew that Dad turned his cell phone off when he golfed. It was the only time he did so, saying that it was his "church time." Church time could last multiple hours, depending on whether he played eighteen holes.

"What is it?" I asked.

"I've been arrested."

A tingling ran up my neck.

"Public intoxication," he said. "I'm at the Cucamonga police station."

"Oh, shit."

"I don't have my clothes."

"Why not? What are you wearing?"

"They gave me this scratchy jumpsuit. It's really big on me."

In the long silence that followed, I could hear a gardener's leaf blower in the distance, Gabe's breathing, and the busy chattering noises of the police station in the background. From the window, a beam of sunlight made the flecks sparkle in the kitchen tiles. I'd detected a note of belligerence in Gabe's tone and wondered if he was still drunk.

"What happened?" I asked, perching the phone in the crook of my shoulder, so that I could pour myself a glass of orange juice from the refrigerator. When I'm scared, I get thirsty.

"I can't call Mom," he said.

"Gabe, what happened?"

He didn't tell me, but I found out later from the police report that he was arrested at Ralph's grocery store near his high school. On a dare, he slid down the aisle in his socks and boxers, his friends recording him on his Samsung camcorder—the same video camera that would get us in so much trouble later. Dad gave it to

Gabe for his twelfth birthday. Gabe used it to record his and his friends' skateboarding feats.

His friends ran away before the cops arrived, taking Gabe's clothes with them. Even so, Gabe refused to rat them out. Because Gabe fell and hit his head on the edge of the shelf and, I imagine, because he was drunk and slow, the cops caught him.

"What should I do? Can you call the clubhouse?"

"That won't work," I said.

"Yeah," he admitted.

"Listen," I said, "here's what you do." I told him about my encounter at the beach with the cop B. Lester, and how once I'd mentioned Dad's name and his connection to Sheriff Krone, B. Lester dropped the charges and let me go. I hadn't told anyone about the experience, and it was strange to hear myself speak about it.

Dad's influence, I told him, and Krone's, extended to Cucamonga. "Let them know about Dad." I said. "It's our Get Out of Jail Free card."

After a strained and confusing silence, he said, "You're kidding, right?"

"No. I'm not."

"The problem," he said, "is that I'm not a coward. I don't hide behind my daddy."

I was shocked. "You're drunk," I said.

"Maybe," he said.

"Now's not the best time," I suggested, "for you to be a self-righteous prick."

But he wasn't up for an argument. "I can't do it," he said in a hushed, sad voice. "I can't. It's so hypocritical. I can't."

"I don't know why not," I said. It bothered me to think that Gabe was more principled than me. "You don't even know what the word 'hypocritical' means."

"That's right," he said, his voice full of hurt sarcasm. "Because I'm not smart like you."

I didn't say anything.

"Even and his books," he added.

"Sorry," I said. I didn't want to encourage him. No one could tease me or poke fun at me like he could.

"I just can't," he said.

"You're calling him for help. Isn't that the same thing?"

He moaned.

I took another sip of my orange juice—too pulpy. I couldn't drink it anymore or even look at it. Cradling the phone again, I took the glass to the sink and poured it out. These dramatic changes in my taste preferences happened all the time during my teens. My favorite foods would unexpectedly disgust me, as if I'd become a different person overnight.

"I don't want that kind of help," he said. "I don't want to use his name."

"It's the same thing," I lied, filling another glass with water. "Help is help. There's no difference. You can't pick and choose."

"Dad wouldn't do that," he said.

"Huh?"

"Dad would hate someone who did that. Used him like that. He wouldn't do it. I want to be my own man. Dad would understand."

"Not true," I said, but he got me wondering. "Dad," I continued, speaking slowly, "does whatever he has to do."

He said nothing.

"Help is help," I said. "It's the same thing. Tell them who Dad is. Let them know." As I spoke, I remembered B. Lester's contemptuous look, and I felt a swirl of self-disgust.

"My head's bleeding," he said, changing the subject. "This nice lady cop gave me a towel."

"Do you need stitches?"

"Probably."

"Does it hurt?"

"Yeah."

"How'd you cut it?"

"I don't know. I fell?"

"You've got to tell them about Dad."

He was quiet.

"We've got to get you out of there. Think about Mom."

"No," he said. He paused, and then added, "It's different for you."

"What do you mean?"

"I mean," he said, "it's different."

"Why?"

"You're close to him."

I laughed. "He's your dad, too," I said, and as I spoke, I remembered telling him this before.

"Not really," he said, in that same sad, hushed tone. A long pause. "Listen," he said, "I'm gonna hang up now. There's nothing you can do to help me anyway."

"Gabe, don't be stupid."

A click—he hung up on me.

I didn't call our mom, deciding to wait for Dad. When he came home at around four, I apprised him of the situation. All business, he made three phone calls in his study. I watched through the crack in his door, but I couldn't hear him. He wore golf shorts and ankle socks, and his legs were skinny and bowed. I was unaccustomed to seeing his leg hairs, the same reddish-gold-gray as his head hair, and I noticed a few bruises on his shin. He tapped his cigarette in an ashtray and then left it smoldering there, forgotten.

As a kid, when I watched him work, his every movement—the way he crossed his legs, held his pen, shuffled his papers—seemed to me to be so smart, deliberate, and important.

Done with the phone calls, he came back to the dining room table and sat beside me. He took his glasses off and rubbed his eyes, his face pink. Then he put them back on. "They've released him," he said. "We've got a court date in three weeks."

"What's going to happen?" I asked.

He set his hands on the table. "He's going to show the judge what a good boy he is," he said. "Show him a list of all the AA meetings he'll be going to, offer to do Caltrans work, pick up trash at the side of the freeway, whatever it takes. At best he'll get this expunged from his record. No one will know the difference. At the very worst, they'll reduce it to a 415 infraction for disturbing the peace. Either way, he'll be fine."

He lit up a cigarette. A long silence while I watched him smoke.

"I told him to use your name," I said.

He looked surprised. "What do you mean?"

Another long silence. He stared at me, reaching to tap his ash into his abalone-shell ashtray. He'd gotten it as a souvenir from a trip to Catalina.

With a sinking feeling, I said, "I told him to let them know who you are, and your connection to Krone."

He shifted in his chair. Then he shrugged. "If I'd gotten to him sooner," he said, "they wouldn't have booked him."

"So that's okay?" I asked. "I mean, what I told him to do?"

"If you think so, by all means, yes," he said sharply. He gave me a heavy-lidded, deep look.

"Gabe said that you wouldn't approve."

He didn't say anything for a moment. Then he pulled the ashtray closer and said, "I can't figure that boy out. He needs to use his head. Krone does what I want and that's the whole point."

8.

GABE CONVINCED ME to go with him to his first AA meeting in Newport that weekend. Dad had a schedule directory, and he gave Gabe a slip of paper that his lawyer had created with ten separate corresponding lines for the dates, names, and addresses of the meetings and the signatures of the meetings' secretaries.

"When they pass the basket," Dad instructed, "put this in"—he waved the slip in front of Gabe's nose—"along with a dollar if you want. You don't have to give any money, but you do have to put this in. Then after the meeting, someone will sign it and give it back to you. That's their trick. They make you wait until the end of the meeting, so that you won't leave. But that's all you have to do. You don't have to speak or do anything else. Just get it done. Ten meetings in three weeks should be more than enough."

"No way," Gabe said. "Not ten. Maybe one or two."

"Just go," said Dad.

We chose a Saturday noon meeting—The Serenity Noon-Timers, it said in the directory—at what was called an Alano Clubhouse, a building within walking distance of Dad's house, near a shopping center.

I'd noticed the building before, and that a throng of people seemed to be constantly smoking near it, but hadn't known what it was, or what the small wooden sign on the front—a circle with a triangle inside—meant. An American flag hung from one of the windows, which wasn't unusual, since it had been only a little over a year since the September 11 terrorist attacks and there were still American flags everywhere.

From the outside, it looked like a typical run-down building. The meeting room downstairs had the feel of a small cafeteria, and there was a meeting room upstairs next to a room with a shabby pool table and a bar area that sold sodas, candy, and chips.

The stairway smelled of cigarettes and mold. "This is ridiculous," Gabe muttered, as I followed him. Though he looked okay, he gave off a faint odor of alcohol. He'd been partying into the morning with his friends in the garage.

While Gabe waited, sullen and silent against a wall, I bought a pack of Trident gum at the bar. A TV propped up in a corner showed George W. Bush standing near a group of politicians, smiling and waving, looking like a frat boy, and a zigzag of static worked its way up and down the screen.

A haggard bleached blond took my money, and after I thanked her, she said, "Aren't you a sweetheart. So polite!"

Thinking that it would make us less conspicuous, Gabe and I decided to sit apart from each other in the long, dark room—the chairs were arranged in an oval with a couple of gray couches intermixed—and took great pains not to look in each other's direction.

I sat near a pink box of doughnuts, a plate of sliced honeydew melon, and a coffee maker that made regular hissing-sputtering noises until it finished brewing and then, giving one final heave, went silent.

A man wearing a noisy windbreaker sat in the foldout chair next to me; he was albino-like, with white-blond hair, nearly without eyebrows and eyelashes. We gave each other acknowledging nods, and then he used his thumbnail to create a ridged pattern along the rim of his Styrofoam cup. The squeaky noise bothered me.

But I didn't move, because a girl who sat across from me—her hair thick and reddish-brown, and her skin a creamy tan color— entranced me, and I had a good vantage point. Double take beautiful. She looked hungover, mustering the occasional pained expression and contemptuous glare. She didn't even pretend to want to be there. She wore cutoff jeans, a tank top, and a leather choker studded with cowry shells. She couldn't have been more than twenty, and she was all attitude, bored smiles, and heavy-lidded eyes. I did my best not to stare.

People kept coming into the meeting long after it started, until the chairs and couches were filled, and people sat at the floor, their backs leaning against the couches and walls. Body-builder types, old and young people, businessmen, fake-breasted women, hipsters, freaky-quiet types, chattering attention seekers, and everything in between.

After some boring, God-centric readings, the sharing began, and hands were raised. Lots of boisterous laughter throughout. Some told crazy and harrowing stories about drinking and drug using, others sounded off about sobriety, and then a young woman began to sob while she spoke about her dead grandmother, but no one stopped her or comforted her.

I hadn't witnessed a person so openly expressing emotion before without reprimand or embarrassment. I looked around the room, and most people seemed unfazed, even empathetic.

A wad of Kleenex got passed—it came to me and I passed it to the next person—until it landed in the woman's lap.

"Thank you so much," she said, looking up and around at all of us with wet and grateful eyes, and then she blew her nose. It was difficult not to be moved.

After a ten-minute break during which both Gabe and I continued to ignore each other and everyone else, the meeting resumed. The secretary asked which of us were newcomers and a couple of people looked pointedly at me. But otherwise no one bothered me.

A middle-aged woman whom the secretary called "the chip chick" tried to distribute plastic chips to people, calling out the number of days of sobriety (thirty, sixty, ninety)—with a long, anticipatory pause, as if she were at a game of bingo—but no one took one.

Then we sang "Happy Birthday" to an old man with a cane who claimed to have four years without drinking. He looked drunk to me, and he sounded drunk, slurring his words as he spoke his thanks, but everyone clapped and hooted for him anyway.

After that, the meeting became somewhat more serious, though people continued to laugh. They talked of loss and pain and shame.

At one point, a man who looked not much older than me said that though he loved his family, he'd never felt like he belonged. "Maybe it's not them, and it's not their fault," he said. "Maybe it's me." My face heated up and my eyes stung; I felt a lump in my throat.

I stole a glance at Gabe. His head was thrown back, his mouth was agape, and he was sleeping, his hand with the slip of paper at his knee.

A basket got passed, and I watched as the two people on either side of Gabe leaned forward to bypass him and let him sleep, passing the basket over his legs.

The meeting ended with everyone rising and forming a circle and, to my horror, holding hands. The last time I remembered holding hands with a person of my own sex (besides Gabe, when we were kids) was on a kindergarten field trip.

Styrofoam-cup thumb-etching albino man reached his hand out and I took it, sweaty palmed, same with the woman in the nurse uniform on my other side.

Gabe startled awake and looked equally horrified as he realized he had to hold hands with the people next to him. Then everyone recited the Lord's Prayer.

My face hot and downcast, I kept silent. This is bullshit, I wanted to say. Having to recite an openly Christian, threatening prayer—deliver us from evil, or else. Death and temptation and trespasses. No, thank you.

I'd been looking for something specific to hate—probably because of my earlier throat-lumping identification—and felt relieved to have found it, relishing the moment.

As people shuffled out of the meeting room, Gabe's eyes met mine in confusion and wonderment. I crossed the room to him and he said, "Fuck, I fell asleep, didn't get my paper signed. Dad's gonna be pissed."

"Calm down," I said, taking the paper from him.

The girl whom I'd been staring at during the meeting looked at us. She was standing near the doorway. I saw that a bit of skin showed between her tank top and her cutoffs. Her head tilted up, acknowledging us. "You on a court card?" she said, her voice deeper than I expected.

"Yes," I lied. "Forgot to get it signed."

She laughed. "Your first meeting?"

"Uh-huh," I said.

"What about you?" she asked Gabe.

He said nothing, didn't even look at her.

But she didn't let his rudeness faze her.

"C'mon," she said distractedly, hooking me by the arm, guiding me to the other room, where a group of men were talking by the pool table. She smelled like vanilla. Tapping one of them on the shoulder, she said, "Hey."

He turned, smiled, and said, "Hey, baby." Somewhere in his thirties, he wore khakis and a faded peach-colored polo shirt.

She nodded at me, saying, "Forgot to get his card signed."

"Not a problem," he said, taking the slip from me. He leaned over the pool table, pulling a pen from his pocket, and while signing the paper he said, "What'd you do last night?"

"Not much," she said.

"You don't look so good," he said, looking up at her.

"Long Island iced teas," she said.

"Don't you know," he said, handing me the slip, "that something bad always happens with Long Island iced teas?" His eyes grazed past me—"What are you, like, in fifth grade?"—and landed back on her.

"Long Island iced teas," one of the other men chimed in, "make me want to fight."

"Me, too," she said.

"Girl fight," another man said encouragingly.

"Or wreck my car," said the former.

"What happened last night?" the paper-signer asked.

She shrugged. "It's none of your fucking business."

The paper-signer said, "What happened to your arm?"

She outstretched her arm and looked at the three intertwined scratches.

"Cat?" he asked.

"I don't have a cat."

"Self-mutilation?" said another, in a tone suggesting he was trying to be helpful.

"I have to go," she said listlessly, pulling me away.

"Okay, Sara," said the paper-signer. "Will you be at the meeting tomorrow?"

"Yeah," she said, not turning around.

I tried to thank her as we walked back to Gabe but she said, "Not a big deal," and then she smiled. "See you around," she said, and she turned and left before Gabe had the chance to be an asshole again.

LATER THAT AFTERNOON, Dad rattled the ice in his cocktail while we told him about the meeting, and Gabe showed him the signature on his slip.

"Good," Dad said, reclining on a chaise near the pool. He took a sip from his glass, his hair toweled into a spindly Mohawk from his swim. He wore his terry-cloth bathrobe; in his hip pocket were the TV remote and his cell phone.

Gabe and I sat in deck chairs.

"I don't want to go back," Gabe said, leaning forward in his chair.

"It's not that bad," I said, musing out loud. "It's interesting, especially in a sociological way." I remembered Sara hooking my arm and her vanilla smell. "Except for all that God stuff and praying."

Gabe gave me a contemptuous look. "And the holding hands," he reminded me.

"Yeah," I said. "Awful."

"Why can't I just make up signatures for the secretaries?" Gabe asked. "I've got the directory. I can add all the details and then have my friends sign. They probably don't check."

"Not smart," Dad said.

"Yeah, I know," Gabe said.

Dad rattled his drink some more, staring at us. A patio umbrella cut the sun in half and shadowed his upper torso, leaving his hips and legs in the light.

"Listen," he said, looking at us fiercely, "I'm not going to spell it out. You need to go to the meetings." He waved his hand, shooing us away.

We went into the kitchen and Gabe paced a bit. Then he stopped and looked at me, his face lighting up with a revelation.

"I've got it," he said. He put his hands on my shoulders and went on to elaborate a plan whereby he'd pay me to go to the meetings and pretend to be him, until I got ten signatures.

I agreed, not because I necessarily cared about the meetings or the money, but because I wanted to see Sara again, and I believed that I'd find her, since she'd told the paper-signer that she'd be back.

We negotiated. Twenty-five dollars a meeting times nine. Not a bad deal. Dad must've known, though he didn't say anything.

I ended up going to more than nine meetings, filling in the back of the slip with the extras. (I started going with Sara.) But Gabe refused to pay me for those, since it hadn't been part of our agreement, even though I insisted it would impress the judge.

Ironically, by the time of his court date, Gabe didn't need proof of the AA meetings. Dad's lawyer used Gabe's head injury as evidence, claiming Gabe hadn't been properly treated at the police station—besides a towel from a cop to halt the bleeding—and that he should have been taken to the hospital, since his cut had ended up requiring three stitches. Dad's lawyer submitted paperwork from two doctors attesting to the severity of the injury and the risk of concussion. All bluster: Gabe hadn't suffered a bit, but the lawyer claimed he'd convalesced for days after, and had experienced dizziness. Rather than risk the threat of a lawsuit, the judge decided that it would be in everyone's best interest to dismiss the charges.

Gabe, in celebration, struck a match to light the edge of the paper listing all my meetings. We watched the spark curl the slip into a blue and yellow flame, until it blackened into ash in Dad's abalone ashtray.

9.

S ARA SAT IN front of me, wearing that same choker with the shells and a different tank top.

I stared at the back of her neck—her hair was in a sloppy bun like she'd tied it in a knot—until I got the courage to tap her arm and say hello.

She turned halfway. "Oh," she said, "it's you." Drunk—I could tell by the way she spoke, her words heavy in her mouth. She patted the space on the church pew next to her. "C'mon," she said. "Sit with me."

She slumped in the pew during the meeting and rested her head on my shoulder.

The speaker, Tom L., a retired policeman, spoke in a deliberate voice. Large but not fat, with a weary demeanor, he wore a rumpled, dark blue suit with a striped tie.

I wish I could remember exactly what he said that night, and why it impressed me so much.

But what I remember is that at one point he said, "Now that I'm retired, I can help people who come to me with troubles, whether it be with the law or something else. So if someone needs my help, you can reach me easy. I get letters and things forwarded to me from the police department, care of Tom L. I'm retired, sure, but they let me keep a postbox. Or just come find me and talk to me. Like this guy"—he gestured to a man in the front pew—"was going through it, and he came to me and he said, 'Jesus, Tom, I don't know what to do,' and I said to him, 'Well, first off, tell me what you did.' So he did, and we figured it out together. He served, what was it?"

The man called out, "Three days."

"That's right. Three days of incarceration for a clear conscience and peace of mind. Was it worth it?"

The man nodded vigorously.

After the meeting, I waited while Sara smoked a cigarette underneath a streetlight that gave off a dirty orange glow. The other smokers congregated near the parking lot, using a couple of dirt-filled coffee cans as ashtrays.

"Aren't you cold?" I asked, since she was wearing cutoffs and a tank top, and the temperature was dropping.

She gave a little shiver in answer.

After she smoked the cigarette about halfway down, she said something I couldn't hear.

"What?" I asked, moving closer.

"I said," she said, "can I borrow some money?"

"How much?"

She looked to the sky as if calculating. "Five hundred," she concluded. I must've looked shocked, because she said, "Kidding. How about a twenty?"

"I only have a ten," I said.

She sighed. "Fine," she said. "I'll take it."

I pulled my wallet from my back pocket and gave it to her. She took the ten out, handed the wallet back to me, and to my surprise, she politely thanked me and said that she would pay me back.

"Don't worry about it."

"No," she said. "I will."

She dropped her cigarette and ground it out with her flip-flop, and then she began to fumble inside her purse, looking for something. She started walking away from me, still rooting in her purse, and then she found it: her keys. They jangled in her hand.

"Wait," I said.

She stopped but didn't turn.

"I'll drive," I suggested, even though I didn't have my driver's permit on me. I didn't want her to drive drunk, but I knew it wouldn't work to call her on it.

With her back to me, she extended her arm; the keys dangled from her hand. I came forward and took them from her—a brass heart keychain. We started walking toward the parking lot.

"What's your name?" she asked.

I told her.

"You're shitting me," she said. "What kind of name's that?" And then she added, "That's not the name on that paper you get signed."

"It's my brother's," I said. It came out before I thought to lie.

We came to an old, faded blue Toyota Tercel with a dented back bumper, and she said, "It's not locked." The driver door creaked open and I sat. She got in on the passenger side. It smelled like cigarettes and vanilla.

After adjusting the seat and mirrors, I tried to act like I knew what I was doing, turning the key in the ignition and revving the engine, relieved it wasn't a stick shift. Gabe and Dad had taken me driving in parking lots and the streets around Dad's house, but I was still nervous.

She stared at me. The car jerked into reverse, and she said, "Whoa!"

"Sorry," I said, smoothing into drive.

I drove slowly, hunched forward in my seat, peering at the road.

"You look like a grandpa!" she said, and then she patted me on the shoulder and said, "Hi, Grandpa!"

We stopped at a Del Taco drive-thru, and she ordered a couple of tacos, fries, and a burrito.

"We'll share," she said, removing my ten from her wallet and handing it to me to pay the cashier. "My treat, Even."

We pulled out of the parking lot. "Turn right at the signal," she said, sorting through the bag of food, not looking at the road, "then left at the next signal."

I followed her directions to her apartment complex in Costa Mesa—THE KON-TIKI, the sign said. While I drove, she ate. "Sorry," she said, between chews, "I can't wait. I'm so hungry."

"I don't mind."

"Park here," she said, the parking lot one straight strip with no place to turn around, and I pulled into her carport.

We stared at each other in the dark, and she said, "How're you going to get home?"

"I don't know," I said. "I hadn't thought about it."

"You might as well come inside and eat," she said, and then she told me that I could sleep on her couch if I wanted. Immediately, I took this as a proposition and felt a stiffening inside my jeans.

We walked through the complex: At its center was a gated pool with a strong chlorine smell, lit up and aqua-colored, wavering with shadows.

Once we were inside her apartment, she switched on a standing lamp and offered me a 7-Up. She set our bag of food on the coffee table and then went to the kitchen for our sodas. I sat on the couch and waited for her.

The apartment was made up of a kitchen and living room combination and a bedroom and bathroom, with pale, blank walls, minimal furniture, and an old TV. Lonely and bare.

"I just moved," she said. "Haven't decorated much."

She sat next to me on her couch and we ate and drank our sodas, the lamplight yellowish and warm. After we finished eating, she didn't speak and took sips from her can. She crossed one leg over the other, and I started imagining scenarios: her brushing against me, then leaning farther into me, and my seizing the opportunity, our age difference obliterated by my skills as a lover. Handling her with expertise and executing our pathway to her bedroom.

I stifled a burp from the carbonation and set my soda on the table.

With all my nerve, I hazarded a full look at her. I'd thought she had brown eyes, but now I saw the green in them, and the little V of a divot on her upper lip just about killed me.

Oblivious, she lit a cigarette, not more than a foot away. I could barely hear the thumping bass from a neighbor's stereo filtering through the walls: Missy Elliott's "Get Ur Freak On."

"Sara?" I said.

She glanced at me, distracted.

"Can I sleep in the bed with you?"

I expected her to be surprised or upset, but her expression hardly changed. She shifted and faced me. "How old are you, Even?"

"I'm almost sixteen." A lie—I had a ways to go until my birthday.

She was silent for a moment. Then she said, "I'm nineteen, Even. I know I look younger, but I'm not."

Though she'd just lit it, she stubbed her cigarette into a half-eaten taco in its paper wrapper. "I may be a drunk," she said, "but I'm not a slut."

"I would never think that," I said. "That's not what I meant."

"Is that right?" she said.

I stared at her and didn't say anything.

"So," she said, her gaze steady and intense, "all you want to do is fuck me?"

"Oh, no," I said, my face heating, sweat in my armpits, "you have the wrong idea. I really like you. I think you're so pretty"— and then I shut up.

I was trying to decide how to leave discreetly when, to my surprise, she leaned her head back on the couch and laughed.

"Good for you," she said, looking up at the ceiling, "good effort."

"I should leave," I said.

"Nah," she said, stretching her arms. She yawned, rubbed her eyes. "Don't go."

She rose and motioned with her hands at me. "Up, up," she said encouragingly. Once I stood, she flipped the sofa cushions off. "Help me," she said, and we yanked at the couch. It creaked open, we stepped back, and it clanked down to become a bed.

I called my dad from my cell phone—just in case he might worry—and left a message, letting him know that I was spending the night at a friend's.

One might assume that my forwardness with Sara would have stunted the possibility of a friendship between us. But oddly, Sara appreciated me for it, as if we'd cleared up any misperceptions and defused the awkwardness of my being sexually attracted to her.

After that night, she spoke to me openly, and we went to meetings together. We got to be close friends.

She worked at an insurance company. Her day life was boring, routine-filled, and efficient. Mexican mother, Irish and German father, no siblings. A horrific home life. She'd left at sixteen, had been on her own since. Independent, tough, and practical.

I could go on and on about Sara. She's really beautiful and strong. She got sober eventually, and she's the one who helped me, for good and for bad, to do what I had to do.

PART TWO

10.

JULY 3, 2003

T HOUGH I'VE BEEN able to recount what happened so far, the events over the Fourth of July weekend are difficult for me to narrate. Nearly impossible. A jumble of images.

Tove Kagan, a girl I knew from Cucamonga, arrived at our dad's house with Crystal Douglas and another girl, Melissa Stroh, at around four in the afternoon on July 3. Tove pretended not to know me. I wasn't that surprised. She ignored me, since I'd left for Newport without saying good-bye to her. In grade school, we'd been good friends. We had history, Tove and I. Gabe didn't know; the others didn't know. Only Tove and I knew, and that was how we kept it. Both of us were sophomores now, sixteen and driving, her little red Dodge Dart parked at our curb. Her eyes brushed right past me, and then she walked to the other side of the pool to a cooler of beer hidden behind a large planter.

In retrospect we didn't know what to say or how to cross that divide from our past into the present: The startling immediacy was too much. So we did what we had to do, and I'll regret it for the rest of my life.

"I'm a Pisces," Melissa said to me. Blond hair and tan body, red bathing suit, bikini ties visible under her white top. The kind of girl who used to be indifferent to me when I lived in Cucamonga. Half-reclined next to me on a chaise beside the pool. More like shouting over the rap music—"I'm a Pisces. Like, we're the type of girls who support our men. We don't need attention. Like, we're vulnerable and kind, but strong. I guess I just, like, understand myself because of astrology. I have a strong sense of myself. It really makes sense if you study it. It's true! Don't laugh! It really works."

She was paying attention to me because of my dad's money. Trying to hit on me. I'd overheard her earlier joking—"Maybe one of us will get pregnant by a Hyde and then we'll be rich. I wouldn't, like, mind living in this house."

Tove arrived in her brown work shirt and black slacks, and I heard her explaining that she hostessed at the Marie Callender's restaurant in Cucamonga, "mostly guiding sweet old people with canes and walkers to their tables." She looked the same, except that she'd highlighted her long brown hair with gold streaks, and she had a woman's body now, not the beginnings of a woman's body, like the last time I'd seen her, in the seventh grade. Holding a beer, talking with Gabe and Crystal, she favored one leg.

"Tove's a good liar," Melissa said, noticing me watching her, trying to keep my attention. "She's a Gemini, and they're the worst. That's, like, the worst sign for a girl, because it means she's manipulative and rude and stuck up."

The Tove I knew had not been any of those things. But I didn't want to argue about astrological signs, so I encouraged Melissa to return to the first subject—"Why do you say that she's a good liar?" I held my hand up to pause her answer, shifted in my chaise, and shouted to Gabe, "Turn it down!"

His head lifted in acknowledgment, and I watched him walk through the open sliding glass doors to the stereo inside the living room and turn the volume down.

I resettled myself on the chaise and nodded for Melissa to proceed.

"She, like, pretends to be her mom on the phone"—she switched to an authoritative voice—"Hello, Mrs. Stroh, this is Tove's mother. Hum, she, like, has my permission to sleep over tonight."

She paused, waiting for my encouragement.

I gave her a smile and a laugh, wanting to hear more.

"I can't even do it," she said. "But Tove, she's, like, really scary-good at impersonating voices and stuff like that, like handwriting. She's really good at making notes and signing parent signatures." She paused and watched Tove and the others for a moment.

The sun inched out from behind the patio umbrella, and I squinted at Melissa while readjusting myself on my chaise. Fully shaded again, I took a sip from my Budweiser.

"She lies all the time," she said, still watching them, pensive. "This one time, she said she knew Eminem. Said they were good friends, told everyone. Lie! And this other time she said that she's a model. Said that her parents told her not to tell anyone, but that her photographs are all over Europe and China. Lie!"

She looked at me, her eyes widening as if in confidential warning. "If I were you, I'd stay away from her."

"Why?" I asked. "It's not that big of a deal."

She shook her head. "It's more than that," she said. "She's, like, really smart"—she reached for her Diet Coke can. She and Crystal weren't drinking alcohol. Earlier, I'd heard them telling Gabe that they were on a diet that prohibited it. "Gets straight A's and doesn't even study! It's not fair. But she's smart *and* she's crazy."

She took a sip, her eyes watching me over her can.

"What do you mean?"

She sighed and set her Diet Coke on the cement. "She parties and drinks and, like, screws all the time. Don't look at me like that! I'm not kidding. She's a slut! You don't know, because you live here, but, like, everyone in Cucamonga knows."

"Aren't you supposed to be her friend?" I asked.

She seemed to consider my question seriously. "Not really," she said. After a pause, she added, "We, like, party together, but that's about it. She's always been really, really, really"—she paused again, grimacing, as if searching for the right word— "weird," she said at last. She didn't say it meanly, but in a philosophical way.

She nodded toward one of Gabe's friends, whom I hadn't met before, a guy named Kent Nixon. Tall, athletic, angular facial features, humorless, tough, on the football team with Kevin Stewart. I thought of them after, and still do, as the Ks.

"She, like, thinks that's her boyfriend," she said. "But he doesn't even like her. He had sex with her in her car last week, right in front of his house. He told me. She brags about giving him road head. She doesn't know they make fun of her. They all think she's a slut. No one wants to be her boyfriend."

I took another sip of my Budweiser and watched Tove. Her head was back in a laugh, and then it moved forward and she gave us a sideways glance with a glimmer of antagonism.

"Does he know," I asked, "that she thinks he's her boyfriend?"

She shrugged. "He doesn't care what she thinks," she said.

LATER, AFTER MIKE arrived and after the sun went down, Gabe and his group of friends left for the garage to play pool.

Mike and I stayed and drank a few beers, swam a little, since the party we'd decided to go to didn't start until nine (varsity girls' volleyball team; the party started when they came back from an away summer practice game), and we had time to kill before it.

Dad came home, turned off the stereo, stuck his head out the open sliding glass doors, and asked if everything was okay. He and Nancy had been at some fund-raising barbecue with Krone and his buddies.

"Yep," I called back. Mike and I were in the Jacuzzi, the water bubbling. The bridge of Mike's nose was peeling from a sunburn, and he kept picking at it.

Behind Dad I saw Nancy leaning over, standing, moving around purposefully as she cleaned, throwing away cans and empty potato chip bags. Just seeing her set off my memory-smell of her perfume.

Dad gave a prolonged reprimand in his gruff voice—"When you leave the doors open, insects get inside the house. Don't forget to turn off those pool lights when you're done. Last time, someone kept them on all night. Keep the noise level down, and make sure to tell your brother to do the same. We don't want more noise complaints."

A few weekends ago, a cop had arrived at our door and in an apologetic manner had asked us to "tone it down, please." An anonymous phone complaint had come from one of our neighbors.

We figured it was Mrs. Libby, the old widow who lived alone in the giant mock Tudor. The one time I met her, she'd offered me an ancient, frosty-looking piece of green ribbon candy from a crystal candy dish by her front door. Though she kept the curtains closed, I often saw her silhouette vacuuming the living room in slow motion.

But later we found out that Mrs. Libby was partially deaf. It was the lawyer couple two houses down. We rarely saw them, since they left at the crack of dawn each morning for the gym and worked late.

Ever since the complaint, Dad had been reminding us about our noise level.

"Okay, Dad," I called back. "Have a good night."

"You, too," he said.

"Hello, Mr. Hyde," said Mike, with a big wave. He liked to make fun of the fact that Dad didn't usually remember his name.

"Who's that?" said Dad, squinting.

"Mike," Mike said.

Dad nodded.

"Hello, Nancy," I called out in the same spirit, knowing that she would prefer to be left alone.

She peered at me from behind Dad's shoulder for a second. A quick smile, possibly my imagination.

Dad slid the glass doors shut and retired to his bedroom with Nancy, on the opposite side of the house. I watched their dark forms as she followed him down the hallway, holding his hand.

Later Dad claimed that his weekend had been consumed by an epic migraine, and he'd sought refuge in his bedroom. The migraine, he maintained, had prevented him from properly supervising Gabe and his friends.

I don't know if he had a migraine that weekend or not. But I like to believe that he did.

DRESSED AND READY for our volleyball party, Mike and I went to the garage, the center of Gabe's universe. It was only 7:30 PM; we still had about an hour to kill.

"We can play pool," Mike said, "and if it's too weird, let's leave."

He didn't like Gabe's friends much, either.

The whole time, I'd been thinking about telling Mike that I knew Tove—imagining what I'd say: See that girl right there? Yeah, her, in the Marie Callender's uniform. I know her. No one knows that we were friends. We used to play together as kids. We had this special class together, because we both read at an advanced level. Now she's pretending she doesn't know me. She used to be so different. I used to go over to her house. I know her parents. Her dad really likes me. I wonder what happened to her? I wonder how she knows Gabe?

And imagining what Mike would say back: Go talk to her. Who cares if she's trying to act cool? She's just intimidated. Look at her! She actually looks kinda scared. C'mon. Let's go talk to her.

But I kept quiet and didn't explain.

When we entered the garage, Tove was lifting a bottle of rum to her lips, leaning against a wall near Crystal and Melissa, who were smoking cigarettes, and who both turned and stared at us. Melissa gave me a quick, unmistakable glare. Then she whispered in Crystal's ear, and Crystal nodded with her eyes on me, so that I'd be sure to know that I was the subject of the whisper—Melissa was angry because I'd ignored her as soon as Mike had arrived.

Kent and Kevin swung their pool cues at each other in a faux sword duel, and Gabe fiddled with a portable television that he'd brought to the garage, using wires to connect his Samsung camcorder. The Beastie Boys thumped loudly from his stereo.

I looked at Mike, asking with my eyes if we should leave.

He shrugged and moved toward the stand of pool cues.

Walking past Tove, I felt a strange sensation, as if she were leaning against me instead of the wall.

But we didn't speak to each other. Not once.

I was racking the balls when Gabe turned off the music and said, "Movie time."

He knelt next to the television.

Everyone quieted down and watched. I glanced at Mike as he chalked his pool cue with a cube of blue chalk.

It took Gabe a minute to get the television working.

The screen flickered. A grainy recording, so at first I couldn't make anything out, but then I realized—as Kevin and Kent hooted and hollered, "Oh, yeah!"—that two bodies were moving in discord, thrusting and jerking, having sex on a bed.

I won't lie: A shiver of excitement and pleasure fluttered through me.

"That's disgusting," Crystal said, and Melissa said, "Oh, my god! It's true! You *did* make a video! Kent, you weren't lying!"

"Tove, that's so disgusting," Crystal said.

I couldn't tell that it was Tove in the video, but my gut sank as soon as I heard her name.

Tove looked stunned. Her skin reddened, and then she said, "Look at me. I'm a porn star," in a sarcastic voice, trying to save face.

My head buzzed with shame, even more so when Tove tried to deflect the attention. Then her head went down and she said, "Turn it off."

Kent said, "There's, like, forty seconds left."

"Yeah," she said, "because that's when I figured out what you were doing."

"You know you like it," he said, sidling up to her and putting his arms around her. "You know you wanted to."

She buried her face in him.

Crystal pulled at Gabe's arm. "He tried to get me to," she said. "I told him, 'No way, get that camera out of here.'"

"What're you talking about?" Gabe said, pretending not to understand.

Crystal laughed and said, "Sicko-freak," nuzzling him. "I don't want to be a porn star," she said in a baby voice.

Kevin walked over to Tove and Kent with a bottle of Jose Cuervo tequila. "Here," he said, guiding the bottle to Tove's mouth, "take a sip and you'll feel better."

At first she swatted at the bottle, but then she drank, her hand moving to wipe the excess from her mouth, Kent holding her.

"Good girl," said Kevin, and then he took a swig.

"Hey, man," Mike said, "she looks like she's had enough."

"Hey, man," Kevin mimicked back, "why don't you mind your own fucking business?"

For a second, everything stilled. I wondered if Kevin would hit Mike, and whether I'd be expected to fight. Then Gabe broke the silence. "Let's go swim," he said, leaning in between them, using his rough monotone voice, similar to Dad's but not as gravelly. I noticed that he adopted it around his friends.

Mike and I went inside to the kitchen. "Your brother's friends are assholes," he said.

"I know."

"That girl's really drunk."

"Yeah."

"That video"—he had no words, shaking his head.

The house was quiet except for the refrigerator's ticking and the sounds from the others filtering in from outside. Through the kitchen window, we watched their dark figures at the pool.

Tove, unsteady on her feet, made her way to the pool's shallow end and sat on the steps in her pants. After a few minutes, she waded into the water, her work shirt billowing behind her.

Kent and Kevin—the Ks—swam around her, kicking and splashing, the pool lights off (I'd followed my dad's instructions, and Gabe and his friends hadn't bothered to turn them on again).

Tove came back to the steps, and Crystal knelt next to her, talking to her.

Crystal and Melissa helped her to the garden area, behind some bushes.

"What are they doing?" asked Mike.

"I don't know."

When they came back from the bushes, we saw that Tove wasn't wearing her pants.

"She must've had to pee," said Mike.

"Yeah."

"You ready?"

"Let's get out of here."

We walked out the back way, past the pool. Dark sky, silver crescent moon, cool breeze, the smell of gardenias. Tove's wet pants dripping on a deck chair. Near the back gate on the path, a curled wet sock, and to the side in the dirt, a black sneaker.

11.

JULY 4

I WENT TO THE girls' volleyball party with Mike and a bunch of
people whom I didn't know, and I woke up at Mike's house,
on the floor beside his bed. A blanket on me and a pillow beside
my head.

"Are you okay?" Mike asked, looking down at me.

"Yeah," I said, though I wasn't.

"You got really fucked up," he said.

"Hmm," I said, gripping the side of his bed to stand. Black dots
flickered in my peripheral vision.

"I got worried, so I brought you home."

I sat on the bed next to him, taking deep breaths. Fragments
of the night came back to me: a long-legged girl giving me a pig-
gyback ride; shots of whiskey from a paper cup; making out with
another long-legged girl in a room full of more long-legged girls
and other people, mostly athletes, to claps and cheers; someone
slapping my back; a close-up of a blue-tinted toilet bowl and my
getting sick into it; riding in the backseat of Mike's Datsun, the
windows opened, a heavy, cold breeze on my face.

"Do you remember what happened?" Mike asked.

"Not really." My temples throbbed.

"You drank too much," he said. "I tried to stop you." He left me for the bathroom. I could hear him running the water, whistling a song I couldn't make out, and then the toilet flushed.

When he came back to his bedroom, I said, "Those volleyball girls know how to party."

"They work hard," he said, "and party hard."

"I guess so."

"Who's Tove?" he asked, sitting next to me again, the mattress collapsing a little with his weight.

A coil of fear ran up my spine. I realized we hadn't introduced the girls earlier, so he didn't know their names.

When I didn't answer, he said, "You talked about Tove."

"When?"

He yawned and ran a hand through his hair. "Last night," he said, "in your sleep, after you passed out."

"What'd I say?"

He watched me for a moment. Then he said, "You said, 'Get out, Tove. Go home, Tove.' Some things I couldn't understand. And I don't know what else, just the name. 'Tove, Tove.' I'm sure that's the name. Who is it?"

I lay back on the bed and groaned.

Mike's mom knocked at the door, cracked it open, and showed her face. "Good morning, boys!" she said. "How do you feel about scrambled eggs?"

Mike stood up. "Thanks, Mom."

"Thanks, Mom," I echoed. It started as a joke, my calling Mike's parents Mom and Dad. But as time went on, I took it seriously, and they did as well, granting me a place inside their home.

"You know," he said, when his mom shut the door, "you don't have to eat Mom's eggs if it'll make you sick."

"I think it might help," I said.

He nodded. "Who's Tove?" he asked again.

It was a moment before I answered. "Just a girl I used to know."

12.

JULY 4

I CAME HOME FROM Mike's, and after briefly talking to Gabe, I slept most of the day, facedown on my bed, oblivious. Gabe told me that he and his friends were going to the beach to meet some girls. The house was deserted, Dad and Nancy gone, no note.

I got up and took a long, hot shower, trying to decide whether to go with Mike to another party that night, or just stay home and take it easy. Mike wasn't a huge partier, but every now and then he went a little nuts.

Peeling and eating three tangerines, I sat in Dad's recliner and watched a special on CNN about September 11 with lots of sweeping, patriotic music; wind-rippled flags; close-ups of soldiers, children and babies; and fireworks shooting off. An earnest, deep male voice intoned: "September eleventh took away our innocence, but it didn't take away our spirit. Our great nation is on the mend, and we're coming back strong. Let's celebrate this Fourth of July like none before. Let the fireworks become symbols of light that will guide our futures, and as the fireworks fill the skies, let hope, courage, and the American spirit fill our hearts."

I decided to call Mike.

"Yeah," I told him. "Let's party."

BEFORE OUR PARTY, Mike and I went to a fireworks show with his family at the Back Bay. We sat in lawn chairs in the dusk on a bluff overlooking the water with hundreds of others also sitting in portable folding chairs or lying on blankets or standing. People around us ate, drank, talked, laughed, listened to radios, strummed guitars, napped, kissed, cuddled, and played with dogs. It smelled like dirt, beer, sulfur, algae, and barbecue.

Mike's parents and sisters sat nearby; we could see the tops of their heads in front of us—they'd let us go off on our own.

"Don't be strangers," his mom had said.

His twin sisters, Michelle and Melanie, in fourth grade, wore white shorts and red, white, and blue tops, with matching plastic beaded metallic necklaces.

His youngest sister, Emily, in first grade, wore red cowboy boots and a plastic diamond tiara.

When I watched television at their house, sitting on the sofa, or when I sat on the sofa for some other reason, Emily would move from where she was and come sit next to me, leaning her entire body into me, and hold my hand.

Their mom would smile and say, "Emily, for heaven's sake: Give Even some space," but their mom knew that I liked it. It was as if they were all comforting me through Emily, wanting me to be okay.

Strange to think that Emily's a high school junior now, grown from that little sober-eyed girl who leaned into me, sensing my sadness and loneliness.

The stars began to prickle to life in the darkening sky. I took a sip from my Coke can, which had a touch of Bacardi 151 rum in it. One of our acquaintances from high school had offered it to us, stealthily pouring from a bottle into our cans, his sweatshirt covering the procedure, before moving on to find his group of friends.

"I can barely taste it," Mike said.

"Yeah," I said, but I was glad, planning not to overdo it again.

At my right side, an older gray-haired woman sat with a star-spangled-sweater-wearing Chihuahua on her lap, and the dog stared at me, pointy-nosed and beady-eyed, its body shivering with intensity.

I tipped my can in its direction, and it continued to stare.

Patriotic music sounded from a distance, echoing in the expanse of the bay.

In the dark sky, a blur of light shimmied upward, stopped, sparkled, and—a beat of silence—exploded, bursting into cascades of blue, red, yellow, and green, fizzling downward, illuminated in the water below. A boom went off, and then something that sounded like staccato gunfire.

Oohs and aahs from the crowd.

I leaned my head back, breathed in the smoky night, and watched the fireworks releasing, sparkling, and lighting the sky, falling in slow motion; changing colors from red to purple to blue to green; disappearing in puffs of gray smoke; evaporating further into nothing; sparks of light shooting out in a bloom, flaring, and dying just as quickly; great looping arcs of color fading, disappearing.

I watched the backs of the heads of the people in front of me illuminated in the blaze of colors. One little boy had his ears covered with his hands and his face down. Near him, a line of senior citizens sat in wheelchairs, their heads tilted the same way. The Chihuahua huddled into its owner, its back quivering.

I closed my eyes, sensing something in the fireworks, something of the danger in just being alive. Living and breathing and existing as a part of this crazy world, not understanding what anything meant. Trying to make sense, struggling. It felt as if I could shatter, and that then I'd be nothing. I'd felt this way a few times before, and it always terrified me, like my body couldn't contain me—or at least all the feelings inside me. It wasn't just the idea of being nothing that scared me, but what it might feel like to shatter.

For some reason, I remembered Tove's wet sock on our path as we'd left the night before. Had I gotten so drunk to try to forget about her?

Then I thought about her parents, my brother, his friends, my parents, Nancy, me. With my eyes closed and head back, the fireworks created patterns on my eyelids.

Dizzy, I brought my head forward between my knees, breathing in my Levi's. The chaos inside my head wouldn't settle.

I took deep, gulping breaths.

I felt a hand on my shoulder. "You okay?"—Mike's voice.

I lifted my head and smiled at him. He had leaned to the side of his chair so that he could reach me, and it looked like he might tip over.

I wanted to say, I'm lost and scared, but instead I said, "Yeah. Still a little hungover, I think."

But I didn't have to explain.

"Hey, Even," he said, tilting his chair back in place, "what do you say let's just take it easy tonight? Hang with the folks, then you can spend the night?"

I nodded, trying to appear nonchalant.

After the show ended, Mike folded and collapsed his chair, and then he picked up trash.

I stayed in my chair for a moment, watching people bring about order, a general bustling of purpose, and then I joined them.

13.

JULY 5

I SPENT THE NIGHT at Mike's house on the Fourth, and so the police left me alone for the most part, since I wasn't home anywhere near the time of the event. Mike's parents vouched for my whereabouts. And we had different friends: All of Gabe's were from Cucamonga, mine from Newport. But later an investigating officer did ask me if I'd noticed anything different about my brother the afternoon of the fifth, when I returned home.

"No, sir," I said; true, for the most part.

Gabe, at the time, weighed about a hundred pounds, and was barely five feet tall at seventeen years old. The Ks, on the other hand, almost a full year older than Gabe, weighed close to seventy pounds more than him, nearing six feet each.

But Gabe wasn't the underdog: What he lacked in height and weight he made up for in craftiness, homing in on weaknesses and insecurities, teasing both Kent and Kevin about their working-class backgrounds, calling them the Fontucky Fags, since both their families had moved from Fontana.

I didn't want to think about the ugly side of Gabe, the horrible things he said to his friends, the ways that he imitated them and joked around, using his cleverness in a bullying manner.

Rather, I concentrated on the brother that I knew and loved so well: charming, friendly, funny, sensitive. Instead I blamed the Ks, bullish football thugs, and a bad influence on Gabe.

I no longer underestimate a person's—including my own— capacity for revisionism and rationalizations.

So I said, "No, sir," and didn't tell the investigating officer that when I came home that afternoon, I sensed something bad had happened. How could I explain that the air inside the house felt different—heavier, perilous, as if still radiating with the crime that had recently been committed?

Gabe and Kevin were talking in the living room. Neither of them heard me come inside through the back door into the kitchen.

Gabe leaned forward in Dad's chair and Kevin sat on the couch. I could see them over the bar that opened from the kitchen to the living room.

Kevin's brow furrowed, as if they'd been speaking about something serious, and I could see Gabe's profile. He was barefoot, and wore his blue long board shorts and no shirt.

I moved a few steps closer to watch and listen, with the risk of being seen.

In a steady, deliberate voice, Gabe said, "Listen, shut up, it's not a big deal."

Kevin bowed his head. He wore a torn T-shirt, plaid shorts, and black Vans with no socks. Next to Nancy's white zippered Bible on the coffee table in front of him (she left the Bible there, I'm convinced, hoping to convert one of us while we watched TV) were the remains of nachos on a paper plate. Gabe's specialty, ready-grated cheese on tortilla chips, microwaved for a minute, topped with Old El Paso mild salsa from a jar.

Gabe settled back in Dad's chair.

Kevin, to my great surprise, stood and walked to him and—to this day, I'm still surprised, but I know what I saw—he knelt in front of the recliner and set his head in Gabe's lap.

Gabe stroked Kevin's dark hair.

It continued.

Holy shit, I thought. What the hell is happening? All I knew for sure was that Kevin and Gabe had done something that they shouldn't have, and that they might be doing other things, too, and that they'd kill me if they knew I was there.

I backtracked slowly, making my way to the door as quietly as possible, wanting a glass of water, but knowing that I needed to escape. The thought of what I'd seen roiled my stomach, and suddenly I had to use the bathroom. It was warm and still out, the sky a hazy white that made me somehow more nauseated.

I circled around the yard, came to the front door, made considerable noise opening it and walking down the hallway. Coughed a few times. When I reached the entry to the living room, I saw with relief that Kevin was back on the couch.

Not able to make it to my bathroom, I released my bowels into the toilet in the half bathroom near the living room. My skin wet with sweat, I flushed the toilet, washed my hands, and then stood before the door, not wanting to exit. The fan made its whirring noise, but I could hear them talking, though I couldn't make out what they said. At one point I heard my name.

But I had nowhere to go. They both watched me come through the door, and Gabe smiled at my apparent discomfort, trying to put me at ease.

"What's the matter?" he asked.

"Nothing," I said.

"You sick?" said Kevin. He said this without real concern or empathy or interest.

"Nah," I said. "I'm fine." I decided to change the subject. "Where's Dad?"

"He's not here."

"Are you sure?"

"Yeah. He's with Nancy somewhere."

I said nothing for a moment. "How was your Fourth?" I asked, thinking small talk might help.

They looked at each other and laughed. I waited until they quieted.

"What is it?" I asked.

"Want to see?" said Kevin.

Gabe wouldn't look me in the eyes.

"See what?"

"Our Fourth," said Kevin.

"What do you mean?" I had no idea. I noticed Gabe's Samsung video camera beside him on the chair. "Gabe?" I said.

For a long, horrible moment, Gabe continued to avoid eye contact with me, setting his hand on the camera.

"What do you think I mean?" Kevin asked.

Then I knew. "You made a porno," I said.

"That's right, *amigo*," Kevin said. "Wanna watch?"

I leaned against the wall, feeling light-headed. "Who's in it?" I asked. "Gabe, are you in it?"

Gabe shrugged. "No one you know," he said.

"Jesus, Gabe," I said. "What did you do?"

"Don't worry," he said.

I stared at him and didn't say anything.

I was ready to ignore what Kevin and my brother told me about making a porno, just as I disregarded the repugnant parts of my brother's personality.

I'd like to say that at this point, I knew that Tove might somehow be involved, and I also knew that I had a moral duty to investigate further, to make sure that she hadn't been hurt.

But I don't recall being torn morally.

Rather, I would like to have forgotten the whole deal.

People love to be indignant. "If it had been me," they like to say, if they suspect that an acquaintance or family member might be a rapist, molester, drug dealer, thief, et cetera, "I would've turned him or her in right away."

But they don't know what it's like. Or they're lying. It's far more comfortable and easy to remain stupid and silent. Like I would have.

14.

JULY 6

MY CELL RANG at 4:13 that morning. I know because I looked at the neon numbers glowing from my alarm clock, my first angry thought being, Who's calling me this early?

Dad and I had watched TV late into the night, like when I'd first moved in with him, no Gabe or Nancy. An episode of *20/20* and then *The Jerk*. Gabe had gone somewhere, leaving with a quick good-bye.

During *The Jerk*, Dad drank two martinis, grunting now and then instead of laughing. At one point, when he got up to use the bathroom, he paused and put a hand on my shoulder and squeezed. He wore a black sweater with a teal blue golf shirt underneath, the collar peeking out.

I snacked on popcorn and drank a bottle of Orangina that I'd found in the back of the refrigerator.

"G'night, Even," Dad said as the credits rolled on the screen, setting his glasses case next to the remote. "Sweet dreams." He smoothed my hair with his hand, and then he left for bed.

An easy sleep for me, and then my cell ringing. I fumbled for my phone, opened it, and stared up at the ceiling.

"Even," said Sara. Crying, unmistakably. A terrified, gulping-for-breath crying.

We still talked a lot on the phone, about everything—school, work, fears, families, ambitions, philosophies, books, movies.

She'd even told me once that she couldn't stop drinking—wasn't sure if she wanted to—and that she also had a problem with cocaine. "You're the only one who knows about the coke," she'd said. "Joe thinks I quit."

Joe was her boyfriend, a local amiable pot dealer who knew both Gabe and Kevin since he dealt to them.

I'd adjusted to being just Sara's friend. I was jealous of Joe, sure, but it was better than not having a relationship with her at all.

I'd met Joe once at a party I went to with Mike. Joe was wearing a cowboy hat, long sandy hair peeking out, handsome, tall, and I'd had an urge to slam him against the wall, but then he left for the other room to drop off a bag of weed.

Sara had stayed in the hallway with me. Her eyes had met mine. She was wearing a cashmere sweater, a soft gray color. Her eyes were luminous, a dark greenish-gold, and she'd smiled and said, "Don't be mad, Even. I really like Joe. But you're my best friend."

During the last phone conversation we'd had, before hanging up she'd said, "I'm really glad that I met you, Even," and I'd said, "I'm really glad, too."

"Even," she said now, on the phone, "help me."

My gut clenched. "What is it? What happened, Sara? Where are you?" I rolled over, sat up, and turned on the lamp. Car accident, I thought, death, limbs torn off, drinking and driving, beaten by her jackass pot-dealing boyfriend.

Blinking, I was relieved to find in the light the regularity and familiarity of my bedroom. But that Sara was crying scared me considerably. She's a tough girl. I'd never seen or heard her cry before, and I haven't seen or heard her cry since.

She gave me Joe's address on Amethyst (he'd rented a house for a week on Balboa Island that summer), told me that I needed to come right now, right this second, no time to waste. She couldn't tell me why. It would take too long to explain.

"Hurry, Even," she said, in a hushed and shaky voice. "Don't tell anyone. Don't let anyone see you. Just come."

I did hurry, wearing jeans and a T-shirt, no shoes, pulling on a hooded zipper-front sweatshirt on my way out, and forgetting my driver's license. Careful not to make noise as I shut the front door; starting the BMW parked at the curb and flinching, wanting it to be quieter. I noticed only a few cars on the road, headlights lighting up the darkness.

I couldn't find a place to park—if you've been to Balboa Island in the summer, you know what I mean—but I finally got a spot three blocks from the house. Running down the street in my bare feet, my teeth rattling and my sweatshirt flapping behind me, I had a strong urge to turn back around.

But I thought about Sara crying and kept going.

She was waiting for me outside the house near the patio, behind a tree, and she came out when she saw me, her hands wrapped around her chest, trembling. She wore a thin pale blue dress—at first I thought it a nightgown—and no shoes.

"Jesus," she said, "hurry, hurry," and she took me to the side of the house, a dark, small space, where something lay wrapped in a pink towel on the ground.

"Hurry," she said, the tears coming, "hurry, hurry. Fuck, shit, I know they're coming. Hurry, Even. What do I do? What do I do? They'll be back for it," and she unearthed Gabe's Samsung video camera from beneath the towel, flipped the little screen open, pressed Play, and handed it to me.

While I watched she spoke, frantic and scared, in one long, jumbled explanation, no longer crying, and not looking at the screen with me, instead looking all around her. "They showed up at about two this morning, your brother and this other guy, and they kept talking about what was on their video camera, sort of like bragging about it, but they wouldn't say what was on there. Then Joe and this other guy said, 'Let's see.' But they wouldn't let them watch. Stupid shits. But then when they left the party, they forgot their camera, stupid fucking asses, dumb shits forgot it. Left it right on the couch. So everyone's asleep, the party's finally over, there's, like, three people passed out on the floor near the couch, but I'm still wired. Did a line, can't sleep, can't tell Joe, he thinks I quit coke, so I open the thing and look at it, and oh my fucking god, what do I do? What is that, Even? Oh my god! What do I do, what do I do?"

What I saw and heard on that small flip screen I still unwillingly see and hear, when I'm lying in bed or at the grocery store, or just taking a walk, whether my eyes are closed or not, because it's imprinted inside me, and it can never go away.

15.

JULY 6

WHILE I WATCHED the video, Sara watched the street, and then she grabbed my arm and said, "Oh, shit, it's them, they're coming!"

We stood frozen, staring down the street. A car's headlights swooped past us in a left turn, and then the car disappeared.

"What do we do?" she asked, taking the camera from me and turning it off. She wrapped it in the towel like a baby.

"I don't know," I said. I felt numb, as if I were under anesthesia. "Why'd you call me?" I said, looking at her. My voice sounded whiny.

She stared at me, some indistinct emotion coupled with a fearful awareness intensifying and connecting us, and then she said with a trace of an apology, "What was I supposed to do, Even?"

A long silence, and then we heard the hint of another car in the distance, and she said, "Hide! Go across the street, behind that bush," and she ran with the camera wrapped in the towel to her beat-up Toyota Tercel, the car engine noise coming closer, its headlights turning down the street.

I did what she said and watched as she set the towel on the backseat, shut her car door, and slipped back inside the house like a ghost.

This time it was Gabe and Kevin in Gabe's truck, and they screeched to an illegal park in the driveway, half-extended into the street. Their car doors slammed, and they ran up to the front door.

My heart banged against my throat, thinking of Sara inside the house and the video camera wrapped in a towel in her car. Was she pretending to be asleep? What would she say?

I could've escaped then, but I stayed and waited, crouched behind the big manicured bush on a neighbor's front lawn. Near the doorway, an American flag shuddered and clanked on a flagpole.

Minutes passed. A few lights came on in the house. Then some more lights, until the entire house was lit up.

It occurred to me that I should take the camera and flee, and I crouch-walked to Sara's car, tried the car door, but she'd locked it, so I crouch-walked my way back behind the bush and waited some more.

I could hear shouting inside the house, but I couldn't make it out, and I didn't recognize the voices. Out of nervousness, I dug inside my pocket, extracting an old receipt and gum wrapper, a couple of pennies and a nickel, and then I inserted the items in the other pocket.

Then all at once the front door opened to Gabe, his hands on his forehead, and Kevin following.

"Shit! Fuck! We're so fucked, we're so fucked, oh shit!" Gabe said, walking along the front pathway, crying and wiping his face.

Joe followed, and a few others, and then Sara, her arms wrapped around her torso, wearing her flimsy dress.

"Are you sure you didn't see it?" Kevin said, pleading.

Joe and the others nodded, and I heard murmurs of "Yeah, yeah, I don't know where it is, don't know where you could've left it."

A few more minutes passed with Kevin's questions and Joe's answers:

"Are you sure you don't know?"

"Yeah, yes. We told you everything."

"Now think back. One more time. Do you remember seeing it?"

"Yeah," Joe said. "I told you. We all did. Gabe had it on the couch. He was sitting there with it. But I don't remember seeing it after you left. I already told you everything. No one knows where it is."

"Where could it have gone?"

"I don't know. Maybe you took it with you and set it somewhere else. Did you replay your steps? My mom used to make me go through my steps again. She'd say, 'Now think, Joe, just go back and think.'"

"Yeah, fucker," Kevin said impatiently, "we did that. That's why we're here."

To my dismay, Gabe and Kevin started walking around the house, peering in bushes, and moving to the cars parked on the street.

Gabe looked into the passenger window of Sara's car, his hands visor-like at his forehead to help him see.

Then to my utter relief, Gabe moved on to the next car.

At one point, Kevin stood in the middle of the street, and I thought he might cross to where I was hiding, but then he went back to the front yard and stood next to Gabe.

He and Gabe stared at each other for a giant, earth-sucking vacuum of a pause, and then Kevin said, "Asshole," pushing Gabe in the chest with his palms, so that Gabe floundered, one hand on the ground, in a half fall, "asshole, asshole, why'd you bring it? It's your fault."

Gabe stood, waited a beat, and then he came at Kevin headfirst in a pummeling body slam. They went down onto the lawn, grasping and fighting, and for a second, on instinct, I stood up, thinking that I needed to help Gabe. It was like watching a lapdog fighting a pit bull.

Joe and some others broke up the fight, separating Gabe and Kevin a good distance, until they both calmed and got their breathing back to normal. Gabe's nose looked bloodied.

I worried that the commotion would wake the people whose yard I was hiding in, but no lights came on. They were probably used to the noise during summer break, or maybe they'd left for another vacation home. No one on the block yelled at us to be quiet or turned on lights or called the police.

Joe pulled a pack of Marlboros from his pocket and shook one out. He coughed, and then set the cigarette in his mouth. Lit it, coughed again, blowing smoke.

"Suppose," he said, done coughing, "it'll turn up. These things always turn up when you give up looking. Like last week, I couldn't find my car keys, got all crazy"—his hand flared for a second—"looked everywhere, yelling about it, 'Fuck, where're my keys!' Remember?"—he turned to Sara, and she affirmed with a nod. A pang went through me, understanding that she couldn't speak out of fear. She didn't want attention. But Joe didn't ask her for more.

"Finally gave up," he continued, "smoked a bowl, ate some fries, and took a nap." He paused, took another drag from his cigarette, blew out the smoke. A rush of admiration went through me for how Joe finessed the situation.

"Then," he said, "I woke from my nap, went to the fridge to grab a beer, and there they were, my keys, waiting for me on the top shelf next to the milk. I'm telling you. That's when it happens. When you give up and let it go."

Gabe's head went down—sad, resigned.

"Worst-case scenario," Joe said, "it doesn't turn up. You can just buy another camera. Shit! I'll help pay for it."

Kevin had been listening from his side of the lawn. I saw him take what looked like a long, deflating, accepting exhale.

Gabe seemed relieved as well, looking up and around, and then moving toward Kevin, no longer worried about getting his ass kicked. I had a flash of Kevin's head in Gabe's lap, and Gabe stroking his hair.

They stood around, discussing the weirdness of losing things and having those things turn up again, until they agreed to go inside and spark up, a peace offering extended from Joe to Gabe and Kevin.

Sara followed them to the front door, the last to go inside the house.

So I waited some more behind the bush, my knees pulled to my chest, feet tucked in and warmed within my sweatshirt, and tried to rest. Listened to the American flag clicking and clacking and flapping at its pole, and waited and waited some more.

The sun began to rise—a flare of light in the dark sky—and then Gabe and Kevin walked out the front door and to Gabe's truck without speaking.

Gabe started the engine, and then he pulled out of the driveway and sped down the street. His brake lights went red at the stop sign, and then he made his turn—gone—the street quiet.

I wasn't sure what to do, when Sara came out of the door and walked to her car without looking at me. She unlocked it, opened her door, shuffled around inside, and got a sweatshirt. She pulled it on, shut her car door, and walked back to the house, still without eye contact.

I waited a few more minutes—I counted to 120—and then I did my crouch-walk again, back to her car.

This time the door wasn't locked, and I opened it slowly. On the towel-covered camera was a note in Sara's block-letter writing:

TAKE IT AND DO SOMETHING. GIVE IT TO POLICE? SHE LOOKS DEAD! YOU SAW IT! THEY'RE WATCHING ME INSIDE HOUSE. I SAID I WAS COLD AND NEEDED SWEATSHIRT. SORRY I CAN'T HELP. EVEN, I'M SORRY. I DIDN'T KNOW WHAT TO DO. I'M REALLY SCARED!

I stuffed the note in my pocket and jog-walked to my car, three blocks down, carrying the camera wrapped in its towel. The air seemed static, and the rising sun cast a shimmering, halo-like purple-yellow on the horizon.

Walking beneath a tree, I looked up to see its leaves trembling and glittering above me, their undersides pale. It smelled of salty ocean and grass. Although I moved quickly, everything seemed to be in slow motion, as if in a movie.

In the home to my left, a light came on. Two houses down, a garage door rattled open, and a car engine started.

After that, I had tunnel vision, not looking around me, ignoring noises, focused only on getting to my car.

When I got home, I opened the back door quietly and went straight to my bedroom, setting the camera beneath my bed with the towel over it and my sweatshirt over the towel. A bread loaf–size lump.

No Gabe at home, I knew, since his truck was not parked outside.

Then I sat down on my bed and thought about what I should do. But I had no idea.

My alarm clock showed 6:04 AM, and I didn't know whether to start my day or try to sleep.

An early riser, my dad usually woke at 6:30 AM and started brewing his coffee soon after. He would be suspicious if he found me up this early.

I wasn't hungry for breakfast, and I felt a numbed panic. Whatever adrenaline had gotten me through hiding and escaping with the video camera had worn off—or was in the process of wearing off—and sitting on my bed, alone, thinking about what I'd seen on that little screen, and about Sara's involvement, made everything seem hopeless and unbearable and terrifying.

I tried reading Salinger's *The Catcher in the Rye* for distraction, but after five minutes or so of the sentences wobbling, I set the book back down.

The very fact of the video camera, and what it contained, and its presence—right under the bed—really freaked me out, as if I'd had something to do with the content, or as if what I'd seen was alive and happening now, on the morning of July 6, not on the Fourth, just by its existence and my awareness.

Then my cell phone rang, and I figured that it was probably Sara telling me what to do, but when I flipped it open, I read my caller ID: BRO.

A burst of fear as I answered, saying, "Hey, what's up?" My voice sounded shaky but he didn't seem to notice.

"You awake?" he said.

"I am now. Where are you?"

An indistinct shuffling noise while he paused, and then he said, "Kevin's."

"What's up?"

He didn't speak but I could hear him breathing into the phone.

"Gabe," I said, because I didn't think I could wait, "what's up?"

"I'm just wondering," he said, "if you've seen my video camera. I can't find it."

"No," I said, my heart speeding. "Do you want me to look for it?"

"Yeah," he said. "That'd be great. Thanks, dude. I don't think I left it there. But can you look?"

"Sure," I said, and instinctively, I pushed with my heel to make sure the camera was far beneath my bed, invisible. "I'll call you if I find it."

"Thanks, little brother," he said. He hadn't called me that in a long time, and it made me so sad.

"I'll be by later," he said. A short pause, and then he added, "Hey, don't look at what's on there if you find it, okay?"

"Yeah, sure," I said. To be honest, I wanted to tell him right then that I knew. I imagined we'd both cry, and that he'd be remorseful. I'm not sure what stopped me, except for an intuitive sense that he wanted only to save his own skin.

"Promise?" he said.

"Yeah," I said. "I promise."

We said our good-byes, and then I sat for a moment, feeling bad for having lied to him. From his voice and request, I knew that he didn't suspect me at all. But I remembered what was on the camera, and any guilt morphed into horror and fear. No matter if I wanted to forget, I couldn't.

I heard the faint noises of Dad in the kitchen, shuffling around, brewing his pot of coffee. He would be in his bathrobe. I thought about taking the video camera to him, showing him. But it scared me, knowing that he might not do anything about it, and that he might destroy the camera.

Thinking back, this was pivotal, and the first time I didn't believe in or trust my dad's decision-making abilities.

Had I gone to him with the video camera, I would have been making a conscious decision to probably let Gabe, Kevin, and

Kent off the hook. But what I'd seen, along with the knowledge of Sara having witnessed it as well, had extinguished that
possibility.

I tried lying down on the bed and deep breathing to ease my
panic, but after a few moments, I gave up and went to the bathroom. I tore up Sara's note and flushed it.

A long, hot shower later, I stood towel-dried in my boxers in
front of the mirror, and with skin flushed from the heat, I watched
myself cry.

16.

JULY 6

I WANTED GABE'S SAMSUNG video camera out of my possession. That was all that I knew for certain. But I didn't know how to make it happen. So I dressed and prepared myself for the day, all the while wondering how to make it through the hours ahead, and how to get rid of the video camera.

I called Mike's cell but it went to voice mail. I called his house, and his mom told me that he'd left with his dad and sisters to visit his grandma in Whittier. "Are you okay?" she asked. "Your voice sounds different."

I made my bed. Brushed my teeth. Tucked in my shirt. Put on my socks and shoes. Each small action felt momentous, as if it would lead to an answer, to a bigger and greater action.

The Fourth had fallen on a Friday, and now a bright Sunday loomed, birds whistling their songs outside my bedroom window.

I thought of calling Tove. But what would I say? Are you okay, Tove? Do you know what happened? Did you black out?

Part of me believed that if she didn't know, she'd be okay. She was okay if she didn't know. Right?

I'm not going to relay what I saw on that video. But I will say that Tove looked dead, which scared Sara the most. So I knew that most likely she had blacked out, and had been unaware of what had happened to her.

I'd had a few blackouts—most recently at the girls' volleyball party—as if what happened hadn't happened, because I had no memory of it. If someone told me, then there might be flashes of memory, like a ghost me had been there instead of the real me.

If Tove didn't know—didn't remember—I didn't want to be the one to tell her. She would be safely unconscious, shielded from the pain. I didn't want her to have flashes of memory. I wanted it not to have happened. She wouldn't want to know.

I thought about her parents—Ben and Luanne—and how they both volunteered in our classes in grade school. Luanne, petite and with brown hair like Tove, deceptively normal-looking, bringing her guitar for sing-alongs. Ben with a patch of grayish-white at the back of his hair, as if someone had settled a hand there, full of chalk, rubbed it in, and then pulled the hand away. He'd been fond of me once and had told me, "If I had a son, I'd want him to be like you."

I remembered sitting in plastic chairs with Tove, first grade or second, listening to her explain her name. "It's a Scandinavian name, the author of my mom's favorite books when she was a kid. The author's a Finn, pronounced *Thou-vé*, last name Jansson, but no one says it right, so I'm just Tove. There's also 'Jabberwocky,' a poem by Lewis Carroll. A tove is part lizard and part corkscrew. It nests under sundials and eats cheese." Then I remembered how

Melissa, that afternoon at the pool, had thought long and hard and then called Tove "weird," and how I'd always suspected this to be a shared trait between Tove and me.

Wouldn't everyone be better off—Tove, her parents, Gabe, the Ks, all of us—if the camera didn't exist? And if it didn't exist, we could pretend—those of us who knew—that it hadn't happened.

With this in mind, I grappled with destroying the camera. Taking a hammer to it. Setting it on fire.

Or I could delete what I'd seen. Delete everything and leave the camera somewhere for Gabe to find. He would be so relieved that he would change his ways. We could pretend that what had been on the tape hadn't happened. It would never happen again.

But it did happen. I'd seen the proof. It was etched permanently inside me. If I destroyed the camera and the evidence, I'd always know.

Then I thought about calling Sara. You're the one that got me into this mess, I would say. You figure out what to do. I'm giving the camera back to you. I want nothing to do with it. Forget about me.

But then I remembered her fear. I wanted to protect her from what we'd seen on the camera, and from having to be involved further. I also liked the idea of being her savior. I wanted to help her.

I had my phone ready and came very close to pressing Sara's number. But then I flipped it shut and put it back in my pocket.

I heard voices coming from the living room or kitchen, two that I recognized—my dad's and Sheriff Krone's—and one that I didn't know.

My dad wouldn't suspect anything from my being awake now, so I decided—since I didn't know what else to do with myself—to join them.

A quick fantasy floated through me. I would give the video camera to Sheriff Krone. He would know what to do. You did the right thing, son, he would say. If Dad protested, he would tell him, This is way beyond a Get Out of Jail Free card, Dan. Appropriate measures need to be taken.

But then I remembered Krone's manipulative and ingratiating manner at Banderos Steakhouse. How he'd swung the blond woman from the bar to face us and pretended to handcuff her, and then slapped her ass. Given me a backhanded compliment, while at the same time letting me know that he controlled my dad.

I couldn't give him the video camera, because I didn't trust him.

With a sick, uncanny sensation, I walked down the hallway to the living room, letting my hand skim the wall.

But they weren't in the living room, so I made my way to the kitchen.

I'd never seen the man who was with Sheriff Krone and my dad, but I knew—even though all three were dressed for golf—that he was Assistant Sheriff Scott Jimenez, Krone's right-hand man. Something about his air of authority, coupled with an attentive and fluctuating deference to Krone and Dad. Slim and brown-skinned, with a classic square jaw and a full head of dark hair, he stared at me for a long second, and then he smiled—his face boyish and handsome—setting his hand out for me to shake. "Well, well, well," he said, with the jovial gallantry of a practiced salesman, "this must be the famous Even Hyde."

The strength of his handshake surprised me.

Sheriff Krone slung an arm around my shoulder and pulled me to him. He made as if to knuckle my head. He knew that I disliked him and was letting me know that he knew while also working at making me hate him more, all for his entertainment.

"Even," he said, crooking my head in his elbow, "how's it going?"

I struggled to free myself without appearing too hostile.

Dad, smoking a cigarette, said, "Leave my boy alone."

To my relief, Krone did, releasing me, saying, "Okay, not a big deal. Just being friendly."

He leaned forward and slapped my back—one last seemingly sociable but intimidating and hostile action.

I felt rather sick and hot, wishing I'd stayed in my bedroom. My eyes wandered around the kitchen, wondering how to escape.

Jimenez reached into his pocket and extracted a small bottle of aspirin, shaking a few into his hand. He swallowed them dry and noticed me watching. "Want some?" he asked, extending the bottle to me.

"I've got a headache," I said, accepting them. I took two with a glass of water from the kitchen sink.

Jimenez smiled at me impersonally, and I felt like a caddy at his country club to whom he'd just granted a favor.

Krone said, "I sure hope you don't get migraines like your pop."

"It's just a headache," I said.

Dad began to cough, his face reddening and crumpling, and I refilled my glass with water to help him. He set his cigarette in an ashtray and drank the water down.

When he finished, he said, "Thanks, Son."

"Smoking," said Krone solemnly, "is a bad habit."

Dad glared at him and said nothing.

"Lung cancer," Krone said, "diseases, all of these things can be prevented."

Jimenez reached for the Newports on the kitchen counter and lit one for himself in solidarity with Dad.

Dad's cigarette smoldered in the ashtray. He looked at it and said irritably, "I've been smoking since I was ten, and I'm fine. You think I don't know what I'm doing? 'Stop smoking, drinking, cut out the caffeine, eat better, more vegetables and greens, less meat, be careful about your cholesterol.' You don't think I've been hearing these things from my doctors for most of my life?" He waved a hand in a dismissive gesture. "What the fuck do they know? How about you mind your own fucking business and not tell me what to do."

A stunned silence, and then Jimenez blew a puff of smoke.

"Jesus," Krone said. "Relax."

Dad shot him a hostile glance. Nobody seemed to know what to say.

We watched Dad take his glasses off and spray the lenses with Windex. He rubbed and polished them with a paper towel, and his eyes looked weak and watery and small, a vague blue, crinkled at the edges. Putting the glasses back on, he said, "Golfing with the Millers?"

"Sure thing," said Krone. He sounded relieved to have a less contentious subject change. "Pretty thing, that wife of his. Dark hair and blue eyes, nice figure, the real deal. She'll be there today.

None of that silicone. Too much makeup, maybe a little less lipstick would be nice. Gets on her teeth. Three sons but she looks
good." He leaned forward, lowering his voice. "A ton of money.
We're talking money like you wouldn't believe. Two helicopters,
a private jet. All of it new money, so they're happy to show it off.
She wants to contribute and he wants to do what she wants." He
laughed, ran a hand over his balding head. "Hell," he said, "I want
to do what she wants."

Dad looked at me, and for a fraction of a second he seemed not
to know what to say or do. Then he said, "Don't talk like that in
front of my son."

Krone smiled at me with sheer dislike.

"*Ándale*," said Jimenez, stubbing out his cigarette in the ashtray. "I don't want to be late."

Sunlight streamed through the window above the sink and
the kitchen felt hot and stuffy. My throat dry, I got another glass
of water.

As I drank, my dad let me know that he'd be back in the afternoon, after a short round of golf.

He ruffled my hair with his hand, and I got that warm sensation
under my sternum.

"You okay?" he said, leaning to speak in my ear so that the
others wouldn't hear.

I moved my head so that he couldn't see the tears welling, and
I wanted to kiss him. "Yeah," I said, "I'm fine."

"All right, Son," he said.

The back door closed, and it got quiet again. Dad's cigarette
smoldered in the ashtray next to Jimenez's extinguished one.

I poured water into the ashtray and watched the cigarette wither and die in a soggy, cloudy mixture of tobacco and ash. Then I rinsed everything in the sink, using the garbage disposal, appreciating its aggressive noise as it ate up the ashtray debris.

My stomach grumbled and I realized that I hadn't eaten in a long time. While making myself a peanut butter and jelly sandwich, I remembered the speaker Tom L. from the AA meeting. How he said that people came to him with their troubles, and he helped sort them out.

In a cold sweat, I ate my sandwich and decided what I would do.

With yellow kitchen gloves, I took the Windex Dad had left out and some paper towels and cleaned the video camera of fingerprints.

I wanted to get one of the boxes in the garage, but I didn't want to go in there. What I'd seen on the camera took place in the garage. It took me at least five minutes to get the courage. But I did it. As soon as I opened the door to go inside, a sensation of great loss and sadness came over me, almost like a physical pain, so that I groaned. It didn't seem quite as real to me—as if before, the event had existed in some phantom reality—until I saw the pool table, the wicker couch, and the pool cue.

I found a box and got out as quickly as possible, my heart thumping.

I set the video camera inside the box and taped it shut. After typing my note—*for Tom L.*—I printed it and taped it to the top of the box.

Then I drove to the police station in an alert hyperdread, still wearing my kitchen gloves.

Tom L. had worked for Krone and retired, and he'd know what to do. I thought of his soothing voice at the meeting, his calm and spiritual demeanor.

They all worked for Krone, but Tom seemed like the best option.

I'd gone to Gabe's AA meetings for him—a slippery slope that I refused to extend—and now it made me angry that Dad had allowed it.

A sense of incensed justice also compelled me to turn the camera over, but that faded rather quickly.

It occurred to me, as I parked the car, that video cameras surrounded the police station, spying on people. I didn't want to be recognized.

So I covered myself with the pink towel, like a cape over my head and body, and took off my shoes. I rushed to the police station with the box in my arms.

From where I'd parked down the street (after putting a quarter in the parking meter, giving me fifteen minutes), the walk to the police station felt long, as I was hunched beneath the pink towel.

A car whooshed past me and honked.

Tired, scared, sweating, my head still hurting, I breathed heavily, wanting to be rid of the camera more than anything.

About halfway there, I panicked. But my feet kept drawing me forward, until I finally set the box by the police station doors, my hands shaking.

No one stopped me or asked me questions, and I rushed back to my car, hidden beneath the towel.

When I got inside my car, I flung the towel aside, removed the kitchen gloves, and for a few moments I took deep breaths, everything spinning in my vision, until the world settled, and I got my bearings again.

Then I went to the Del Taco drive-thru and ordered food. I parked in the lot and wolfed down three bean-and-cheese burritos. Nervous still, yes, but it felt like a great boulder had been lifted from my shoulders.

When I got home, I turned off my cell phone—Mike had left a message—and sat in front of the big-screen TV in a daze, watching one stupid show after another (*Baywatch* reruns, *Celebrity Boxing*, *The Jerry Springer Show*), my head throbbing, until Dad came home late in the afternoon.

His sparse hair windblown into a cliff-like wedge, he had a flush of sunburn across his nose, and he wore his clown-like golf attire: a white-and-peach-striped shirt and pastel plaid pants.

He seemed pleased to see me, and I got that warm feeling underneath my sternum again.

"This isn't like you," he said, "to waste your day. You're no couch potato."

He asked if I wanted to go for a walk with him, and when I didn't respond, he said, "It's a beautiful afternoon, Even, let's go. Up, up. Get up. Time to move."

The sun, low in the sky, extended our shadows on the sidewalk.

We walked for a long time without speaking, all the way to the boardwalk overlooking the beach, where we could smell the fire pits mingling with the ocean air and hear the people, intermixed with the noises of the waves crashing and swooshing in retreat. A crowded Sunday, people prolonging their Fourth of July weekend as long as possible, the beach crammed with towels and umbrellas, and families camped in the parking lot on the islands of grass, grilling and barbecuing.

I watched some kids running in the wet part of the sand left by the outgoing tide, seagulls pausing above them in the wind, flapping their wings but getting nowhere, screeching into the air.

"Jesus," said Dad, "look at the circus."

The walking had helped, but my head still hurt, and it felt strange to be with my dad, as if everything hadn't really happened and wasn't happening now. At any moment, I might wake and realize that the video camera—all of it, the walk now with my dad—didn't really exist.

Dad stopped near a bench where an old couple was sitting, looked me in the eyes, and said, "Is it a girl? Is that what's bothering you?"

My face burned with shame. It just about killed me that he wanted to help, and that he'd guess something so innocent, so I looked out at the horizon and shook my head.

He seemed to understand that I didn't want his attention, and he focused on the horizon as well. "Look," he said, pointing to the left.

Seven pelicans in a triangle formation—three on each side and one in front—swooped and glided with the breeze, until they skimmed the ocean.

"Isn't that something?" Dad said. He faced me. "Even," he said, "I know something's bothering you." He paused, gave a short cough into his fist, then continued, "I know I'm not the most attentive father. I may not be that good of a parent, but I care about you and your brother. I want you to know that I'm always here for you. If you need anything, I'm here. I didn't have that. As you know, I didn't really have a father to look out for me. That's why it's so important to me. I want it to be different for you."

"Dad," I said, "can we talk about this another time?" Every once in a while, he got in one of his earnest moods. I just wasn't up for it.

A long silence, and then he said, "Sure, of course. If that's what you want."

"When you think something's right," I said, "but you might have to hurt some people in order to do it, what do you do?"

He looked at me, considering. Then he said, "That's a tough question, Even. A real dilemma. I suppose it depends on the situation."

AT DINNER THAT night with Dad and Gabe, I didn't do anything stupid or say anything I shouldn't. But I talked and ate way too much in compensation, trying to appear lighthearted.

Nancy had made the lamb roast and potatoes the month before, and Dad thawed it from the freezer and warmed it in the microwave. A freezer-burn taste lingered, but I ate and ate.

We sat at the dining room table instead of in front of the TV, a rarity. Dad even lit a couple of long candles. Gabe pushed his plate in front of me without my asking, and I ate in Pavlovian response, finishing his meal as well.

Much of my chattering centered on sports and TV shows and real estate and business, things that I didn't really care about. I told a few stupid jokes.

Entertainer Even, my brother called me that night, and he and Dad watched me with a bemused interest.

By the time I went to bed, I felt delirious from smiling and talking and eating and being someone else. I lay down on my bed without changing into my pajamas. As I flipped my shoes off without untying them, listening to them thud against the floor, a few tears trickled down my face.

I lay on my side, my stomach bloated, and stared at an oblong slice of moonlight on my wall for a long time. Then I closed my eyes and went to sleep.

17.

JULY 7

WHEN I WOKE late the next morning, I knew that the police would arrest Gabe that day, knew it deep inside me—only a matter of time now—my fault for turning over the video camera. I sat in bed, watching the minutes flip-change on my alarm clock, and listened to the wind rustling the trees outside my window, not wanting to get out of bed to face Gabe or our dad or what would happen because of what I'd done.

I'd had a terrible dream just before waking, abstractly involving the severing of a dog's head. All from a headline I'd read in the newspaper weeks before, concerning a man who had chosen to prove his love to his beloved by beheading her canine companion.

But the dream dissolved when I woke, leaving me with the reality of what I'd done and how I'd wronged my kin. One of the side effects of removing the video camera from my life had been relief, but there was another far less satisfying one: With the camera gone, it was no longer so much about what I'd seen as about what I'd done.

A deep melancholy settled over me like a heavy blanket that I couldn't remove, one that would stick to me like another layer of skin. I didn't know this at the time—thank god, or I might have taken irrevocable measures—but it would not lift for years.

Most teenagers have a sense of immortality—something about the immaturity and plasticity of our brains at that age, I'd read—but not me. I've always been one to ponder death, to feel its nearness and my own fragility, freaking out at the feel of my own blood pulsing in my temples, and at the contemplation of my organs working in their orchestral complexity to keep my organism functioning.

One little flaw in the system, I knew, and the whole enchilada can end, just like that. Death, death, death, all around me, and in my life, always the constancy of death. Life, I'd come to believe, was about hiding awareness of this beneath the veneer of acceptability, functionality, imperviousness, and now I didn't think I could do it anymore.

One time, at around age nine or ten, not a teenager yet, I'd told my dad about my death awareness, and he'd said, "You've got the soul of an artist, Even. It's normal for someone like you. Of course you think about death and stuff like that," which made me feel better.

I thought about Gabe now. Would he have done the same thing to me that I'd done to him? I doubt it. But would I ever have done what Gabe had done? God, no.

What made me different from Gabe?

One time, when I was three, Gabe dared me to shove a marble up my nose to see how far it would go, and I did. We had to go to the hospital for the doctor to pull it out, and Gabe cried the entire time. "Why'd you listen to me?" he asked afterward. "Don't ever listen to me."

I called Sara that morning, knowing that she'd already be at work. "Even," she said, and I was so glad to hear her sweet, whispering voice that I felt like crying.

"Are you okay?" I asked.

"When my alarm went off this morning," she said, "I didn't know where I was, what day it was, or why I had to wake up."

I told her what I'd done with the camera.

"Good," she said.

"Why?" I asked. "Why are we doing this?"

"Why?" she said, as if amazed that she had to answer this question for me. She paused. "Because," she said, her tone softer and slower, "Even, we both saw what they did to that girl. They can't do that. It's wrong."

I started to tear up a little, relieved that she couldn't see me, and I said, "I'm just like him."

"No," she said.

"He's like another me—except he's mean to people sometimes. Maybe he just gets mean when he's drunk. I don't know."

"Something must've happened," she said, "to make him like that. Trust me: You're not like him."

We agreed to talk later.

"I haven't told anyone," she said.

"Me, neither. I want to tell Mike."

"Is that a good idea?" she asked.

"I don't know."

"I wonder who that poor girl is?" she said.

I almost said, She's my friend, the first girl I kissed, and a weirdo like me, but decided to keep quiet: It was not something I wanted to acknowledge.

It took all my courage to rise from my bed that morning and brush my teeth in the bathroom, avoiding my foaming-toothpaste mouth in the mirror.

But I caught a glimpse, leaning over to spit in the sink. Judas, traitor, jackass, rat, backstabber, double-crosser, tattletale, squealer, snitch.

I don't know what I expected. I suppose I hadn't thought my actions through to what they would generate. But there I stood, my heart thumping in my chest like someone was pounding a fist inside me at the thought of having to leave my bedroom and encounter the repercussions of what I'd done and the people I'd wronged. My disloyalty. Even worse, the hypocrisy that I would have to participate in to hide this awareness.

So in my new role as lying hypocrite, I made my way to the living room, where Dad, dressed in his bathrobe, sat reclined in his chair, watching a golf tournament that he'd taped at a volume far too loud.

"Aren't you going to work?" I asked.

He shrugged. "Maybe later," he said, not turning his head from the screen, smoking a cigarette, a Bloody Mary on the table beside him. "Woke with a sore throat." The screen glowed a leprechaun green with the grass course, and the commentators spoke in hushed and reverent tones, as if they were discussing the supernatural.

"Where's Gabe?" I asked.

"Gone," he said. "Left this morning, back to Gina's."

Gabe didn't get arrested that day. The hours passed and I waited and nothing happened.

Maybe, possibly, maybe, I thought, just maybe Tom L. found it in his heart to find another solution, one that I couldn't fathom, and all would be okay.

In the afternoon, our home phone rang. Still in his bathrobe, remote peeking from his pocket, and with cigarette in hand, Dad picked up the cordless phone in the kitchen, walking into the living room, where he muted the television, and where I sat on the couch eating a nectarine.

Standing, he gave monotone monosyllabic answers in his gruff voice ("Yes." "No." "Negative." "Wrong."), all the while staring at me while he spoke, and then he said, "You're wrong about that, sir. Gabe wouldn't do that."

I set my half-eaten nectarine in its paper towel on the table, fear climbing the back of my neck.

"I don't know what you're expecting me to do," he continued, "but it sounds to me like you've got enough to worry about with your daughter."

As Dad paused to listen, I tried to calm my panic, understanding that most likely it was Ben Kagan speaking to him on the phone.

"No disrespect"—Dad paused to inhale on his cigarette—"but," he exhaled his smoke, "let's think about this for a moment. She came here, to our house, and lied to you about it, and you're telling me she's lied to you many times before, and now she's claiming that she slept with my son, and you're telling me to keep him away from her?" He paused, as if to let this sink in, and then he said, "How do you know she's not lying about this? Perhaps you need to keep *her* away from *him*."

With that, their conversation ended. Dad hung up the phone and then he leaned over to smash out his cigarette in the ashtray on the coffee table.

"Do you know much about this girl, Tove Kagan?" he said, reaching into his robe pocket for his pack of Newports.

"No," I said, keeping my voice calm. "I had some classes with her in grade school. Why?"

"That was her dad." He lit another cigarette with a Bic lighter. Exhaling, he stared thoughtfully at it. Then he looked at me and said, "Haven't I told you and Gabe to always wear protection?"

In fact, we'd not had that conversation, but I was so shocked that I nodded.

"What's Gabe thinking, messing around with this girl? Sounds to me like she has a bad reputation. Lies to her parents."

"I don't know," I said.

"The dad says that he knows you. Said he has respect for you."

I felt a rush of claustrophobia, along with a sensation that the walls were closing in on me. "I barely know them," I said, my face hot. "I had classes with her, and her parents volunteered a lot. That's all."

He grimaced. "Kagan," he said. "Sounds Jewish."

"Don't know," I lied.

He nodded. "Sounds like they can't keep a lid on that girl. A wild child."

"What'd he want?" I asked.

He'd just taken a hit from his cigarette, and I waited for him
to respond. "You've got to be careful," he said at last. "You and
Gabe. We need to have a talk."

"About what? What'd he want?"

He sighed wearily. "Well," he said, "the thing is, Even, you're a
trusting boy, but people will try to take advantage. They know that
I have money, and that you're my son, that Gabe's my son. Girls
are going to go after you. They're going to want to get pregnant by
you. So that they can get my money. They see it as an easy street,
a shortcut. That's just the way it is." He squinted at me shrewdly.
"Do you understand?"

Surprised by his explanation and unprepared for it, I stared at
him and didn't say anything.

"It's about money," he said, sensing my disbelief. "It always is.
The sooner you learn this fact, the better."

"How do you know he wants your money?" I asked.

He leaned forward to ash his cigarette, his face thoughtful.
"I'm not sure," he said. He cleared his throat, and then he said
that most people always wanted something from him, and that it
came down to money ninety-nine point nine percent of the time.

18.

JULY 7

AFTER TURNING OFF our home answering machine, I went to my bedroom with the handheld cordless kitchen phone and lay down on my bed, trying to make sense of it all, startled by my dad's lecture, and by his conversation with Ben. I still thought of him as Ben, and not Mr. Kagan, since he and Luanne had insisted that we students call them by their first names. A flash of a memory came to me: Luanne leaning over to help me paste glitter on a paper-plate holiday wreath, her hand on my shoulder, my sense of pride. "Beautiful, Even. Look at those colors."

I planned to keep the phone from Dad's reach, and I put the ringer on mute. As if by kidnapping our home phone, I could ward off the future.

Did Ben know what had happened? What had Tove told him? What did Tove know? I imagined the Kagans sitting at their dining room table, Ben and Luanne interrogating Tove.

I opened a book—Robert Penn Warren's *All the King's Men*—but set it down almost immediately and went over and sat in my desk chair by the window. I thought, or rather tried not to think, about the Kagans, while staring through the crack in my curtains at the fat palm tree in our front yard, the sun glittering on its fronds.

I remembered the inside of the Kagan home, and how a breeze would come through their open window. One wall composed entirely of a bookshelf, and flowers and plants everywhere—dead, dying, and fresh—on desks, tables, windowsills, and counters. Fragrant, and another scent heavy in the air, one that I now know must have been sandalwood incense. Everywhere I looked, something unusual to see, something that wanted to be touched: porcelain figurines, knickknacks, strange-looking clay sculptures, pieces of dried-out wood and rocks and seashells.

In third grade, Tove and I watched musicals in the late afternoons at her house, and when we finished, the light outside the windows would be darkened to a day-ending blue. *Grease*; *West Side Story*; *Hello, Dolly!*; *Guys and Dolls*; *Oklahoma!*; *The Sound of Music*; *Singin' in the Rain*; *Mary Poppins*.

I'm not a musicals type, but at the time these strange hybrids of forced optimism and story lines, with accompanying soundtracks and lyrics, fascinated me. I couldn't believe things like musicals existed without my knowledge, and I wouldn't have been exposed to them if not for the Kagans.

"I'm agnostic," Ben told me once, around the time I was in fifth grade. "That means I have no idea," he added, "whether there's a god or not." He owned a watch-repair business called Tick-Tock, but he fixed other appliances as well.

"What about your religion?" I asked.

"Religion," he said, "is the opiate of the masses."

For a few long seconds, I tried to wrap my head around what he'd said. It's one of the most paraphrased statements of Karl Marx's, but I'd never heard it before, and I thought he'd simply come up with it.

"You're Jewish," I said.

"That's right," he said. He smiled. "I'm Jewish. Luanne isn't, but I am."

I didn't say anything.

"Know any Jews, Even?"

"None," I said.

"You do now," he said. "You know a Jew now." And in my head, I repeated: I do now; I do now; I know a Jew now.

"For me," he said, "it's not a religion. It's about culture."

I wanted to tell him that I was also an agnostic. As soon as he'd explained, I'd decided. But I wasn't sure how to pronounce the word, so I said nothing.

My comforter jiggled, startling me, the phone vibrating beneath it, and I rose and picked it up. The area code from caller ID showed that it was from Rancho Cucamonga, and I let it ring at least twenty more times.

I've thought about it—why'd I answer when I knew that it was probably Ben? How stupid. What could I have been thinking? And I've never come up with an adequate explanation, besides Ben's persistence in not hanging up, and my curiosity.

"Even," he said, his voice tinged with affection when he heard me on the phone and not Dad, "what a nice surprise. So good to hear your voice. It's been years!"

"I shouldn't be talking to you," I said, terribly upset, understanding immediately my mistake in answering. Unthinkable that I should betray my family more than I'd already done.

"It's okay," he said in a pleading tone. "Don't hang up. Please."

I said nothing, feeling myself break into a sweat.

The line went silent, and then he said, "Are you still there?"

"I'm here."

"Listen," he said, "I'm sorry to bother your family. I really am. I wouldn't be calling if it weren't so important. We've been having trouble with Tove. I'm trying to figure out what's going on."

I didn't know what to say.

"Maybe," he suggested, "I can tell you what I know, and then you can tell me if you have anything to add?"

When I didn't respond, he said, "It's like a puzzle. Your dad thinks I'm accusing him of something. I'm just trying to figure out what's going on."

"I don't know anything," I said.

"That might be," he said, "that might very well be."

"I should go," I said.

"The thing is," he said, "we found out that she lied to us about her Fourth of July weekend. She said she spent the night with Crystal and another girl, but we found out later that she didn't. We know she spent the Fourth at your house. We contacted her friends when she didn't come home and we found her car outside her friend's house. She wouldn't leave." He paused, took a breath. "I couldn't get her to come out until I threatened to call the cops. That's how bad things have gotten, Even."

He paused again, in case I wanted to respond, and when I didn't, he said, "Anyway, she finally came out, and I took her home. She admits that she spent the Fourth at your house"—his voice took on an embarrassed, discreet tone—"and that she and your brother"—he coughed—"got together," he finished. "But that's all we know. I'm trying to piece the rest."

"I spent the Fourth at my friend's," I said.

"She said that she didn't see you." He laughed in false merriment. "Hey," he said with sarcasm, "she told us the truth!"

It wasn't funny, and I didn't respond.

"Sorry to bother you and your family, Even," he said in a gloomy tone. "I'm just trying to figure out what's going on."

"That's okay," I said. "I have to go now."

"All right," he said.

We said our good-byes and I didn't speak to him again until over a year later, when we happened to be in the same courthouse bathroom during a break at the trial.

A ridiculously inane and brief conversation that did little to mask our deep discomfort: a mutual, agreed-upon complaint concerning the lack of paper towels. That he spoke to me at all was, I realize now, significant.

GABE ARRIVED LATER that afternoon in a foul mood. "Even," he said, kicking at my legs outspread at the couch, "get out of my way." He took the remote from me and switched the channels, sitting in Dad's recliner.

I'd been watching Hitchcock's *Rear Window*, and though I'd seen it before, I got rather involved at the midpoint. But I felt exhausted and guilty and not prepared to fight him for television control.

So we watched what he wanted, *The Anna Nicole Show*, a depressing reality series—every ten minutes or so deluged by commercials—depicting the drug-induced downfall of a plus-size model.

"She's so hot," Gabe commented, when Anna wobbled into her kitchen, high as a kite, lipstick smeared around her mouth, and sat in a chair. A close-up of her globe-like breasts, and then her staring-into-space face, lips parted with lipstick-flecked teeth, her cheek on her closed fist, an elbow on her kitchen table.

"Gabe."

He glanced up absently.

"Gabe, change the channel. This is stupid."

He stared back at the screen. "Fuck you," he said, waving me away with a tired hand. "Leave me alone."

I saw red. I did. A blazing red as I went for him, tackling him, slinging him to the floor, where we wrestled, my thigh grazing the edge of the coffee table. "Fuck you," I said, feeling the spittle fly from my mouth, "you fucking dick piece of shit!"

"Fuck!" Gabe said. "Jesus, Even, calm down."

He loosened my grip and crawled a few feet from me. Squatting and staring at me, he breathed heavily. His hair looked like the feathers on the back of a turkey, standing straight up, as if also wondering what to make of my outburst.

We stared at each other, not knowing what to do. I'd never exploded like that before and it scared me. My arms and legs still tingled with adrenaline, and it took a long time for my breathing to settle.

"God, Even," he said at last, using the same aggrieved, under-appreciated tone as our mom. "I didn't know that you wanted to watch that movie so bad. Next time, just tell me."

AFTER OUR FIGHT, Gabe tried to get me to stay—"We'll watch the movie together! I'll watch it with you!"—but I went for a long drive on the 55 freeway instead, to nowhere in particular, only in the direction of Saddleback, a saddle-shaped landmark formed by the ridge between the two highest peaks of the Santa Ana Mountains. Despite my love for the ocean, when troubled I revert to my Cucamonga roots and seek refuge inland near mountainous terrain. As a kid, I used to like to imagine myself mounting the mountain-saddle like a cowboy on a horse.

Looking at the landscape in the copper glow of smoggy sunlight, I wished I could go back to my childhood vision and ride away like John Wayne.

But instead I turned around and came home.

Dad and Gabe sat in front of the TV, finishing a dinner of pork roast, biscuits, potatoes, and corn.

Gabe gave me a wary glance and said, "Hey, little brother," to let me know that he didn't hold a grudge.

I couldn't eat—the smell made me sick—so I went to Dad's bathroom and procured two of his sleeping pills from his cabinet.

One would have done the job, but I took the second just in case, and pocketed a few Demerol for the future. The mere thought of having another dog-beheading dream, or of not being able to sleep, scared me.

When I came back into the room, Dad was giving Gabe the same lecture he'd given me earlier, about being cautious and always using a condom, since people—girls—would try to take advantage. He mentioned the phone call from Tove's dad. I could see only the side of Gabe's head as it went down.

The sleeping pills kicked in quickly, and soon I slept, as if someone had taken a mallet to my head.

19.

JULY 8

I WOKE EARLY ON Tuesday to a quiet house. Dad wasn't up yet to brew his coffee. I sat at my desk chair for a few minutes and waited to hear him. I would've liked to have slept much longer, but the sleeping pills' efficacy seemed to expire in a burst of wakefulness. Outside my window I saw the early-morning, lilac-colored sky and the front lawn sparkling with dew, and I heard a few birds singing to each other.

The neighbor's fat tabby cat, Walrus, sauntered past, pausing to give me a deliberate stare. I tapped my fingers on the glass. Walrus's hair rose on his back, and he sprung from view.

I tried not to, but I thought about the video. A flash went through me, a hit of a visual of Tove and my brother—implanted as clear as if I were seeing it again—and in a trance, I slapped my cheek hard to make it go away.

I rose and watched in morbid fascination in the bathroom mirror as the handprint on my face went pink, pinker, ending in red.

I wanted something—I didn't know what it could be—to relieve my anxiety. Then it occurred to me that this might be the way it would be from now on: permanent, tireless, endless isolation and unease.

But later that morning—after my hand-slap mark faded, and after I showered and dressed—Mike stopped by for a visit.

"You're not answering your cell," he said, slouching in a chair in the living room. "And you're not checking your messages. Your phone's turned off. What's up?"

His face was flushed. He'd been working out at the YMCA beforehand, his sideburns and some of the surrounding hair still wet with sweat.

Sitting on the couch near him, I ran a hand through my hair, not sure what to say.

"No, it's cool," I said. "Everything's fine."

"Really?" he said, trying, not very successfully, for sarcasm. A flash of anger and impatience crossed his face, surprising me.

We didn't speak for a long time. He picked his fingernails, something he did when he was uncomfortable. It was like he knew I was lying and he couldn't look at me.

I felt taken aback. "I'm sorry," I said finally, my voice saturated with emotion. I wanted to let him know about everything. But I didn't think I could tell him. That he cared meant a lot to me.

"Sorry for what?" he said.

"I don't know," I said. I could hear Gabe in the kitchen, opening and closing cabinets, making himself something to eat. Dad had already left for his office.

Mike listened to Gabe's noises as well, and he noticed something in my observance, saying, "It's Gabe, isn't it? What happened?"

"What?"

"What happened with Gabe? Your face's really red right now."

"It's not Gabe," I said.

He went quiet again, picking at his fingernails.

"You don't know me as well as you think you do," I said. "There's nothing going on."

He looked at me but said nothing.

Gabe walked through the living room, nodding at us in passing, eating a slice of toast, and I felt my body stiffen.

After Gabe left, Mike continued to stare at me, and I saw that he knew I was full of shit.

I had to look away, overcome with a rush of emotion, afraid that I would cry or do something stupid.

My heart sped in panic, and I felt as if the blood were draining from me. For a second, the walls and furniture seemed to slip and shift in my vision.

"Oh," he said, as if to help me, "I almost forgot. Emily's birthday is today. She wants you to come to dinner tonight. She asked me to ask you."

I laughed in relief. The idea of escaping into their family appealed.

"It's not her birthday party," he said. "That's next weekend. So don't get a big head. You're not invited to that. This is a family dinner."

I threw a couch pillow at him and he caught it lazily with one hand, and then—when I wasn't looking—he whipped it back at me. It hit my shoulder and then skittered behind me on the floor.

We both raced to retrieve it, each grabbing a corner, wrestling for control. I laughed along with Mike, and it surprised me a great deal.

Gabe passed through the living room again on his way out the front door. He gave us a sullen stare, and then he left. We heard his truck start and then move down the street.

"Something bad happened," I said.

Mike waited.

It took a while but I told him. Everything I'd been hiding inside me came out. Mike made it possible. He got the whole story.

Every now and then he looked at me with a pained, sorrowful expression. He spoke only twice to say, "Slow down, you're talking too fast," and "Oh, shit, Even, this is awful."

Somehow, I got off track and told him about how Tove had been my first kiss—fourth grade, behind the handball courts—and how I wished I'd told him about her that night at our house, before we'd left for the girls' volleyball party.

"Promise you won't tell anyone," I said when I'd finished.

"Sure," he said. "What are you going to do?"

"Wait."

He invited me to the beach ("A swim in the ocean always helps me," he said), but I declined.

He hugged me before he left, saying, "Let me know what you need. If I can do anything, let me know."

When he released me, I could see the tears in his eyes. "That poor girl," he said.

After he left, I lay on the couch and watched *Wheel of Fortune*. I felt better, but I also worried that Mike would let his parents know, and that they'd tell my family what I'd done.

I zoned out in front of the TV. One of the contestants on the game show—a giggly black woman with dimples—was about to solve the puzzle. But she spun and landed on Bankrupt—that awful *Waaahoooom* falling bassoon sound—leaving the puzzle for the greedy, bespectacled lawyer.

"I'd like to solve the puzzle, Pat," he said, blurting out the answer in a self-satisfied voice to lights and music and applause.

Unable to stand it, I switched the channel to a remake of *Carrie*, not recognizing any of the actors, and settled in for the entirety. But it was so dull that I fell asleep on the couch.

When I woke in the afternoon—the room stuffy and somewhat dark (no lights on) and the TV off—my dad was standing with his back to me, wearing khakis and a yellow collared shirt, his hands clasped behind him. He stared out the sliding glass door toward the pool and the garage.

I knew something was wrong immediately, and I sat up. "What's going on?" I asked. "Why are you home early?"

"Even," he said, not turning around, "I'm afraid there's been some trouble." His voice had a detached quality that spooked me more than his words.

I didn't respond, waiting for him to continue.

A very long pause, and then he said, "I need a favor."

"What?" I asked, with a rush of dread.

He turned to face me and said, "I want you to admit something first."

I would've admitted to anything to appease him right then. But it scared me to no end to think that he might be talking about my turning over the video camera.

"Okay," I said, "what?"

He didn't answer right away, pausing to take his glasses off and wiping them with his shirt. To anyone else, he might've looked emotionless, but I could tell that he was upset. His eyes looked unprotected without his glasses, small and strange.

He put the glasses back on, then fumbled in his pocket for his crumpled pack of Newports, lighting one with a shaky hand.

After flicking the match, he placed it in the ashtray. He took a few anxiety-reducing drags, blinking at me.

"Admit," he said finally, cigarette knuckled between his pointer and middle finger, "that as your father, I know more than you. That I'm smarter than you."

Involuntarily, I laughed, not expecting a contest of intellect.

He gave me a long, patient stare. A thin ray of sunlight struck the side of his face and torso. He took a pull on his cigarette, and the smoke came out of the side of his mouth in a hazy-dirty puff.

"Okay, sure," I said, clutching a couch pillow to my chest. "You're smarter than me," I said, and I believed it, too.

Silent for a moment, fixing me with his grim stare, he flicked his ash onto the floor (something I'd not seen him do before; he'd always been careful to use ashtrays). Then he said: "Take the wicker couch from the garage and get rid of it."

I was too stunned to say anything.

He continued to smoke and observe me. "Just take it somewhere," he said. "What about your friend, what's his name?"—he hit his forehead with the heel of his cigarette hand, trying to remember—"Matt—"

"Mike."

"Mike. Take it to Mike's or someone else's. Just get it out of here."

"Why?" I asked, but I knew that he'd just asked me to remove crucial evidence.

"I got a rather alarming phone call," he said, "at my office. A couple of detectives"—he looked down—"from Cucamonga."

"Oh, god," I said.

He glanced back at me, reticent. "Your brother's in big trouble this time," he said. "I'll bet it's that crazy girl, the one from that crazy Jewish family. The detectives came to Gina's house to get Gabe this morning, but they called me, and he's coming here. They're all coming here, since what happened, they've determined, took place in our jurisdiction, which is good—it's great, really—since we've got Krone and Jimenez looking out for us."

"What did the detectives want?"

"They have his camcorder," he said. "Gabe told me it got stolen. It's got Gabe's name and Gina's address on the warranty. That's how they knew where to go. There's some video on it—something bad, something happened in our garage on the Fourth, it's time-stamped on the video. I won't say what they said it shows. But it's bad."

He shook his head and took another hit from his cigarette. "Gabe," he said, blowing smoke, "actually thought the detectives were returning it. He said to me on the phone, 'Dad, honestly, it got stolen, and I thought they were being cool and giving it back to me.'"

He paused to share an incredulous stare with me.

Then, quite unexpectedly, the doorbell rang, and rang again, and someone knocked less than a second later, impatient.

We looked at each other, my dad swearing under his breath, and then he said, "Whatever you do, don't panic. It's going to be okay, Even. I'm going to take care of everything. I promise."

20.

IT TURNED OUT to be Assistant Sheriff Scott Jimenez at the door, in his full uniform, so that it looked to me at first like a costume, along with a lieutenant. "Hello, Dan," Jimenez said, giving my dad a significant look. He directed a less intense expression at me and tried, with little success, to lighten his tone. "Hello, Even."

The lieutenant, a small man with a beefy, muscular form, who reminded me of a French bulldog, coughed, as if to say, Don't act too chummy. Remember why we're here.

"What do you want?" Dad asked.

At first, Jimenez was officious. They were acting, Jimenez said, as "representatives from the Sheriff's Department to protect the department's interests."

"Okay," Dad said skeptically.

"We're on your side," Jimenez said, reaching out a hand and placing it on Dad's forearm.

The lieutenant shook his head and said in a stiff voice: "This isn't about teams or sides or loyalty or any of that"—a disapproving nod at Jimenez's comforting hand.

Jimenez placed it back by his side.

"We're representing," the lieutenant continued, "the interests of the Orange County Sheriff's Department. That's all. Nothing else. Because you're a major supporter of Sheriff Krone and a well-known public figure in the department and community"— he nodded at Dad—"we're here to ensure that the interests of the department are maintained, and that's it. Nothing more, nothing less."

"I'm more than a major supporter," Dad corrected him.

"Be that as it may," the lieutenant said, "we're here in the capacity of ensuring the department's interests and reputation."

"What does that even mean?" asked Dad impatiently.

No one seemed to know how to answer.

We stood in the entryway for a few awkward moments until Dad invited them inside, and we sat across from each other in the living room.

"Listen," Dad said, lighting up a cigarette, "I want to talk to Krone and I want to talk to him now."

Jimenez looked down and didn't say anything.

"That's not possible," said the lieutenant.

"We need," Jimenez said in a whisper, looking up and directing his statement at Dad, "above all, to keep up an appearance of objectivity."

Dad's face paled. He nodded, and then he offered his packet of Newports to Jimenez.

Jimenez declined while looking at the lieutenant.

"I'll tell you one thing," my dad said, sucking in his smoke, "no son of mine is spending even one day in jail."

Jimenez and the lieutenant stared blankly at him and said nothing.

Dad suggested that he and Jimenez talk in private in the kitchen, but the idea was promptly squelched by the lieutenant—"No way, nu-unh, not okay."

"The detectives are from the Cucamonga Police Department," Jimenez confided. "Gabe's main custodian is Gina, so they went after him in Cucamonga. They're on their way here now."

Although Dad already knew this, he groaned.

"That'll change," Jimenez said, his voice soothing, "since the alleged crime took place here."

"In the garage?" Dad asked.

Jimenez nodded.

"Do I have time," Dad asked, "to clean up some things?"

Jimenez stiffened, and the lieutenant said, "Not a chance. You didn't just say that. That's a serious crime. No one, and I mean no one, just heard that." He stared at each of us, and we all confirmed with nods. As if it was afterthought, he added, "Besides, the detectives will be here any second."

We stared at each other, and then I focused my gaze near the floor, concentrating on a corner of the lieutenant's pant leg, black sock, and shiny black shoe.

By the time the Cucamonga detectives arrived with Gabe, stoop-shouldered and puffy-eyed, in baggy jeans and a purple T-shirt, Dad had a better idea of what to do, thanks to Jimenez.

Jimenez had also given him a slip of paper with the name and phone number of a lawyer. "This man," he claimed, "is a wolf."

No one seemed to notice that Gabe was high, probably on medication. I could tell by the way that he rubbed his hands together. He sat next to me on the couch, and at one point he leaned against me without seeming to notice.

He didn't smell of alcohol or pot or act inappropriate. But there was a particular flatness to his speech and demeanor, and his eyes had an almost imperceptible sheen, as if they were coated in clear plastic wrap.

Both Cucamonga detectives had sandy brown hair. The greatest distinction between them was that one had acne-scarred cheeks.

The lieutenant gave the detectives the same spiel he'd given my dad and me earlier about why he and Jimenez needed to be here.

They shared a few shrewd stares during the lieutenant's explanation but otherwise didn't seem upset.

Yet much later, in statements, both detectives claimed that Jimenez's actions at our house were "extremely inappropriate" and "the beginning of a long chain of preferential treatment," saying that Jimenez gave Dad "legal and criminal advice for a horrific crime."

On the advice of Jimenez, who happened also to be a lawyer, I learned that afternoon before the detectives arrived, Dad didn't allow Gabe to be interviewed or questioned, except concerning the identity of the victim, whose welfare, they all agreed, was of paramount concern. The detectives were eager to check on her.

It surprised me that they let me stay in the room and listen, but everyone seemed to forget my presence, and I didn't say anything to remind them.

Gabe, who'd earlier admitted to the Cucamonga detectives to being in the video, claimed that he didn't know the victim. "Nope," he said, shaking his head, "no idea," he said, all of them exchanging glances.

But then he gave them the Ks' names, phone numbers, and addresses.

After Jimenez pointed out that the video in question had been shot at Dad's house, the detectives admitted that the investigation would soon be turned over to the Newport Beach Police Department.

Dad—with an approving nod from Jimenez—consented to a search of the garage, to be done the following morning.

Shortly after the Cucamonga detectives left, the lieutenant and Jimenez left also, and Gabe said, "Oh, my god. Can this really be happening?" and began to cry.

For a moment, we were all too shocked to say anything, and then Gabe burst out in a half sob: "Oh, god! I'm so sorry!"

Dad came to the couch and sat between us, putting his arms around Gabe—in a way that we hadn't seen or experienced since our childhoods, and even then very rarely—and let Gabe burrow into his shoulder. The only noise for a long time was Gabe's sniffling and sucking in the air as he wept.

Dad petted Gabe's hair—something I'd not seen him do before to Gabe, only to me—murmuring, "It's okay; it's gonna be okay."

Then finally Gabe pulled away, wiping his face with his hands, and said, "I'm so sorry, Dad. I'm really, really, really sorry. I messed up. I messed up so bad. Do you hate me? I'm so sorry. You hate me!"

Dad steadied Gabe's head with his hands, directing him to look into his eyes. "You're my firstborn," he said, his voice breaking with emotion. "I could never hate you. Don't you ever say that again, ever, do you understand?"

When Gabe didn't respond, he pulled Gabe's face closer, so that their foreheads almost touched.

His tone conveyed severity and concern. "Don't you ever, ever say that I don't love you," he continued. "You're my life. I haven't been there for you. I know it's been hard. This is my fault. Mine. But I'm going to make it up to you. But don't you ever say that I don't love you, ever again. I can't take that. I can't. It's not true; it's not right. Do you understand?"

He shook Gabe's head a little, and finally Gabe nodded, the tears spilling out.

"Listen to me," Dad said, releasing Gabe, "the both of you. We're going to fight this, and everything's going to be okay. I give you my word."

We both nodded. We'd not seen our dad cry before like he was now, his eyes shining.

My vision swam with the tears pooling in my lower eyelids, and I swiped them with my forearm, feeling a whirlpool of emotions: guilt, grief, anger, and a surprising relief at the connection between Dad and Gabe, so long in coming. But why had it taken this to make it happen?

And then, overpowering all my feelings, a sense of the disappointment my dad and brother would feel toward me once they knew what I'd done. I hated letting them down more than anything.

"Oh, god," I mumbled, unable to contain my emotions any longer, wanting to tell them about my bringing Gabe's video camera to the police station, to get it over with. "Oh, god, oh, god, I'm so sorry. I'm so sorry!"

But Dad hooked me into his arms before I confessed, and I, like Gabe before me, released my tears into his shoulder, the material of his shirt still wet from Gabe.

BEFORE DAD HOLED up in his office to call his lawyers, he had a couple of stiff drinks and made a phone call to Nancy at her Newport Bluffs apartment. Reclined in his chair, his third drink on the table beside him next to his cigarette propped in an ashtray, he said, "That's right, honey. I like the yellow one." A little tipsy, eyes and cheeks bright. "The blue one is okay, but the yellow is better. I don't know about the black. Doesn't seem right. Yes, yes. I'd go with the yellow."

Gabe and I sat on the couch and listened. We didn't know what else to do.

More murmurings of approval, and then he said, "Okay, honey, that's right. Smooches to you, too."

After he hung up, he said, "Didn't have the heart to tell her. She's upset. She wants to know which dress to wear to her charity event." His head went down, a smile spreading. "To be honest"— he shook his head in pleased incredulity—"I don't even remember what the dresses look like."

WE ORDERED A pizza to be delivered. I made a quick phone call to Mike and explained what had happened, and why I couldn't make it to Emily's birthday dinner.

He put Emily on the phone, and she asked me to sing "Happy Birthday" to her, so I did.

When Mike got back on the phone, he said, "If you need anything, I'm here."

Gabe and I were eating slices in the living room when we heard a thumping noise from Dad's office, and then Dad shouting, "Son of a bitch!"

Red-faced, he came into the living room, searching frantically for the remote. "Where is it?" he said. "Where, where? Hurry!"

Gabe found it wedged between the couch cushions and handed it to him.

He flicked between the stations, landing on the local news, muttering, "Son of a bitch."

To my horror, I saw Tom L. on the screen, talking to an over-animated female newscaster, who wore bright red lipstick and had her hair slicked back in a ponytail. But what horrified me the most was that as they spoke, boxed in the corner of the television screen and titled "MYSTERY VIGILANTE," a black-and-white image replayed, over and over: grainy security camera footage of someone hunched beneath a towel, setting a box down in the police station doorway. Shot from above, with the time and date spooling beneath the image, and then blacking out.

Replaying—toweled figure setting the box down, blackness, replay. Toweled figure setting the box down, blackness, replay.

Because I knew that I was under the towel, it seemed that everyone must know. My hunch, my bare feet, the visible trim of my jeans. The hand-trembling passing off of the box.

"If anyone has information," said Tom L., in his soothing voice, "please contact us at the phone number that we listed. We would really like to speak with the person who brought us this video camera. If you know who it is, or if that person happens to be watching right now, we need your help. A serious crime was committed. We need as much information as possible."

"Can you tell us," the smiling newscaster said, seemingly aroused by the possibilities, "what crime took place on the tape?"

Tom L. shook his head. "I'm afraid not."

The newscaster—I swear it—gave a lower-lip-jutting pout.

"I will say," said Tom L., "that in my entire forty-three years of law enforcement, I've never seen anything quite this disturbing."

This perked up the newscaster. She said, "You heard it, folks! Please call the information line if you can help. Thank you, Lieutenant Lawrence, for taking the time to talk with me, and for your incredible career of service."

"Thank you," said Tom L., reaching to shake her hand. The newscast went back to the regularly featured co-anchors.

Dad flicked the TV off, and we all sat silent for a moment. Then he said, "That son of a bitch hiding beneath a towel"—he paused, sucking in his breath, overcome with his emotions; once composed, he continued in a far more controlled and steely voice—"I'm going to find out who it is, and then I'm going to destroy the bastard."

Even though I was sitting, I had a vertiginous sensation, and I could feel the sweat from my armpits trickling down my rib cage. Dad seemed to be waiting for one of us to respond, and I knew that Gabe wouldn't.

When everything stopped spinning, I concentrated on Dad's forehead, locking myself back into the world. I said—or rather forced myself to say—"All right, Dad. Everything's going to be okay."

PART THREE

21.

F ROM THE MOMENT I set foot in Newport Beach, I'd felt a freedom from my mom and brother. I was Dad's son; Gabe was
Mom's son. But now that was over. It didn't matter where I lived.

Mom had told me once that I seemed more like Gabe's older
sister—whiny and wise beyond my years—than his younger brother.

I couldn't help but think about this as Sara talked.

"I saw the tail end of the news," she said, "just happened to
be flipping channels, but then I stayed up for the replay at eleven
thirty. Oh, my god. Seeing you underneath my towel, dropping off
that box . . . I couldn't sleep. I scrubbed my kitchen floor"—she
gestured toward her kitchen—"got on my hands and knees, using
paper towels. Look how clean it is. It's never been that clean, not
even when I first moved in."

Mike and I crooked our necks to observe her kitchen, and then
turned back to her.

Mike had not met Sara before, and I could tell that he thought
her pretty. But she overwhelmed him, as did our situation. He'd
been the one to insist that we meet and discuss what had happened,
and how he might help. Now in her apartment he seemed not to
know what to say.

Music from one of her neighbors filtered through her window, Beyoncé and Jay Z's "Crazy in Love," God help us. I got up and closed the window, which muffled the noise.

Sara sat across from us on a dining room chair, legs crossed, barefoot, and she tapped an unlit cigarette against her palm. She never did light it. She wore her cowry shell necklace, and her hair was in two braids, pulled back from her scalp so that her face seemed more open and vulnerable and childlike. When she talked, she looked to my right, as if she was afraid to meet my eyes.

"I used to tell Even," she said to Mike, "that he thought way too much about his family. 'Just wait,' I'd tell him, 'when you turn eighteen, you can go away, never come back, go to college,' because I knew he had to break free from them first. That's when all the good things would start for him.

"I had to get away from my parents, and once I did, it really helped. I didn't fit in my own life before. They're so messed up, my parents. There wasn't any way for me to be around them without being messed up, too. You know? You've got to get away sometimes first, just to separate and figure things out. Not that I've got everything figured out."

She glanced at the AA meeting directory on her coffee table. "I'm going to meetings again," she said as an aside.

She paused and her shoulders went down. "Now Even can't get away from them. I'm almost sorry that I called him, because now he's stuck. Even if he leaves, he's stuck now. He'll always feel responsible."

Another long pause, and then she set the cigarette on the coffee table. "I didn't know what else to do," she said.

I resented Sara's assessment. I wanted to tell her: At least I'm not estranged from my family like you. I still have my family.

I felt like everything was unreal—part of some crazy-ass dream—and that soon I'd go back to my old life: a mild alienation from my father mingled with a staggering affection and respect.

With Gabe, a shared sense of omnipresent despair, and the feeling that we would get through life together, that we understood and loved each other no matter what, and so we wouldn't be defeated.

As for my mom, I loved her but that was it. I didn't much like her or want to be around her.

Mike's voice broke the silence: "I have to ask"—he shifted his weight on the couch—"I have to"—he shook his head—"it's just, what's on that videotape? Why'd he go on the news to try to get Even to come forward? There's got to be something on there that's really bad—not that rape isn't bad—but what happened? I mean, god, what's on there?"

For the first time that afternoon, Sara's eyes met mine. Her face paled, and I wondered if mine did as well.

She took a deep breath, and then she said, still looking at me, "Picture something so terrible that for the rest of your life you don't know how you'll deal with it."

A long pause, and then Mike asked, "Where were her friends? Why didn't anyone stop them?"

"They're not really her friends," I said.

I saw that Sara had shut her eyes.

Mike bit his cuticle and started fiddling with his fingernails.

Sara went into the kitchen.

I sank into the couch, as if lead weights had been sewn into my clothes.

When she returned, she set a glass of water near me on the coffee table. She also brought over a plate of Oreo cookies.

"Did something happen to him?" she asked, sitting again. "I mean, when you were kids or something. Did someone molest him or something?"

I shook my head, but later I remembered a pimply-faced babysitter who had Doritos breath. Gabe and I must've been ten and nine respectively. He forced Gabe into the bathroom with him, and when they came out, the babysitter had a towel wrapped around his waist, and Gabe wouldn't tell me what had happened. Gabe also made sure to keep me away from the babysitter, making me play in another room. When the babysitter knelt to get a tennis ball from this little pond that we had in our backyard, Gabe pushed him in. "I don't like him," he said. The babysitter had to wash his wet and muddy clothes and dry them before our parents came home—smirking and thinking it funny, he walked around the house holding sofa cushions to cover his penis and ass—and he made it just in time, pulling on his jeans as Dad parked the car in our garage. The next time the babysitter came over, Gabe threw a fit, and our parents decided not to use him after that—not worth the hassle.

"It's his friends," I said. "Gabe doesn't have good friends like me."

I meant them, and they both knew it.

"Why don't you tell him?" Mike said. "Tell your dad. Tell your brother. Tell them why you did it, what you saw, and explain."

While they waited for my answer, I drank down my water and set the empty glass on the table. Then I said, "It would hurt them too much," and added, "and it would hurt me too much."

"What about your mom?" Mike asked. "Can't you tell her?"

"She'd hate me."

"Are you afraid of disapproval?" Sara asked. When I didn't answer, she said, "Your mom's, dad's, or Gabe's—or all of them?" I still didn't answer, and she said, "God, Even, don't you get it? They should be afraid of yours!"

"That's easy for you to say," I said, angry and hurt. "I don't know who I am. I'm sixteen. I'm still just trying to figure out who I am, and you expect me to know?"

No one spoke for a moment.

"I'm not telling them," I said, "I won't do it."

"Okay," Sara said, "but I'm not really talking about the camera. It's about more than the camera, Even."

"Maybe," said Mike, "we should get back to the reason I wanted to meet. What can I do," he continued, "to help you? What can Sara do to help?"

"Don't tell anyone," I said.

"What else?"

"I don't know."

"Listen," he said. "How about I say that it's me? That I turned in the camera?" Mike had obviously been thinking about it, and he seemed to have convinced himself.

"At this point," Sara said, "it's not so much about the camera anymore."

"Mike," I said, remembering Dad's threat from the night before, "you can't do that."

"Why not?" he said. "I don't care what your dad and brother think of me." He laughed. "Half the time, your dad doesn't remember my name."

That got me to laugh. But then Sara said that she'd looked up some things about my dad, and that she thought he might be dangerous.

"I know he's your dad, Even, but he's done some shady stuff. I mean, it's on the record."

"You don't know anything about business," I said, my face heated. "He's a self-made man. He got to where he is because he's smart."

"He is that," she agreed, looking away from me.

The last thing that Sara said to me before we left was: "I know that you admire your father, Even. But he's not a good guy. You're better than that."

When I got home, I locked myself in the bathroom and hit my fists against my arms and legs, hard enough to bruise them. Then I heard Dad calling to let me know that it was time to eat dinner, so I stopped.

22.

THE REPORTS THAT our dad spent over nine million dollars on Gabe's defense are not true. It's not true that he hired a dream team similar to O. J. Simpson's, consisting of twelve lawyers (two from Simpson's own defense), a team of private investigators, and a public relations expert.

Not entirely true, that is. If I'd ever questioned the power and usefulness of money, I no longer did.

Gabe's head lawyer, Jonathan G. Cavari, Jimenez's so-called wolf and a good pal of Sheriff Krone's, had earned a reputation as a dogged, ruthless fighter. Well-tanned, with oil black wavy hair, he owned a mansion in Newport Beach and a fleet of luxury cars. He came from a tough New Jersey neighborhood and liked to remind people—in his New Jersey–heightened accent—of his street-savvy working-class roots.

Dad asked me to come with him to Gabe's initial consultation with Cavari.

Cavari knew how to make people turn and take notice of him, and everything about him—the way that he dressed and talked— spoke of intimidation and success.

Cavari sat at his desk, smoking a fat cigar, his black eyes fastened on Dad. In front of him was a thick file with TOVE KAGAN written in permanent marker across it.

It was a gaudy office filled with lots of modern, expensive-looking sculptures and ugly oil paintings of what looked like Italian landscapes. On the walls were diplomas and a certificate for a martial arts class. The wall behind Cavari had been decorated with plaques and photographs of him with his arm around various celebrities: some whom I recognized (Corey Feldman, Larry Hagman, Donna Mills, MC Hammer), some who looked vaguely familiar, and some whom I didn't recognize.

Our chairs—upholstered in burgundy leather—fart-squeaked against our thighs and butts if we moved too much.

"This girl came to your house, alone, without her girlfriends, on the night of the Fourth," Cavari said to our dad, "knowing full well that she would have sex with all three of these boys. Now that there's a porno—which, by the way, she wanted to make—and now that her parents know, she's crying rape, because what else can she do?" He shook his head in exaggerated disapproval, and then added, "The lying little nympho."

Dad took a puff on his cigar (a gift from Cavari), his expression solemn.

"She," Cavari said, tapping his cigar ash in a crystal ashtray, "should be the one charged with rape, for forcing herself on these three young, decent men."

Cigar smoke hung in the air, and I could see Gabe's foot—propped on his knee—shaking restlessly.

"Look," Cavari said, setting his cigar in the ashtray, "I know this is difficult. But before I go on, I need you to understand something—all three of you." He paused for dramatic effect, taking a sip from a squat cut-crystal glass.

"That's good Scotch," he said. "You sure you don't want some?"

Dad grunted a no.

Cavari took his cigar and regarded its tip, and then he eyed each of us.

"This is war," he said, his voice grave. "She's your enemy. Her lawyer, her family, her friends—they're your enemies. If we're going to win—which, by the way, we will, because I always win—you need to hate them." He paused for us to take this in.

"I don't care," he said, "if they have a terminally ill mother or a child with cancer"—he fisted his hands and pretended to rub his eyes, as if wiping away tears—"boohoo! I don't care!"

He smiled angrily and leaned forward. "Make no mistake. They want to destroy you. But we're going to destroy them first. You need to hate them." He looked at each of us intently. "Do. You. Understand?"

"I understand," Dad said.

Gabe nodded.

When I didn't speak, all three of their faces turned to wait for my response.

"I can't hear you," Cavari said to me in a lilting, cajoling voice, cupping a hand to his ear.

"Okay," I said, barely audible.

He gave me a look of contempt. "Now's not the time," he said, slowing his words, "to be a pussy. Now's not the time." He pounded a fist on his desk. "Do you understand?"

"Yes," I said, my face burning.

He gave a belabored sigh. "Better," he said, wheeling his chair to a file cabinet. "A little better." He opened the cabinet and sifted through its contents. "We need warriors, not pussies," he mumbled. He pulled out a folder and opened it, wheeling himself back behind his desk.

"This," he said, running his index finger down a page, "is our time line." When he reached the bottom, he lifted his hand and licked his index and middle fingers, using them to turn the page, and then he began the process of dragging his finger down it again. This went on for a few minutes. Then he said, "I want to go over the time line in a very general way, Gabe."

Gabe's foot stilled with the attention. I knew that he'd abused his anxiety medication again, since his face was very pale and his eyes—though glossy—had a startled quality that the pills couldn't erase.

"Now," Cavari said, "she lied to her parents and said that she was spending the night at Crystal's, the night of the third of July. She also impersonated her mother in a telephone conversation with Melissa Stroh's mother, so that Melissa could also come with Crystal to your house on the third to swim and hang out, correct?"

"Yes, sir," said Gabe.

Cavari smiled. "Such good manners," he said. "How could anyone think a boy such as this"—he shook his head sadly—"could do what they're saying he did?"

Because there's a video, I wanted to say. I've seen it.

"Okay," Cavari continued, "one of these girls, this Crystal Douglas, is your girlfriend, correct?"

"No, sir," said Gabe.

"Hmm," Cavari said.

"We just hang out," said Gabe.

"I understand." Cavari looked back at his time line. "Don't want to tie a man down. Young and handsome, no need to get tied down, no, no," he said, while scoping the page.

"Now, Tove," he looked back at Gabe, "drank about ten swigs of Bacardi rum, along with the other girls, and you and Kevin and Kent, and you all got drunk."

"No, sir," said Gabe. "Crystal and Melissa said they were on the Atkins Diet, and they couldn't drink. They seemed real serious about it. I only drank beer and smoked pot. I don't know about Kent and Kevin. But I didn't get that drunk."

Cavari took a pen and scratched notes on the paper. "So Tove," he said, "made a video with Kent Nixon in late June, and you watched this porno together on the night of the third? Correct?"

"Yes, sir. Nixon made the video of them. I tried to take one of me and Crystal but she wouldn't let me."

"But Tove gave her permission and participated. Correct?"

"I don't think that she knew. When she figured it out, she told him to stop."

Cavari coughed. "Were you there?" he asked.

"No, sir. I was in another room."

"So you don't know that she told him to stop."

Gabe nodded in confused agreement.

"At this point, when you watched the video on the third, Tove had consumed a shot of tequila?"

"I don't know, sir."

"Did she say anything?"

"She said, 'Look at me. I'm a porn star.'"

Cavari beamed. He scribbled frantically, saying, "That's wonderful."

"She was being sarcastic," I said.

Cavari stopped writing and looked at me. "Excuse me," he said.

"She was trying to make a joke, because she didn't know what else to do."

"How would you know?"

"I saw her and heard her. Me and my friend Mike. We left for a party after."

Cavari scribbled again. Then he said, "No offense, son. But whose side are you on?"

I felt like he'd punched me in the gut.

A long silence as I stared at the grainy pattern of the wood floor and the fringe trim of what looked to be a flashy southwestern-style rug.

Then I heard my dad say, "Leave my boy alone," and Cavari said, "No one told the detectives that you were there. Let's keep this between us."

Dad's hand squeezed my shoulder.

"Tove," Cavari continued, his tone weary, "then went into the pool wearing her work clothes. At some point, her friends helped her go to the bathroom behind a bush, and they removed her pants at her request, so that she could urinate. Correct?"

"I don't know, sir."

"When Tove returned to the pool, she sat at the shallow end, took off her top, and then she had sex with Kevin Stewart. Correct?"

"To be honest, sir, I don't know. I was doing my own thing with Crystal at the other end of the pool."

"You were having sex with Crystal in the pool?"

Gabe looked away.

"So, if you're being honest, you don't know if Tove was having sex with Stewart, because you didn't see, because you were busy having sex as well?"

A quiet "Yes, sir."

"Honesty," Cavari said in a contemplative voice. "Let's think about this word. 'Honesty.' 'Honesty.' Honesty is about what you know in your heart of hearts, even if you're not sure of specifics. The emotions"—he thumped a widespread hand on his chest—"make it true."

Although Gabe seemed confused, he nodded.

"At around one in the morning," Cavari continued, "you all smoked pot in your bedroom, and then everyone left your bedroom except for you and Tove. Correct?"

"Yes, sir."

"Crystal and Melissa fell asleep in Even's bedroom?"

"Yes, sir."

"Wait, what?" I said.

Gabe faced me. "Yeah," he said. "They looked at some of your books and photos and stuff."

I hadn't known that anyone had been in my room, and it really bothered me to think of Crystal and Melissa poking around and invading my privacy.

Cavari gave me an annoyed passing glance, letting me know that he had no concern for my feelings.

"Tove," he continued, "fell asleep in your bed. You woke her and began rubbing her thigh. Then you removed her boxer shorts"—he laughed. "Does she think she's a man? Boxer shorts?"

He waited for us to laugh with him, but no one did. "You and Tove had consensual intercourse. Then you attempted to penetrate her anally but she denied your repeated requests, orally copulating with you instead. Correct?"

Gabe was silent, his face red.

"Gabe," Cavari said, "I know this is difficult for you, but stay with me."

Gabe nodded.

"Are you sure she didn't consent to anal sex?"

Gabe said nothing.

"Think about it," Cavari continued. "She's a liar. You might be remembering wrong. It certainly would help you if you did have anal sex, because that's the kind of slut that she is."

Gabe barely nodded.

"She left your bedroom. She then had consensual sex with Nixon in the living room, and she orally copulated with him as well. Correct?"

Gabe was done. His head was down and he was done.

"Let's move on to something else," Cavari suggested. He closed the folder and picked up the manila file with Tove's name on it. "Aha!" he said, flipping a page. "Listen to this from the police report."

He lifted the page and cleared his throat. "When confronted by her parents, Tove Kagan admitted to them," he read in a deadpan voice, "that she had consensual sex with Gabriel Hyde, but withheld the fact that she had sex with Kent Nixon. She relayed the events from the night of the third as if they'd taken place on the night of the Fourth of July, because she had no memory of the Fourth. She said that she didn't want to disappoint her parents any further, and she felt that they would be less disappointed if she told them about Hyde." He paused to roll his eyes.

"Yeah," he said bitterly, "because the Hydes are rich and the Nixons aren't," and then he continued reading in an expressionless voice: "When she admitted to the police and her parents that she knew of the videotaped events occurring on the evening of the Fourth of July, she thought the police were referring to a videotape Nixon had recorded of her and Nixon having sex in late June. She assumed she was being confronted with evidence from this tape."

He paused again, taking on the voice of a girl: "Oh, no! I would never let anyone videotape me having sex! Oh, no! I would never have sex with more than one boy in a night. That's bad!"

He shook his head in disgust, and then he continued to read: "The night of the third, Kagan had sex with Hyde and Nixon. Before that, she claims that she was intoxicated in the pool, and that her friends had taken off her pants. Kevin Stewart swam to her and tried to initiate sex. He pressed against her and she could feel that he was erect, but she pushed him away.

"Yet Crystal Douglas and Melissa Stroh claim that they saw Stewart and Kagan having sex in the pool, and that after, Kagan spoke to them and said to not let her have sex with anyone but Nixon, because he was her boyfriend." He snorted derisively.

"So," he concluded, "she says it's only two boys, but we all know she had sex with all three of these boys the night before, and then she comes back—alone, without her friends—the next night for more. This girl is insatiable! She's insatiable! But when her parents find out, when her porno surfaces, she decides to call it rape."

He paused to give any of us an opportunity to respond, and when no one did, he continued to read: "Kagan woke up the next morning, on the Fourth, feeling sick to her stomach, extremely tired, and with a headache. She and her friends left the Hyde house in her car, and during the drive, she denied having sex with Hyde since Douglas was present and was Hyde's girlfriend.

"But as soon as Douglas got out of the car, she told Stroh that while having sex with Hyde, she thought only about how wealthy her children would be if she got pregnant.

"After dropping off Stroh, she stopped at a McDonald's and ate part of a cheeseburger and a few fries. Then she slept in her car in the McDonald's parking lot for several hours before going to work for her 2 to 7 PM shift at Marie Callender's restaurant.

"Hyde and Stewart called Kagan at work, inviting her and her friends to return to Hyde's house that evening. Stroh and Douglas could not go. Kagan initially declined, saying that she still felt tired and queasy. They begged her. She said only if her friends came, but after they continued to plead, she agreed. She said that she wanted to prove her loyalty to Nixon, and that she only wanted to be with him, not with his friends.

"She again lied to her parents. When she arrived at Hyde's, Nixon and Stewart and Hyde were playing pool in the garage. She drank a beer, then asked for hard liquor, stating that she wanted something that would get her drunk.

"Stewart left for about ten minutes and returned with a Styrofoam cup. She asked what it was and he told her that it was a 'Bombay.'" Cavari paused to take a drink from his Scotch.

"Here's the thing," he said, setting his glass down. "The prosecutors are going to say that Stewart drugged her, and that's why he was gone for ten minutes. But we're going to say that he didn't, and that the drink contained 8.5 ounces of 94-proof gin, and that Tove gulped it down. She also took a hit of marijuana from a pipe being passed around."

He went back to reading in his flat voice: "She began to feel dizzy and sick when she tried to stand up.

"Her last memories of the evening were of Stewart sitting down on the couch next to her and Nixon standing at the pool table talking to her. She momentarily awoke later when she hit her head on the side of the couch. She also remembered vomiting into her hand. The vomit spilled all over, soiling her clothes and hair.

"Her next memory was of Nixon waking her in the morning for a ride home and asking her where she put her keys. She didn't remember getting into the car. Next she found herself in the passenger seat in front of Nixon's home. Nixon had left for his job at the Shell gas station. She was dressed, her car was hot, and the windows were cracked.

"Nixon's mom came outside and gave her a bottled water. Kagan could smell the vomit and urine on her body. She called Douglas and asked if she could clean up at her house before going home.

"At Douglas's house, Kagan undressed to take a shower and, when her bra fell out of her pants, she realized for the first time that something must have happened. She felt sore in her pelvic area when she went to the bathroom. And then she saw the blood. She was afraid to look or examine further, knowing that something was 'very wrong.'

"After her shower, she talked on her cell phone with Stewart and asked him what happened the previous night. Stewart laughed and responded, 'Why? Are you sore?'

"Kagan's parents discovered she'd lied about her plans that Fourth of July weekend. To locate her, they contacted her friends and eventually found her car parked outside of Douglas's house.

"Kagan refused to leave the house until her father threatened to call the police. She admitted to her parents that she'd lied about spending the night at Douglas's house that weekend. She did not tell her parents she had no memory of the night of the Fourth."

Cavari closed the file, heaved a sigh, and stacked it on top of the folder. "Blah, blah, blah, blah, blah," he said. "I'm a victim. Let me destroy these boys' lives so that my parents don't know that I'm a lying, alcoholic slut."

Dad held the cigar between his fingers, as if he'd forgotten about it, the ash about an inch long.

Gabe passed a trembling hand through his hair. Everyone, it seemed—except for Cavari—was embarrassed.

Dad seemed to startle to consciousness, tapping his ash and setting the cigar in the ashtray. "What do we do?" he asked.

"I'm glad that you asked," Cavari said. "We tell the jury that this is a lying, alcoholic slut. That these rape allegations are a travesty. Just like the Kobe Bryant case. That girl consented, and this girl did, too. Kobe's not going to jail, he's no rapist, and this terrific young man sitting right here is not a rapist, either."

Dad's face had gone red.

Gabe said, "What if I admit that I was wrong? What if I say I'm sorry? I'm a juvenile. So I won't go to jail, right? Maybe I could apologize, and that would be good."

Cavari took a puff on his cigar and nodded. "That's a nice thought, Gabe," he said. "I'll bet that you'd like this to go away, to be over with. But that, my friend, is not the way the world works." He looked at Dad, as if to say, Tell him.

"He's right, Gabe," Dad said. "That's not the way the world works. We've got to fight."

"Look, Gabe," said Cavari, with a measure of severity, "I know that you want to make things better. I know that you feel bad. But I don't see how ruining your life makes anything better. I don't see how that serves anyone's interests."

I'd broken into a sweat without realizing it, and my shirt was clammy against my back. For some reason I said, "How do you know that Kobe Bryant isn't guilty?"

Cavari ignored me. He didn't even look at me. He said, "The most damning piece of evidence is the video. First, we're going to try to block admissibility by claiming that law enforcement doctored the images. It's a long shot, and if it doesn't work, then we need to convince the jurors that although Tove looks unconscious, she willingly had sex with these boys."

"What are our chances?" asked Dad.

"Good," Cavari said without hesitation. "Very good. With a little pressure, the Kagans might drop their case. I mean, they might come to their senses and see that it's futile to go forward.

"If not, we can convince a jury that this was nothing more than a teenage sexcapade, a case of sex that got a little bit out of hand."

He reached for Tove's file, opened it, and thumbed through the pages. "We've found out from our investigators," he said, closing the file, "that Tove's parents sought medical and psychological help for her, because of her rebellion. She repeatedly left the house without telling them where she went, got in trouble, and lied compulsively. Too bad she's a straight-A student, but we can work around that. Her relationship with her father is very strained. Very bad. They don't get along at all. Her friends are already turning on her. We've got them in our pocket. They'll say that she's a liar and a slut, and that she consented. She claimed that she wanted to be a porn star, so of course she agreed to make a video with these boys."

He closed the file and gave us a triumphant smile. "We'll win," he said. "I know it."

23.

NOT LONG AFTER the meeting with Cavari, I began to spend more time at Mike's house, eating dinner there at least twice a week. Then school started in September, and I came over after school almost every afternoon, even if Mike wasn't home (he had some sort of athletic practice going on all the time). I never did find out how much Mike told his parents about my involvement in my brother's case.

The Woods had a separate, windowless room with a sliding glass door near the garage, where Mike's mom kept her sewing machine collection (unused for years) and other stuff. It took about a month, but she emptied it out and sold most of it at a garage sale. Mike's dad put a futon, an old desk, a standing lamp from Target, and a chair inside. The room had a small bathroom with a standing shower and a tiny sink and toilet.

"Yours," Mike's dad told me, with an arm slung around my shoulder, as we stood outside the room one afternoon. "As soon as we get it fixed up." The Santa Ana winds whipped and flapped the curtains against the open sliding glass door, along with a clanking cord.

"You've got a lot going on at home," he said, "and this can be a safe place."

Jerry Wood is an ordinary-looking man with thick silver hair that he keeps groomed in a close cut, and his eyes seem almost always wet with emotion—the only way I can think to describe them.

"Whenever you want," Lori Wood added, "it's here. We'll get you a key." She held her billowing skirt down with her hand, her hair whipping around her head. She, like Jerry, is ordinary-looking, but to me, beautiful, her eyes weighted with kindness.

I thanked them, calling them Mom and Dad. Light flashed through my head so that I couldn't see for a second, from gratitude.

I don't want to sound too dramatic, but the Wood family and their generosity helped save my life.

But I had to wait for them to fix up the room for me, and during that time, Cavari came to Dad's house often to talk strategy. He hired focus groups to test trial strategies and a public relations expert and private investigators, all with Dad's approval and financial backing. He explained over and over that Tove—or the Alcoholic, Lying Slut, as she came to be known in Dad's house—was a whore who loved giving blow jobs and enjoyed doggy-style sex and anal intercourse, so that these things became like facts. She dreamed of becoming a porn star, he said, craved group sex, and liked to give road head and swallow. Everyone knew that she'd faked unconsciousness as a porn technique. Some people were into that—snuff-like porn. Not only had she been an enthusiastic participant in the video, she'd been its initiator and director, Cavari said.

Remember that ridiculous speech on the USS *Abraham Lincoln* aircraft carrier? When Bush said, "In the battle of Iraq, the United

States and our allies have prevailed," all the while standing beneath a festive MISSION ACCOMPLISHED banner? Remember how before-hand, for the photo ops, Bush swaggered around the carrier in his high-tech flight suit?

One afternoon, Cavari, in his loud, didactic voice, said of his attempts to get Tove and her family to drop the case, "Soon, my friends, I'll be saying 'mission accomplished,' I'm sure of it."

Later that same afternoon, Sara and I got into this weird fight on the phone. She asked me, genuinely concerned, "How are you feeling?" and I told her, "There's only one question I hate more than 'What are you thinking?' and that's 'How are you feeling?'"

She said I was trying to be a dickhead, but that I couldn't be one, because I wasn't one, and I told her that maybe she didn't know a dickhead when she saw one.

After that, we stopped speaking for a long time. Looking back, what she said about my dad and my connection to him bothered me, and that she'd put me in this predicament.

No matter what she claimed, I also believed that I was too close to the source, too similar to my brother and father for her.

NANCY CAME OVER to Dad's one afternoon with about six or seven other women from her Bible study, in efficient pantsuits and chunky gold jewelry, to engage in a group prayer for our family. To me, the fact that Dad agreed to it revealed how far he'd gone off the deep end.

"I don't want to," I told him.

"You don't have a choice," he said.

So I joined Dad and Gabe and the women.

We stood in a circle in the living room, our heads bent, our eyes closed, arms around each other's shoulders and waists. But I kept my eyes open. Nancy's heavy perfume clashed with some of the others'. I had to stifle a sneeze.

They took turns praying out loud for our family's suffering, for us to endure, for Jesus to be with us. "Jesus, Father," Nancy said, "keep Gabe and his family strong," accompanied by murmurs of "Yes, Father, Jesus, be with Gabe and his family. Let them feel your strength."

But it wasn't until they started praying for Tove's soul that I got hot and uncomfortable. "Jesus, Father, we pray that Tove will drop the charges, and that she will admit her lies. Let Tove come to you for forgiveness."

The air was so heavy with bullshit I didn't think I could take it much longer. A few hot tears slid down my face, but I stayed silent and waited for the prayer circle to end.

The next morning, I packed a bag with some of my clothes and left it in my locker at school, so that I wouldn't have to come home.

After that, I pretty much lived at the Wood's house and slept on the sofa in the living room until the other room—the one they'd emptied and furnished for me—was ready for me a week or so later.

When I got the key—and the room was mine—it was so wonderfully quiet and private. I spent enormous amounts of time in there: reading, napping, doing my homework, listening to music, and being alone.

Dad didn't take it personally, since he was preoccupied with Gabe, of course. He attributed my absence to the stress of the upcoming trial, and I couldn't go live with Mom, since I went to school in Newport.

I made sure to make an appearance now and then, so that Dad wouldn't make me come back.

Dad insisted on sending a check to the Wood family each month for the expense of feeding and caring for me (I don't know the amount, but knowing Dad, it was substantial).

One Saturday afternoon, I stopped by the house to pick up a few things that I'd forgotten—my electric toothbrush and a T-shirt that I liked—using the key hidden beneath a rock. Dad wasn't home, and Gabe's truck wasn't out front.

In Dad's office, looking for scissors to open a tightly sealed package of almonds, I came across a file from Cavari titled VIDEO EVIDENCE. I sat at Dad's desk and read:

> The purpose of this document is to depict the events in the videotape recorded on the evening of July 4th through the eyes of potential experts for the prosecution and the defense.

PROSECUTION:

The first scene depicted Gabriel Hyde trying to remove Tove Kagan's jeans as she held a can in her hand. Dr. Patrick Fuentes, certified in neurology and sleep medicine, interpreted the events depicted. Fuentes focused on symptoms Kagan displayed to support his conclusion that she was unconscious throughout the events shown in the video.

Fuentes found particularly noteworthy Kagan's comment at the beginning of the video, declaring, "I'm so fucked up." These were the only words Kagan spoke. Fuentes explained that Kagan's silence during the events depicted over a period of 20 to 29 minutes demonstrated a "certain loss of higher brain function as a result of her intoxication."

Fuentes pointed out that although the recording lasts 14 minutes, the elapsed time is closer to 20 to 29 minutes because the tape was paused at different times so that Kagan could be repositioned.

After a pause on the videotape, the next scene depicted Kagan nude on her knees with her head in the lap of Kevin Stewart, who is seated on a couch, with Hyde kneeling and entering Kagan from behind as she orally copulates with Stewart.

Fuentes explained that in this position, Kagan could not support her weight, but rather was wedged in between Stewart's pelvis and Hyde's legs, with one of Kagan's arms hanging limply at her side.

Fuentes noted Kagan's movement in this position was the result of Hyde thrusting, and when Stewart no longer held her, Kagan slid off the couch.

She hit her face on the couch, taking no defensive action. Fuentes pointed out that when Kagan raised her head, it flopped back down, indicating that she could not sustain movement.

Fuentes opined that Kagan's "rag doll" movements—limp limbs and flaccid muscles—objectively signaled her unconsciousness.

When Kagan was moved into position to orally copulate with Stewart, who was standing with his pants down trying to guide Kagan's mouth onto his erect penis, she fell onto his penis, provoking a gag reflex. Kagan moved her arm to her face, which Fuentes explained represented purposeful action accompanying the natural gag reflex to a noxious stimulus.

Fuentes said that Kagan's condition prevented her from understanding verbal communication.

Following a pause in the recording, the videotape resumed with Kagan on the pool table and Kent Nixon penetrating Kagan's vagina with his hand, and then Stewart penetrating her vaginally with his penis before ejaculating on her stomach.

Fuentes pointed out that while Stewart was on top of Kagan, she remained passive and unresponsive, lowering her hand toward her pubis in a similar way to her earlier gag reflex, but that she was unable to sustain the movement because of the level of her intoxication.

Fuentes said that Kagan's lack of movement for over two minutes despite the penetration demonstrated Kagan's "significant level of sedation and intoxication."

The next scene depicted Nixon penetrating Kagan's vagina with a pool cue. Fuentes explained that although this constituted significant stimulation, Kagan's only reaction was to flex her right leg slightly, further demonstrating her severe intoxication.

Fuentes also noted that Kagan registered no response when the boys penetrated her with their fingers. When Stewart pinched her nipples, she reacted by moving both arms toward her chest, in response to a noxious stimulus.

At this point in the videotape, Hyde vaginally penetrated her with the pool cue.

Fuentes described how Kagan made a "nonpurposeful" roll when penetrated, which he described as merely a physical response to the thrust of the pool cue.

Kagan was then repositioned facedown on the pool table and Hyde used the pool cue to penetrate her anus.

After another gap in the videotape, the recording resumed with Kagan being slapped hard on the buttocks. Stewart then used the pool cue to penetrate Kagan again, this time vaginally.

Toward the end of the videotape, Fuentes drew attention to what he believed was Kagan's incontinence on the pool table.

Fuentes concluded, "It is obvious to anybody that she is not aware of her environment here. You don't have to be an expert to understand that when a person appears to be asleep or sedated so significantly that he or she looks like they are behaviorally asleep, they are not responsive to their environment, and they don't know what's going on around them. It's not rocket science."

DEFENSE:

Dr. Harold Fisker, a certified neurologist, described Kagan's movements in the videotape as responsive, demonstrating conscious, learned behavior.

Fisker explained that there are five different levels of consciousness, ranging from alert, which Fisker described as normal, to comatose, at the other end of the spectrum, which he described as totally unresponsive.

Based on his observations, Fisker described Kagan's level of consciousness on the videotape as "obtundation," which means a person retains the ability to function, albeit with impairment.

Fisker explained that if one asks an obtunded person a question, such as a math equation, a delay may occur, but with the proper stimulation, the person can respond appropriately.

According to Fisker, an obtunded person maintains conscious control of their movement and discernment. Fisker explained that an obtunded person would have the ability to refuse to consent to the activities depicted in the videotape.

Explaining oral copulation as a learned behavior, Fisker concluded that the video segments of Kagan orally copulating with Stewart demonstrated conscious thought and purposeful movement.

Similarly, Fisker explained that relaxing the sphincter muscle is also a learned response, so that when Hyde entered Kagan's anus with the pool cue, he could do so only because Kagan consciously relaxed her sphincter muscle, allowing for vaginal and anal penetration.

Fisker also explained that when the "liquid escaped" from Kagan's body, Kagan's movement of her leg away from the liquid indicated voluntary control.

Similarly, Fisker inferred that the liquid stopped escaping when Kagan chose to stop it.

Fisker stated that unless a person overrides the naturally contracted sphincter muscle, it would be impossible to insert a pool cue into a person's anus without causing injury.

Fisker stated that the absence of injury to Kagan's anal canal supported the conclusion that when Hyde inserted the stick into Kagan's anus, she was cooperative and aware of what was happening.

Dr. Ralph Hoffer, a colleague of Fisker's, offered another theory, stating that Kagan's obviously diminished consciousness might have been self-induced because of her post-traumatic stress disorder.

Kagan has low self-esteem and she's morally conflicted, which can cause acute situational distress.

Hyde, Stewart, and Nixon, he stated, could not be guilty of rape by intoxication if Kagan had voluntarily willed herself into a coma.

I SHUT THE file, closed my eyes, and sat there for a long time, thinking about what I'd read. How much were Fisker and Hoffer being paid by my dad to come up with this defense? (Quite a bit, as it turned out.)

I remembered what I'd seen on the video camera, and hearing Kevin as he tries to get a blow job, saying to Gabe, who's having sex with Tove from behind, "Yes! Right there! Right there! Keep her with the fucking lips. You're making her eat my fucking dick off, dude. Come on! Fuck that shit!"

A close-up of Gabe's face and chest as he says to Kevin, "Let's switch up now."

"You think so?"

"Yeah, let's sit her down."

I remembered Gabe grabbing Tove's hair to keep her head from wobbling. He lets go, and her head snaps back, and then she falls face-first onto the couch.

"You done?" says Kent.

Gabe asks, "Do you want me to take your spot now?"

After the couch scene, Tove's on the pool table, her head lying on the hard edge, her eyes closed.

She looks asleep while Kevin fucks her. The roving camera shows no facial expression, and her arms flop.

Kevin comes on her stomach, and then wipes his penis with her bra and tosses it to the floor.

Gripping my head in my hands, trying to shake the images and not wanting to remember the pool cue, I didn't hear someone come into the office.

"Even," the voice said. "Even, are you okay?"

I turned in my chair to see Gabe holding a bottle of Coors loosely in his fingertips.

An awful silence, and then he said, "You look really pale." He smiled.

"Oh, sure," I heard myself say. "I'm fine."

He tipped the bottle and took a long, gurgling pull. Done, he said, "What's that?" gesturing with his empty bottle toward the file.

"Nothing," I said, but he was already moving toward it.

"Were you reading this?" he asked, scanning the content.

I explained that I'd glanced at it.

An ominous silence descended.

Then he shut the file and said, "I remember it different."

Too stunned to ask what he remembered, I said nothing, but he continued, "She got on the pool table by herself, and her eyes were open at times. She had to know."

"Gabe," I said, "this is bad."

"I know," he said. "I regret what happened, the whole thing, believe me. We were all so fucked up. It just got out of control." He paused, and then he added, "I'm the one that stopped it, when I saw her peeing on the pool table."

My heart thumped wildly. "You want a medal?" I said.

To my surprise, he laughed.

"Is it because you hate Mom," I said, "and resent having to take care of her, especially right after the divorce and when I moved out?"

"You think I hate Mom?"

I waited.

"I don't hate Mom, Even. I don't hate women, if that's what you think. I don't think about it that much."

After a pause, he continued, "If you're going to go that route, I'd say it's more about Dad—about wanting to punish him, some sort of crazy, destructive thing."

"What happened with that babysitter?" I asked.

"What are you talking about?"

"That time, in the bathroom, when you came out with him, something happened."

"You think," he said, "that because I was forced to suck some babysitter's cock, that's what makes me a monster? Is that what you tell yourself?"

I had trouble looking at him. "I'm trying to understand," I said. "What'd she ever do to you to deserve that?"

"You act like you know her," he said

I didn't answer.

"Would it make you feel better," he asked, "if I told you that it's not really about her, and it never was?"

"What do you mean?"

"I don't really understand it," he said, "but it's like I was show-ing off for them—for Kent and Kevin—and they were showing off for me, and it got super-crazy, like some tribal, weird thing that got out of control, but I didn't mean to hurt her, or anyone. I don't know." His voice got quiet. "Believe me, I'm sorry. It just got out of hand. I'm really sorry for what this has done to everyone. All of the money Dad has to shell out for my defense. Everything."

"Are you sorry for what you did?"

"Of course," he said.

The fact that he'd opened up to me was more than I'd expected. In the past, I'd concealed certain feelings and concerns from him—judgments—based on a dynamic between us that seemed natural and important to maintain. I hadn't wanted him to believe that I was ashamed of him. I'd wanted to keep him positioned above me, as the older brother, where he belonged. Now I couldn't anymore.

He noticed something of this revelation in my face, because he said, "All I want—all I've ever wanted—is to be a good person," and when I didn't respond, he sat on the floor and his hands went to his face.

I left the room, wondering how much of his tears came from self-pity. Like our mom, he could be hugely dramatic. I no longer trusted him. But that didn't mean I didn't love him.

24.

THE HOLIDAYS PASSED in a blur, and then a few weekends after New Year's, Mike and I went to a party at a junior's house while her parents vacationed in Costa Rica. A Christian who was on the dance team, Kathleen Duren was blond, tan, skinny, with near-perfect tennis ball–sized breasts, and everyone thought she was hot. She also had a manic neediness and seemed to be constantly performing—her walk, talk, eye rolls. She made me nervous. After he graduated, Mike ended up dating Kathleen for about six months of torment and confusion, until she broke his heart. I Googled her out of curiosity the other day: She calls herself a performance artist and poetess and posts titillating naked selfies—glitter and letters from the alphabet and paper money stuck on her body—on her blog, called *Women Objects* along with simplistic, feminist-minded poetry ("she loves her cum and draws pictures on the mirror with it"), all in the name of art and feminism. Within a few minutes, I understood that what she really desires is art's perverted cousin, attention.

THAT NIGHT AT Kathleen's party, her friend shouted at me over the music and noise, telling me, between hits on a joint, about how she became a vegetarian: "It started after I saw *Babe*. I love that movie. 'That'll do, pig,' the guy says. 'That'll do.' Oh, my god! Forget it! I can't eat pig after that."

She took a long inhale from her joint—her eyes widening—and then passed it to me. After her exhale, she continued, "Then I started thinking about how things that I ate had eyeballs and hearts, and parents and faces and souls, and I got really freaked out."

I don't remember her name. Tall, blond, skinny, and also a member of the dance team. Though technically not as hot as Kathleen (slight buck teeth), she had an earnestness that appealed to me.

I hadn't been with a girl in a long time and was ready to try, seeking the pleasure and distraction of an inconsequential hookup.

Though I ate meat, I nodded in solidarity, taking shallow, superficial hits from her joint to be polite.

Someone tapped my back.

I tried to ignore it but then the tapping became a far more forceful hand on my shoulder.

The media had begun feeding on the case—calling the Ks and Gabe the Hyde Three—and I became paranoid that someone might ask me about it. So far, besides the occasional stares, I'd been left alone.

Annoyed at the interruption, and worried that it might be someone confronting me, I turned, surprised to see Sara's pot-dealing boyfriend, Joe, wearing his cowboy hat, his face a mess: black eyes, bandaged nose, split bottom lip with a track of black stitches poking out like insect legs.

"Oh, shit," I said. "What happened?"

He gave me a grimacing grin that looked like it hurt. "Fuck if I know," he said. He had to lean forward and talk in my ear because of the noise, his boozy nicotine breath tickling my skin.

"Minding my own business," he said, "walking to my car in the 7-Eleven parking lot, and I got jumped. A big motherfucker. Starts pounding me into the street, right next to my car. Kicked my stomach, bruised my ribs."

He paused, leaned back, and gave me a strange, knowing stare. Then he came forward to my ear and said, "I said to him, 'Take my money,' and I tried to give him my wallet, 'Take my watch,' but he didn't want that. He just wanted to fuck me up.

"After he beat the shit out of me—I'm not kidding, man, he beat the shit out of me, pounded me into the ground—the dude spits in my face and says, 'That's what you get, rat.' Dude called me a rat. I'm a lot of things, but I'm not a rat."

I glanced back, worried that the vegetarian, pot-smoking blond might be listening, but she had already struck up a conversation with someone else. I watched her for a second as she leaned forward and laughed, touching the other guy's arm, and then I turned back to Joe.

"Jesus," I said, "I'm sorry," and I was, knowing that he possibly got the beating meant for me.

But he couldn't hear me, and took my elbow, guiding me to an alcove near the dining room that was less noisy.

I repeated my apology.

He gave me his hurt-looking grimace-smile and said, "Yeah, man, it was bad." A brief pause, and then he said, "I've got to get out of here. I'm going to leave soon." Dead serious, he gripped my forearm. For a confused second, I didn't understand, thinking that he was making way too big a deal out of leaving the party. But then he said, "I've got a cousin and some family in Canada, and a friend in Mexico also says that I can crash with him. I'm not sure where I'm going. But I'm leaving. It's bad, bad. They're coming after me. Got pulled over the other day for going sixteen miles per hour in a fifteen-mile-per-hour zone, and the police officer hands me a ticket, says that I was going thirty-five, and he says to me, 'Be careful, the law doesn't look kindly on heroin dealers.'"

He let out a long, distressed sigh. "You and me both know," he said, "that I deal weed, maybe a few pills. I've got to pay the bills like everyone else."

A small group of people were sitting in a circle on the tile floor doing whip-its in the kitchen, and one of them shrieked with laughter. We waited for the noise to die down.

"But I've never sold heroin or crystal meth or crack," he continued. "I won't touch that stuff, won't sell it. God, no. Call it principles, I don't give a fuck. A little cocaine, some speed, maybe once or twice and then I stopped, but I never sold that other shit, ever, and I won't. But this cop's letting me know that he doesn't care. They can nail me for anything, and I've got priors, for loosey-goosey stuff, a shoplifting, a public intoxication from riding my bike fucked up on the boardwalk."

"They can't do that," I said stupidly.

To my surprise, he took my hands in his own. "I can't go to jail," he said. "You need to do something for me."

I felt sick and rather hot—and weird, to be holding hands with him. "What?" I asked.

"Sara," he said, looking at me, his voice firm. He clutched my hands tight and pulled. "Don't let them fuck with her. Don't let them hurt her."

In a stupor, I nodded.

He released my hands and let out a bark-like laugh. "Fucking A," he said. "Fucking A! Everything's going to be all right!"

"Did she tell you?" I asked.

Immediately, his disposition changed, as if I'd slapped him. He stared at me, incredulous.

"Do you know what happened?" I persisted. "Did she tell you?" In my defense, I hadn't told anyone besides Mike about the video camera and was anxious to have a shared moment. Besides, I was pretty sure Joe already knew.

He took his hat off and ran a hand through his hair. It frightened me to see that his hand trembled. "Shut up," he said quietly. "Don't be a dumb shit." He shook his head. "You fucking dumb ass," he said.

"I'm sorry," I said.

He nodded, still chagrined, and put his hat back on. He could barely look at me. "How're you going to help her," he said, "if you can't keep your fucking mouth shut?"

"I can," I assured him. "I can keep it shut."

"Okay," he said, without much confidence.

He was quiet for a few moments as he watched me, considering, then he said, "She's had a tough time already, a hard life. She doesn't need this. She's scared."

"I know," I said.

"Do you?" he said—a pause. "If they can do what they did to that other girl, think about what they can do to Sara."

He lit a cigarette with a Zippo, clicked the lighter shut, and stood smoking, watching me with an expression of frustration and worry. Then he said, "I'm leaving tonight. They think it's me, and let them think that if they'll leave her alone." He looked around him and said, "She likes you, trusts you. Listen, someone might be following me. I don't know, maybe I'm paranoid. But I need to leave. I don't want them to see me talking to you. She's going to call you in about a week. Wait a bit first, after I leave. Just in case. You're going to meet with her and help her. You're going to tell her that you can keep your mouth shut, and then you're going to keep it shut. You're the only one that she can talk to about this. Tell her that you'll protect her, and then do it. Tell her that you can protect her from your dad and your brother."

"Okay," I said.

His hand went to my arm and gripped me for a second, and then he left quietly out a side door.

I LEFT MIKE at the party and returned to my room at the Woods'. It was small and comforting, like a cave, a stack of books beside my futon, and I cracked the sliding glass door to give myself some air. The air had that misty-rain feel, barely coming down. I listened—the rain was too soft and vaporous to make noise. I could barely hear the television coming from the Woods' living room.

Though I hadn't inhaled much from the vegetarian girl's joint, I now felt stoned. I lay on the futon. The sheets and comforter were from a queen-size mattress, and the excess material spooled around my legs. It felt like I could hide there forever.

I opened my laptop and checked my email. The Internet was slow compared to at Dad's house, but I had nowhere to go. There were fourteen emails from my mom. I read the first:

FROM: Gina Hyde
TO: Daniel Hyde, Gabriel Hyde, Even Hyde
DATE: Saturday, January 18, 2004 4:17 PM
SUBJECT: Gabe and Trial

Now we're going to trial right after the school year ends. Summertime. I'm telling you, this whole thing is a bunch of nonsense. You boys are going to get dragged in the mud. You have the rest of your lives, in two or three months, no one would have remembered what happened or cared about one out-of-control moment that happened when a bunch of teenagers engaged in a bit of foolishness. Tove Kagan, if she'd been smart, would have just taken some money and forgotten the whole thing. She's got her whole life ahead of her, and nobody dwells on past mistakes. The whole thing is so ridiculous. This girl slept with all three of you boys the night before. She's easy. We had a name for girls like her when I was in high school but I'm not going to say it. She came over that night expecting to have sex with you boys. You went over the line with the pool stick and because you weren't thinking, add to that alcohol, and that's a bad combination. But I have always taught you boys to be good boys. If a bunch of girls had stripped you naked and done things to you, would they go to trial? NO. Had the video never came out, no one would be trying to destroy you poor boys' lives. You are supposed to be sacrificed and go to prison and be irrevocably damaged because this girl likes to have sex with you and then it got out of hand? Ask yourself, a girl her age already so sexually active? That says to me one thing. Bad parents. You boys were presented with a forbidden opportunity and you did what boys will do. You grasped the opportunity and didn't realize the seriousness of your actions. You didn't even know you might be breaking a law! Every high school class has a low self-esteem girl that will have sex with anybody. So you boys are going to go to prison because of that? And this girl, had this video never been discovered, would have continued to be a slut as a result of who she is. Now all you boys are going to be picking up your shattered lives for the rest of your lives because of who she is. Not right. That's why I'm so glad we're fighting this thing.

Proverbs 1:8
Listen, my son, to your father's instruction and do not forsake your mother's teaching.

Love,
Mom

I read the second email, which I saw that she'd sent five minutes after the first:

FROM: Gina Hyde
TO: Daniel Hyde, Gabriel Hyde, Even Hyde
DATE: Saturday, January 18, 2004 4:23 PM
SUBJECT: Money

This is for Gabe but I'm sending it to YOU TOO. Make no mistake. This is about money. I'm just a regular middle-class woman, while your father has reaped the benefits of having worked his whole life to become a successful businessman. Yes, we've had our difficulties, and I'm sorry for the pain we've put you boys through. I'm sorry we couldn't save our marriage. But your father is a good man. He is guilty of loving you children too much and not being able to be with you enough.

Tove Kagan is a rebellious and troubled young woman. She and her family have a reputation for being greedy. She viewed you as a way to escape her horrible less than great family and life. She saw that your father is rich and lives in wealthy Newport Beach and she saw an opportunity. She wanted attention. If seducing you and your friends would give her that, she was willing to do it. You, like all young men with raging hormones, thought only about your immediate sexual gratification with a willing young woman but definitely used exceedingly poor judgment in having sex with her. All four of you teenagers willingly participated in behavior such as drinking and having sex in which you are too young to engage in. Yet my pastor was explaining to me that young people do not always use good judgment or think of the consequences of their actions. But why punish you boys more? You're already being punished for what you did that night because now people will know. That's enough. It's going to get worse, now the newspapers are going crazy. Did you hear any more about that 48 Hours television show? I think it's a good idea that your PR lady said to have a show about teenage sex because then you could teach other boys not to go out of hand like you and to be careful. You are a polite, quiet, loving young man. I know that you will show that on 48 Hours and that people will understand that what you did is not worth ruining your life for one little mistake. Sure you were searching for your identity and acceptance, but I never did feel good about that Kevin Stewart and I never met Kent Nixon before.

They don't come from good stable Christian homes. I don't want you to be punished more.

Chronicles 16:11
Seek the LORD and his strength; seek his presence continually!

Love,
Mom

I deleted the remaining twelve emails, shut my computer, flipped off the lamp next to my futon, and stared for a long time at the shadows on my ceiling. Then I must have fallen asleep because the next thing I knew I was at a party and there were people everywhere and I saw Joe's cowboy hat and went to him.

He pointed to a door and his face was not his but Gabe's face but with a stitched lip like Joe's. I opened the door and went inside and there was someone—a girl—on the bed with her back to me under the covers and she whimpered, so I went to her and got beneath the covers.

Then I understood that it was my futon and that the girl was the vegetarian girl from the party and she wanted to have sex with me and I wanted to have sex with her and that I didn't want it to be her but I wanted it to be Sara.

What happened next was so awful that I don't think I can write it. But I will tell you that it wasn't the vegetarian girl from the party and it wasn't Sara and that I started doing things to her that I'd seen on the video camera.

I shot up from the futon with a scream and awakened, sweating and breathing hard, and for some reason, my hands went to my throat, where I felt the bumping thrum of my pulse.

I collected myself and looked around the room to remember the safe feeling that I got from it, repeating in my head: Not real, not real, not real.

25.

KNOWING THAT WHAT Gabe and the Ks did to Tove was wrong didn't alleviate my guilt and self-hatred for having turned over the video camera. I had two conflicting sensations: My life was over; my life had just begun. I felt that every person could see through me and know that I was a traitor. At the same time, to have taken such an action proved an independence from my family and that I didn't belong to them. I realized now that I'd always wanted that freedom, and that I had it. That I'd told no one (except for Sara and Mike)—to have a secret of that magnitude—made me strong, and gave me a feeling of power.

One way I survived those months before the trial was by obsessing over how not to tell anyone about what I'd done or letting anyone find out, while at the same time fantasizing about coming clean or being found out.

I didn't sleep or I slept too much, barely ate, and drank almost every night and took drugs.

I wanted to be alone. Yet when alone, I became prone to a general neurotic anxiety and self-loathing that I hadn't experienced before.

I sometimes abused the prescription meds that I stole from my dad's medicine cabinet, promising myself that I'd quit once the trial ended. High on Demerol one night, I attacked a rose bush and scratched up my fists and arms.

I shoplifted recklessly, daring security to catch me. I found out how difficult it was for a white, clean-cut teenager to get caught— even mugging for the security cameras. Everything that I stole, I gave away. If I was caught, I imagined that under interrogation and with the sway of authority, I might confess my role in Gabe's case, and the waiting and anticipation would be over.

One afternoon, I walked into Target, took an iPod, dismantled it from its packaging and security bar with a knife from the kitchenwares department, and walked out with it. Then, when stopped at the signal to leave the parking lot, I passed the iPod through my opened car window to a man in a wheelchair with a cardboard sign on his lap that read DOWN AND OUT PLEASE HELP.

"God bless," he said, with a big, semitoothless grin, reaching a sun-cracked hand out to me.

For a few days, I trailed Tom L., waiting in the parking lot for him to leave his AA meeting. I'm the man you want, I wanted to tell him. I gave you the video camera. I've never seen anything that disturbing before, either, and I'm not a cop! I'm the brother of the perpetrator and the son of the protector of the perpetrator!

He lumbered to his Buick, sat, shut his door with a whack, and started the engine. Careful to stay a few cars behind, I followed him. He lived in Costa Mesa in a two-story light blue house with white windowsills and a picket fence. The garage door opened and swallowed him up.

But I waited for him the next morning before school, a block down, parked and sipping a Coke. When he pulled out of the garage, I followed him through the fog to the YMCA where Mike went to lift weights, and watched him lumber from the parking lot in his sweat suit with stripes down the legs. A gut, and a wide cowboy-like walk, swinging his arms.

I thought about going back to the AA meetings, just to hear the people talk. But I didn't go.

I spent hours in pointless reflection, turning over my family's history, looking for cracks that I'd missed, trying to understand how everything had happened and what it meant. No matter how much time I deliberated, I couldn't figure anything out, like a dog chasing its tail.

My refuge and comfort had been reading. Now it didn't do much good. I would try but the sentences evaporated after I read them. I couldn't get them to sink into meaning.

But when they did, and when a book resonated, such as Dostoyevsky's *Crime and Punishment*, which I cracked open for a couple of days, it overwhelmed me. I'd read it before and enjoyed the thrill of the fiction, but now it left me shaken with identification, and I had to put it away.

Every cruel and stupid thing I'd done came back to haunt me. How I used to wipe my boogers on my bed frame as a child, collecting them in some sort of gruesome fascination, a trail of dried, bumpy snot along the wood post. Our maid, Juanita, finally cleaned them one afternoon, shooting me a disgusted look. The three times I'd kicked our beloved dog and made him yelp, before he'd been hit and killed by a car. How once I'd gotten Gabe in trouble by claiming he'd shattered our parents' bathroom mirror. I'd done it with a rock, for no reason. And plenty of other worse humiliations.

By myself a lot those months, I took long walks along the Back Bay and watched the joggers and bikers whir past me.

I went to the movies alone and spent afternoons sneaking into one stupid movie after another, until I'd finally leave six or seven hours later, the sky dark and littered with stars.

It seemed that I hadn't properly noticed life before—everything was more intense and alive and relentless and always, always, always tinged with sadness. The sky was larger and deeper and the sun brighter and the grass greener and the stars more sparkly. How hadn't I noticed before?

I felt strangely liberated and fascinated by the sheer impossibility of just living and breathing and being alive.

Instead of wearing boxers or pajamas, I slept naked. I didn't like the feel of clothes on my skin at night and started wearing an old, tattered robe that I'd bought at a garage sale.

I lost about fifteen pounds and had to poke new holes in my belts. I developed a habit of having to smell foods before I ate them. Things that I used to crave (chocolate, mustard, dill pickles) I couldn't stomach.

I realized that it used to matter to me what people thought about me, but that I no longer cared so much whether they liked me or not. It just didn't matter.

If someone handed me a pill at a party, I no longer asked what it was. I just swallowed it and waited to see what happened.

Mike said that I was isolating myself, and that I should make more of an effort to be around people. I didn't want to be around people.

Sara shared my secret, and I knew now that she understood my situation in a way that I hadn't wanted to acknowledge.

I waited for her to call—like Joe had told me to do—and she never did. I thought about her constantly.

"Should I call her?" I asked Mike.

"I don't know," he said, so I left her alone.

But then one afternoon, about two months before the trial, Mike brought me an article from the OC Weekly by this reporter named R. Sam Michaels. Michaels had hooked into the Hyde Three case with a vicious determination, and no one—not Gabe's PR lady or his lawyers or other reporters—could sway him to take a more neutral position. Dad hated him.

The article claimed that a young woman who lived near the Jane Doe of the Hyde Three gang rape case ("Jane Doe" was a pseudonym for Tove Kagan), and who knew who Jane Doe was—a girl who looked like Jane Doe, especially in the dark night—had been attacked, to the point of needing plastic surgery. Nothing could be proven, no connection made, but only, the woman asserted, when she had yelled that she wasn't Tove (the paper hadn't used Tove's name) did the large man ("a big mother-fucker," I remembered Joe saying) stop his beating and flee.

I set the article down, quiet for a moment, and then I said, "Holy shit."

Mike said, "Do you think it's true?"

I nodded. The feeling of doing the right thing by turning in the camera had been accumulating slowly—so slowly that I'd hardly noticed it—but now it locked into place.

I'd question many things from here on out, but I never questioned myself about this again.

A certain relief came from my certainty, but alongside it was a deepening loss of respect for my father, mother, and brother, so that for a long time it just felt like a huge, sorrowful defeat.

"Call Sara," Mike said, but he didn't have to tell me. I'd already reached for my cell in my pocket.

She said that she'd meet me at my room at Mike's later that afternoon.

I dressed, washed my face, and gave the room a harried cleaning: tucking the sheets and bedspread under the futon, restacking my books, arranging my shoes in a line on the floor.

I couldn't stay still; I was wandering around my room, picking at my skin, looking at my books and papers without really seeing them.

As I was giving myself a final look-over in the mirror—slicking my cow-licked hair back with my fingers—I heard a light tapping at the glass door and jumped forward, on edge with anticipation.

I turned and Sara stared through a crack at the curtains at me, her eyes alive with her smile.

Sliding the glass door open, I said, "Oh!" and she said, "Even!" and she stepped inside and we embraced. We stayed that way for quite some time.

When she pulled away, I saw that she'd also lost weight, and her cheeks were sunken. She looked as if she'd just gotten out of bed, her hair tousled like she hadn't bothered to brush it, and she wore no makeup. Her sweatshirt came down over her wrists, and the hems of her jeans—long and frayed—were tucked under her flip-flops

"This is nice," she said, looking around my room. "They let you live here?"

"As long as I want," I said. "I'm lucky to have it."

We sat on my futon and she put her hands on her knees; her cheeks were flushed. She shivered. She saw that I noticed and she said, "I'm so glad to see you, Even, but it scares me, too."

I told her what Joe told me to tell her—that I would protect her and that I would keep her safe from my dad and brother, no matter what happened—the words came as Joe had directed, and when I finished, she gave me a blank look and said, "Thanks, Even," but I couldn't tell if she believed me. She went silent for a moment, and then she said, "Joe told you to say that."

I didn't say anything. Regardless of what Joe had told me to say, I didn't think it was right for her not to trust me. I felt a genuine desire to protect her. It must have shown in my face because she said, "I know you will, Even. That's why I'm here."

We talked for a long time, and she said that she hadn't called me, because she felt bad about involving me by getting me to take the video camera. "I know," she said, "that it's worse for the girl, always will be—for Jane Doe—because I saw what they did to her on that videotape. Nothing compares. But I realize that you've suffered, not as much as her, but that there's something very real and deep and true in your suffering because of what I made you do. She—Jane Doe—at least she has her family to stand by her, and she has the moral high ground. What I asked you to do, Even, it's shaken all your foundations. You're probably going to have to lose your family over this, and she can keep hers."

She paused, thought some more. "I just hope," she said, "I really, really, really hope, long term, we're talking big picture, Even, that you'll end up surviving to become a better man. Do you think it's possible?"

"Jane Doe," I said, "her real name's Tove Kagan. We used to be friends."

"Oh, god, Even," Sara said. "You know her?"

"My first kiss," I said, the words heavy in my mouth.

She wanted to hear more, so I explained my connection to Tove.

Then Sara told me that she couldn't stop thinking about her— "about Jane Doe, I mean Tove"—and that she'd been reading books. "There's this thing called rape culture," she said, "and it's everywhere if you notice it. Most girls," she said, "don't come forward, because when they do, they just get shamed and victimized again."

"I read," she said, "that your dad won't settle."

"He tried to give the Kagans money," I said, "to not go to trial, but they declined. I don't know how much. But Dad claims he didn't really want a payout anyway, because it'd imply guilt, 'like what happened to Michael Jackson,' he said, 'paying off those kids' parents.'"

"Wow," she said. "That's crazy."

We went silent for a moment, and then she said, "What's she like?"

"Who?" I asked, though I knew the answer.

"Tove."

"Dad's defense team underestimates her," I said. "And her family. They don't understand—too busy calling her names and stuff—that she's strong, independent, and really stubborn. Her parents will keep uniting behind her, and they won't cave. I'm sure of it. All that bullying just makes them more determined."

"But what's she like?" Sara asked. "What was she like when you knew her?"

I told her that as kids we played Clue and Go Fish and Old Maid in her bedroom. Tove would lie on her stomach on the floor, propping her head in her hands, elbows bent. She taught me how to dance to what she called "crazy music," a CD of hers, and it *was* crazy: beeps and bops and synthesizers. "Just let your body go," she said, turning off the lights, "let it do whatever it wants, let it feel," and in the dark, she took big steps, waving her arms and hands like an octopus.

"Now close your eyes," she instructed, and then I danced, the music invading me: free and wild and no one but Tove watching.

"Didn't your family know," Sara asked, "that you were friends?"

"They never asked where I went, and I didn't say."

I told her about the forts in the backyard that we built with blankets and cardboard, and how we pretended to be inside submarines.

We created a recipe for alligator eggs: balled Wonder Bread, green food dye, microwaved for thirty seconds, sprinkled with egg whites, and dotted with brown sugar.

She dared me to eat one, and I did, salting it first.

"She wouldn't wear pants for the longest time," I said. "Refused. Only wore dresses and skirts."

"Why?"

"She said pants were 'too restrictive.' But that changed in middle school. She wanted to be like the other girls."

"Did she lie a lot?" Sara asked. "I'm just curious. I read an article that said she's a compulsive liar."

"She told these really great stories about gypsies and pirates and stuff. But she didn't really lie. She just told these crazy stories."

I couldn't really explain to Sara how everything that Tove said and did seemed to come straight from her heart. This had frightened me a little. Tove had seemed unafraid, and the only time her voltage lessened was when her father was nearby.

"My dad's a jerk," she'd once told me. "He wishes I were a boy, and not me. He likes you more."

A great affection for Tove welled within me and, just as quickly, a giant sorrow. "I don't understand what happened," I said. "I mean, what happened to her? How'd she get so messed up?"

Sara said, "Even, she's rebellious, that's all. Girls go a little nuts sometimes. Especially when they're smart. It just happens like that. Who knows why. She was experimenting, trying to find out who she is, what she likes, what she wants. Sixteen years old, you know? Too smart. And she went a little nuts. Maybe she slept with them the night before they raped her, and if she did, so what? Maybe they were trying to get back at her, since she'd cheated on that one guy she thought was her boyfriend. I don't know. I know they're going to attack her for that in court, but my god, she's just a girl, and she went a little nuts, but now she'll never be okay, after what they did to her."

"I wish I could talk to her," I said.

"What would you say?"

"I don't know," I said. "I'd tell her I'm sorry."

We were quiet for a moment. Then Sara said, "Whatever happened to my pink towel? You know, the one you hid beneath in the police video footage. What'd you do with it? I hope you burned it."

Her question surprised me. I had a vague memory of putting it in my laundry basket.

"It's at my dad's," I said, and as I spoke, I knew that I'd blown it.

"Even," she said, "we have to find it. That towel's from when I was a kid and went to camp."

"So?"

"My name," she said, "is written on the tag. The camp made us write our names on everything we owned. They'll know it's mine, and when they find out, they're going to come after me."

26.

W E DROVE TO Dad's and sat silent and motionless, for a few moments parked at the curb. Sunlight filtered through the tree we'd parked beneath, creating lozenge-shaped spots of hazy gold. Birds twittered.

"Gabe's not here," I said. "No truck. But Dad's home. I see lights on inside, and he's a fanatic about saving electricity."

Sara flipped open the visor mirror and gave me a nervous glance. "I'm going with you," she said. "There's no way I'm waiting."

"Do you think that's a good idea?"

She didn't answer, instead opening her door and getting out.

The front door was unlocked. We entered and I called out hello, and Dad said, "In here," so we walked to the living room and found him in his recliner, watching golf and smoking a cigarette.

At the sight of us, his expression became gentle and inquiring, and I knew he was happy to see me. Since I'd moved into the room at Mike's house, Dad appreciated my visits, trying to talk me into staying longer.

He lifted his recliner to a more upright position, muted the TV, and said, "Even! What a surprise!"

My gut wrenched with guilt, disgust, and affection, and I said, "Hey, Dad, this is my friend Sara. We just thought we'd come by and say hello and see how you're doing."

Alongside a cocktail glass filled with melting ice, a plate on the table next to him had a fly circling it. I knew it was the remnants of creamed chipped beef on toast—half-eaten and an abstract, arty-looking mess—and that Dad had made it from a Stouffer's frozen packet.

"Hello, honey," he said to Sara, lifting himself from his recliner and setting his cigarette in his ashtray. His loose khakis had bunched around his waist—he'd also lost weight—and were fitted by a belt. "It's so nice to meet you," he said, and then, to Sara's bewilderment, he stepped forward and embraced her.

Dad, with the emotional lubricant of a few cocktails, could be quite affectionate; I hadn't warned Sara, so she appeared stunned.

She looked at me over his shoulder, aghast. Her eyes widened, as if to say, What the fuck?

When he released her, she said very formally, "Nice to meet you, too, Mr. Hyde."

"Please," he said, "call me Dan."

"Nice to meet you," she said, pausing before adding, quite awkwardly, "Dan."

Dad rested in his recliner, with us across from him on the couch. He usually smoked with a grim, tight-lipped resolution, as if to get it done with, so that he could spark up another (by this time, his one-pack-a-day habit had skyrocketed to three packs). But this afternoon, all his mannerisms seemed slow.

"I don't know if you're aware, Even," he said, "but your mother got in some trouble with the police over there in Cucamonga, for putting up fliers around the neighborhood."

A silence, during which I struggled between wanting to know more and not wanting to know more.

"What kind of fliers?" I asked finally, the latter desire losing out to my initial curiosity.

A sigh, and then he said, "Asking for information about Tove Kagan, I mean Jane Doe, whatever, any so-called information that might help our case. Digging up stuff from the neighborhood. Gina denied they're her fliers"—a grave chuckle—"but it's obvious since her phone number's on them."

I glanced at Sara—her face was ashen.

"Anyway," Dad continued, "Gina took them down. All of them. She's trying to help—God bless her—but these kinds of things make it worse. 'Just follow what the lawyers tell us,' I keep telling her. 'The PIs will get all the information we need.' It's just hard for her to sit and watch events unfold. She wants so badly to help Gabe. But the Kagans can go after us for intimidation, get more money, those greedy bastards, if Gina doesn't calm down and stop with these tactics."

"Okay, Dad," I said.

"The Kagans," he said, "have hired a PI. They think they can fight us."

"Okay, Dad," I said, "Let's talk about something else. How's your golf game?"

"Gabe's on home study," he said to Sara.

She nodded.

"Couldn't finish out his senior year," he said. "Such a shame. Too many people know. All the media coverage. Gina's going to make him walk for his diploma, hold his head high, and cross that stage with the rest of them."

He ground out his cigarette and lit another, saying, "This *48 Hours* thing should help. They're going to air it before the trial. They've been over here filming and interviewing us, and they're going to help us."

"Dad," I said, "let's talk about something else."

"Even," he said to Sara, "doesn't want to be interviewed," and then to me, "It's your choice."

"How much have you had to drink?" I asked, hoping to draw his attention to his inebriation, so that he'd stop talking so openly in front of Sara.

"When Gabe calls," he said, ignoring me, "the first thing he tells me, and the last before we hang up, 'I love you,' he says, and I tell him, 'I love you, too, Son, it's going to be okay, Son, I love you, too.'"

His eyes welled and he wiped each one with the palm of his hand.

"Why," he asked Sara, "am I talking about this horrible business? Please. Excuse me, honey, for being inconsiderate. This trial is making me a crazy old man. I apologize, honey, I really do."

I FOUND SARA'S towel folded in the cabinet of my dad's bathroom, the lone pink one in a sea of blue, and there on the tag was her name written in permanent marker with a child's scrawl, just as she'd said it would be. I grabbed it, along with a few Demerol and some sleeping pills from his medicine cabinet, which I put in my pocket. All the while Dad and Sara gabbed in the living room. Their voices came to me in a pleasant murmur. I tried to be quick, worried that Dad would say some more inappropriate shit. To be safe, I placed the towel in a paper bag so that my dad wouldn't see it, along with some apples, cheese slices, Wheat Thins, cans of 7-Up, and a pilfered pint of vodka from the freezer, telling Dad that we planned on picnicking at the beach.

"You two have a good time," Dad said, standing on the porch walkway and fishing in the pocket of his khakis for his crumpled pack of Newports. "It was really good to meet you, Sara."

"Nice to meet you, too," Sara said, giving him a little hug, "Dan," she added.

"If you wait another ten minutes," he said, "Gabe will be here. He's on his way."

"That's okay, Dad," I said. "We'll see him another time."

"Sure, sure," Dad said.

When Sara couldn't see him, Dad gave me a wink, his head bowed as he lit his cigarette from his Bic's feeble flame. Sending me a private signal, letting me know that he approved—I could almost hear him saying, Now that's one good-looking broad—and my face went hot.

Whereas before I might have relished his approval, I didn't want him to look at Sara, much less comment on her appearance.

Something of the mess that Gabe had created seemed linked to how Dad worried about our reflecting on his masculinity. Not so much about our welfare, but about this idea of being Men with a capital M. It pissed me off.

I knew that Dad's eyes stayed on us as we walked down the cement walkway. In the sun-warmed cocoon of my car, after our doors whacked shut, for a minute we both watched him watching us as he stood on the porch and smoked. His hand went out in a wide wave and I waved back, though inside I was thinking, You asshole.

"God," Sara said, as I started the car. "That was weird."

I didn't say anything, driving slowly down our street.

"I never, ever," she continued, "ever, ever, would've thought that I'd kind of like him."

I heard myself sigh.

She looked at me and said, "Now I feel like I understand better why you might've wanted to be like him. Why you said that you sort of worshipped him."

"Not anymore," I said, "no way."

I thought we'd finished, but she was still thinking about him, her eyes and face full of reflection, and she said in a tone of wonderment, "I never thought he'd be so, like, well, vulnerable and sensitive or something. He just seems so lonely and sad, and sort of, well, kind of sweet."

"Oh, he's delightful," I said.

She watched me for a moment of silent judgment, and then she changed the subject, asking, "Where're we going?"

I didn't answer, pulling the car to the curb near the beach. The sun marked the horizon with a small orange dot, and spectators on the bluff waited for the sunset. We looked at each other for a moment, and then she opened her car door and stepped out.

I followed her, carrying the bag down the sloping walk-way, until we found a spot near a vacated bonfire that was still smoking.

I found a piece of driftwood and stoked the leftover charcoal and wood in the fire pit, so that the fire rose back, flames leaping and sparking.

We settled in the sand, cross-legged, and I kept an eye on the bonfire, occasionally stirring it with my stick.

Sara rummaged through the paper bag, pulling out the Wheat Thins and opening the box. The air felt misted with ocean and it smelled of seaweed. "Here," she said, handing me a cheese slice cradled between two Wheat Thins.

We ate and drank our 7-Ups and watched the sky darkening, speaking little, listening to the *boom* of the waves, and I cracked open the seal on the pint of vodka. We passed it between us, taking sips, and it helped keep us warm.

At one point, with a courage born of alcohol, loneliness, and selfishness, and the intimacy of the evening, and, in all honesty, probably as a foolish reaction to my dad, I leaned toward her and tried for a kiss.

She stopped me with a hand at my chest, saying, "Even, please."

"Why not?" I said. To my chagrin, my voice sounded whiny. Trying to remedy this, but only further embarrassing myself, I said, "Sara, I'm pretty sure I'm in love with you."

For a long time, she didn't answer. Then she said, "Even, I love you, too. But not like that."

"Then like how?"

She looked at me, her gaze soft and kind. "I have a boyfriend," she said. "You're too young."

"He's in Toronto," I said. "Age doesn't matter."

She didn't respond. We watched each other for a long time, and then she looked away. In the firelight, I saw that her hair was speckled with tiny drops of wet from the ocean.

"Is it because of my brother?" I asked. "I know you think I'm different, but is it because we're related? I'm part of him and he's part of me?"

"No," she said softly, still not looking at me.

After a considerable amount of time, she looked back at me and said, "You want to know how I met Joe?"

"Sure," I said, though the last thing I wanted was to drag more of Joe into our conversation.

She laughed just at the thought of recounting the memory, and a twinge of jealousy went through me.

"He knew my coke dealer," she said, "and I met him through him, but when I started doing so much cocaine, Joe told my dealer not to deal to me anymore, so he stopped, wouldn't take my money.

"I got mad, yelled at Joe, and he said, 'You're better than that,' and he got me to go to my meetings. When I quit cocaine, he sent me a bouquet of roses."

"You said the same thing to me," I said, "not that long ago, about my dad. That I was better than that."

"I know!" she said. She smiled, her teeth gleaming in the firelight, and then she closed her eyes and said, "I miss him so much."

I still remember the way she looked that night, with her eyes closed, and the light from the fire on her face, thinking about how much she loved Joe and missed him.

When she opened her eyes, she said, "He saved my life," and then added, "I didn't care about myself anymore, and he got me to care, he made me care. Can you try to understand?"

I nodded, somewhat ashamed that I'd tried to take advantage of the situation with Joe gone, but also aggrieved that she didn't want me when I so clearly wanted and needed her.

Before we drove back to my room at Mike's, she threw her pink towel into our bonfire, and we watched as it shriveled and burned. A quick flare of flames and then, almost instantaneously, it darkened and blended into the ash.

27.

THE *48 HOURS* episode aired about a month before the trial and within the final weeks of my junior and Gabe's senior year.

Sara, Mike, and I watched it on Sara's crappy television at her apartment. She had to fool around with it so that we could get a decent picture, smacking its side a couple of times. We saw the credits rolling for *CSI* and then, after what felt like ten minutes of commercials, the theme song for *48 Hours* started—the episode was titled "Kinky Teen Sex Gets Out of Hand"—and Lesley Stahl, wearing a light blue pantsuit, and with a smoky spotlight on her, walked to the center of a dark room, saying, "Gabe Hyde spends part of his time living a life of paradise in Newport Beach, California. His father, Dan Hyde, is a multimillionaire who owns a beautiful house near the beach in affluent Orange County."

Her purple-red lipstick had smeared a tad past her upper lip, and she tucked a lock of glossy blond hair behind her ear. "Gabe lives with his mother, Gina Hyde, in San Bernardino County during the rest of the week. His younger brother, Even Hyde, Gina explained, chose to live with their father in posh Newport Beach, but Gabe stayed with her."

I groaned, and Sara said, "Do you want me to turn it off?"

I waved my hand for her to be quiet.

Dad stared out at me from the screen and, gruff-voiced, said: "Gabe's just an average teenage kid, very sensitive, very emotional. Just a good, sensitive kid."

A Lesley Stahl voice-over as the camera panned from Cucamonga to Newport: "It's a long freeway ride from the glamour of Newport Beach. But Gina says that middle-class America is where her sons learned their good old-fashioned values."

"I'll get you a beer," I heard Sara say.

"We've talked about sex," said my mom from the screen. "We've talked about drinking. We've talked about respecting other people's rights."

"But," intruded Lesley, "as correspondent Bob Langley reports, Gabe's sense of morality would be put on display on the Fourth of July, and the evidence would be recorded on tape, by a camera given to him by his father for his twelfth birthday."

Bob Langley, white-haired and serious, walked along the beach boardwalk with his hands in the pockets of his slacks, saying, "Before the infamous videotape was made, Gabe had made other typical teenage films with Kevin Stewart and Kent Nixon, his friends in Rancho Cucamonga. All three boys had parents who split up, and all three shared at least one teenage interest: an obsession with sex."

"You open a newspaper, or a magazine," said Gabe, sitting across from a sympathetic-faced Bob Langley at the dining room table at Dad's house, "a girl is standing there, half-naked, if not more than half-naked. You turn on the TV—it's the same thing. Everything portrays a sexual message, because sex sells."

"What kind of message?" Bob asked.

A pause as Gabe shifted in his chair. "That it's all right to have sex," he said. "Even kinky sex."

"Crystal and Melissa, Gabe's high school friends," Bob said, walking along the boardwalk again, "know him as the boy with one foot in the door of wealth and privilege. They say they're not promiscuous at all. They admit that their life in the suburbs isn't bad, but they'd much rather be in a place like Newport Beach. They're too young for bars or fancy clubs, but the 'in' place is to be at a good house party—especially at the big, glamorous house Dan Hyde owns—where the parents don't monitor every move the kids make."

"Bullshit," Sara said, putting a Coors in front of me. "Those tramps could get into any bar or club, wearing their miniskirts and flirting with the bouncers."

The scene cut to Crystal and Melissa, sitting across from Bob at a picnic table in some park.

"We go to parties," Melissa said, "and girls are, like, getting drunk and, like, hooking up with whomever. And then in the morning, it's like, 'Oh my gosh.'"

"Hooking up," Crystal added, "could be from, like, kissing to, like, having sex. Parents don't, like, exactly know what's going on when their kids leave the home."

The program cut to a commercial, and no one spoke but we exchanged glances. Sara went to the bathroom. Mike got a beer from her kitchen. We sat and waited for the commercials to end.

"On July third," Bob said, the show resuming as he strolled on the coast near the crashing waves, "Hyde invited some of his friends from Rancho Cucamonga, including Melissa and Crystal, to his dad's house in Newport Beach. They hung out in the backyard pool and started drinking."

"We said, 'Okay, we're going to bed,'" explained my dad to Bob, sitting across from him at the dining room table. "'Everybody's gonna be outta here real quick, right?' 'Yeah, yeah, yeah. We're just wrapping it up.'"

A montage of blurred figures—presumably teenagers—drank and smoked and danced and kissed as Bob intoned: "But after Dan and his longtime girlfriend, Nancy, turned in, the party out by the pool would continue late into the night, and Gabe and his friends would get involved in something they would soon come to regret. It had nothing to do with Melissa and Crystal, but a girl who had come along with them. She was someone who Kent had gone out with a couple of times."

"She was, like, one of our friends," said Melissa, "where we were like, 'Wow, she's different than us.' She kind of, like, crossed the line at certain points with certain people."

"Flirtatious," Crystal added. "Very flirtatious."

Voice-over: "According to Gabe's friends, it was a wild night."

"She ends up, like, getting completely naked," said Melissa, "and then Kevin is, too, and so they are at the edge of the pool, like on the step part, on the stair or whatever to get into the pool, and they, like, start having sex."

"I had sex with her about five hours later," said Gabe, across from Bob at the dining room table, "and about twenty minutes after that, Kent had sex with her, all within a five-hour time span."

Bob stopped his walk to face the camera, hands still in his pockets. "Dan Hyde had no idea," he said, "what had gone on. Besides, his son could always be trusted. There were no warnings in the past, no indicators. Things that night got out of hand, but no one could predict what would happen the next night and how it would ruin so many lives, as it was all captured on tape. For Gabe, the next morning, the Fourth of July, hit like a hangover."

Gabe said, "I was pretty much just in that state of mind that 'Yeah, I'm having intercourse with a girl.' So, of course, I'm a guy. Of course it's good."

"He claims," explained Bob, "it wasn't till later that morning, when he spoke with Kevin and Kent, that he realized how wild the night had been."

"I thought I was the only one," said Gabe, hands folded on the dining room table. "But all three of us thought we were the only one."

"If Gabe and his pals were really angry," Bob said, "or even embarrassed, they quickly got over it. By nightfall, they were ready to party again. And a phone call went out to the girl from the night before. The girl was intrigued enough by the invitation to pass it along to her friends, who decided not to go. So the girl told her parents she was spending the night at a friend's house and headed to Gabe's house. Did Gabe and his friends think that they would have sex with her again?"

"I think that thought crossed my mind," said Gabe. "We're teenage guys; we're seventeen. Of course, it's typical of a male to think that."

"Gabe and his friends," Bob added, "say they were completely drunk when the girl showed up. And while all this was happening, Dan and his girlfriend were in the main house. Dan, a migraine sufferer, was incapacitated with a migraine."

"The bottom line with us," Dad said, his voice lowering, "is that we think that the kids are here under our control, under our supervision, that there's a better chance they're going to be safe."

"But Dan once again left the kids on their own," Bob said, beginning to walk the beach again, "and trouble started as soon as the girl walked into the Hydes' garage." He stopped, faced the camera. "Then, in a decision that would change everything, one of the boys reached for Gabe's camera and began filming everything. Gabe says they started having sex with the girl, only this time they were all together."

A female figure hidden behind a curtain shadow-danced seductively on the screen, and then it cut to a commercial for Scott toilet paper.

Sara shook her head at me, and I nodded in agreement. Mike took a sip of his beer.

"I wish I hadn't quit," Sara said. "I could use a smoke right now."

When the *48 Hours* theme music started again, it showed the curtained woman dancing, and then it cut to Gabe sitting at the table, and he said: "She started taking her clothes off and just pretty much saying, 'Oh yeah, I'm fine with all three of you guys,' and stuff like that."

"In the garage," Bob asked him, "there was a pool table, and the girl sprawled on top of it?"

Gabe nodded.

"And the sex was far from ordinary?"

"Kinky sexual acts," Gabe said. "There was a pool cue."

"What made you all think of doing that?"

"Curious guys, I guess. Curious, drunk kids. And she was okay with it."

"From your point of view," Bob said, "everyone knew what he or she was getting into that night. Did the girl ever say no?"

"Not one time," said Gabe.

Sara stood and shouted at the TV: "That's because she was too fucking drunk to talk, asshole!" She sat down again, saying, "Sorry, I can't take this."

"I know," said Mike. "How'd they get them to film this?"

"The PR woman Dad hired," I said.

We watched Bob Langley strolling along the beach again, saying, "Sometime before dawn, Kent drove the girl back to Rancho Cucamonga, which might have been the end of the story. But then Gabe got careless. The next night, he brought the video camera with the tape they had made to another friend's house, and he believes he left it there, where it was stolen. No one knows exactly how the video camera got into the hands of retired lieutenant Tom Lawrence. The lieutenant pleaded for more information on the news. Video footage"—and there I was again, under Sara's towel, my shaky-handed delivery of the box—"was replayed of a man covered in a towel depositing the camera at the police station. But the man never came forward.

"Dan Hyde, a prominent supporter and figure in the sheriff's department and many others believe that the someone—the mystery vigilante—actually had a more base reason for turning over the camera: a political vendetta against Hyde and Sheriff Krone."

"It makes me sick to my stomach that they'd use my son to get to me, and make him suffer," Dad said. He shook out a match and threw it into his abalone ashtray, then he inhaled on his cigarette.

"He could go to jail for this," he said, "because of me. Because of who I am. I don't condone what happened at all; I don't. But it's not a crime. It's been made a big-fish-type case right from the start. These types of cases can mean career advancement for a lot of people. I'll tell you: It sickens me."

"Turn it off," I said, by this time staring at the bottle of Coors in my grip instead of the TV screen.

Mike shifted forward from the couch and pressed the Off button with the sole of his shoe.

28.

AFTER THE *48 HOURS* episode aired, it seemed that everyone knew about the Hyde Three case. R. Sam Michaels began to churn out one article after another in the *OC Weekly*. "Untouchable and unreachable," I heard Gabe's PR lady say of Michaels. Michaels wouldn't acknowledge her or her press kits, and "no one really knows who he is," she said. "There are almost no photographs of him. He keeps a very low profile. I'm not entirely certain that he's not using a pseudonym."

One afternoon just days after the *48 Hours* episode, Mike and I went to the girls' varsity volleyball game against our rivals, Newport Harbor, in their school gym. Mike had become interested in a girl named Karen, a pretty brunette with dark, sad eyes who played setter on the offense.

Since his car was in the shop because of a faulty transmission, Mike had talked me into driving him. It was the least that I could do, he said, trying to be funny but falling a little flat, considering that I lived at his house and borrowed his parents as my own.

We watched as the girls grunted and sweated, their shoes squeaking on the floor, ponytails swinging, and when the game ended (I don't remember who won), Karen and her friend Tina came over and thanked us for coming. A shy and pretty sophomore, Tina had a smile full of braces of alternating purple and blue bands. She reminded me of a nervous colt, not fully grown into her lanky body. I'd met her before at the volleyball party and liked her.

We flirted awkwardly that afternoon ("You don't remember me, do you?" I said, knowing that she did. "I do!" "No, you don't"), and all the while she pressed the brush-like end of her long, dark braid between her fingers.

Meanwhile, Karen and Mike held hands for a few minutes—looking goofily into each other's eyes—until the girls' coach blew his whistle, calling them for a team huddle, before they had to board the bus back to our high school.

They trotted away from us, Tina throwing me one last shy, sweet look over her shoulder, and we watched in appreciation their firm legs and backsides in their shorts, their shirts knotted at their sides.

"She likes me," Mike said, happy, as we exited the dank gym into the bright sunlight. I felt happy for him, and for my good luck with Tina, and this was the overall feeling between us as we approached my BMW in the parking lot.

"Oh, shit," said Mike, the first to see spray-painted on the passenger side of my car in scraggly, large red letters: RAPEIST SCUM.

It felt like getting slapped in the face, but almost immediately I had another sensation of stoic calmness, as if somehow I deserved this public shaming. I made an attempt at disassociation with the comment: "At least learn how to spell 'rapist.'"

"What's that?" Mike asked.

Something had been placed beneath my windshield wiper, and I unhooked it: a clipping of an article by R. Sam Michaels, one that I'd already read, outlining the most ridiculous defense strategies for the Hyde Three, including a detailed account of a former porn star as a potential expert witness testifying that Jane Doe wanted to make a necrophilia-themed porn. (The defense team never did call on Sheila Morgenstern, a.k.a. Nikki Foxx, star of over one thousand porn films, including *Jail Bait*, *Gang Bang Girl*, *Fur Burger*, and *Both Ends Burning*, but she remained on Dad's payroll just in case.)

I handed the article to Mike.

"What's this?" he asked, scanning it with disgust.

As I faced my car, my back prickled, as if everyone was staring. The person who had tagged my car, I somehow knew for certain, was watching me.

"Let's go," Mike said, looking around the parking lot.

We got into the car, and Mike wadded the article and threw it on the floor mat. "It's not like it's your fault," he said.

"Guilty by association," I said.

He shook his head. "Whatever," he said, "but you're not a rapist. Uncool."

I started the car and drove, bouncing over a speed bump in the parking lot, and trying to ignore the stares and pointed fingers from the people leaving the volleyball game and also a crowd from a huge track-and-field event that had just ended.

I couldn't get out of the parking lot quickly enough, since I was bottlenecked behind a line of SUVs trying to exit through the one way possible.

Then I heard a loud groan from Mike. His head went down to his hands, clearing my view so that I could see what he had just seen from the passenger side: the bus with our girls' volleyball team on it, their faces at the widows—pointing, talking animatedly—and there, toward the back of the bus, the grim and sad faces of Karen and Tina.

Looking back, I can pinpoint this as the moment I decided to get out of SoCal as soon as possible. The very next morning I scheduled an appointment with my guidance counselor, a large, kind woman with nerdy black glasses, so that we could more seriously discuss my college opportunities back east, or anywhere, really, but in state. ("Are you sure, Even?" she asked, tapping her pen on her desk. "You know, there are some fantastic universities right here in California." I stared long and hard at her in answer, and she didn't press me again.)

When we finally made it out of the parking lot, I rolled down my windows, letting the breeze thrash us, a rushing noise like going down a river. At Mike's suggestion, we drove to the elementary school where his mom worked.

She'd been rearranging her room, getting ready for summer, taking down her grade schoolers' pictures and their names, which had been stapled across a wall. When we walked inside, she smiled until she saw our bleak faces, and then she said in a panicked voice, rushing to us, "What is it? What happened?"

"Mom," said Mike, "it's okay, calm down."

She looked to me, and I confirmed, "It's okay, Mom. Everything's okay."

She followed us to my car, which was parked at the curb. Hands at her hips, she stared for a silent moment at the spray-painted message, and then she said—and by the way, I loved her even more for this—"Whoever wrote this uncreative and crude and completely erroneous statement was not one of my students, since the idiot can't spell worth shit." I'd not heard her curse before.

We went back to her classroom, and she unrolled a large piece of green construction paper from its spool—a *zzzzip* noise as she cut it with a blade of an opened pair of scissors—and then we went back to my car, where she instructed us to hold the paper over the offending graffiti while she duct-taped it into place.

Dad paid for a new paint job, saying that I could get whatever color I wanted to replace the original Alpine White shade.

Without hesitation, I chose black.

29.

K NOWING SOMEONE INVOLVED in a notorious case such as the Hyde Three, for some people, seemed a little like knowing a celebrity. For the first time in my life, people sought me out. I became popular at my high school, but for all the wrong reasons. I preferred blending into my environment, being the observer and not the observed. I'd worked hard for my invisibility. But now people knew me. I became a salacious anecdote, not a person. I felt the constant stares and heard the whispers of the students and teachers around me those last weeks of the school year before the trial began in that summer of 2004.

As I made my way to my classes, I heard plenty of unsolicited opinions in the hallways and in the quad.

"Even!" someone shouted as I crossed the cafeteria. "How about a game of pool?" Then someone else, "Yeah! How'd you like a pool cue up your ass?"

"Hey, man," said a junior who happened to be our class president, pulling me aside by my elbow before I opened the door to biology, "that girl, Jane Doe, should be thanking your brother and his friends." A smile. "Now she won't have hang-ups about sex, huh? Anything goes."

"That's so fucked up," said a girl I'd never met, who happened to be listening. She glared at me and said, "You should be so ashamed."

"I am," I told her. "I live in shame. Shame and me are best friends. It's my first, middle, and last name. Shame Shame Shame."

She looked horrified.

Another time, a popular senior named Heather Potter said hello to me, and then she asked me if I wanted to hang out sometime.

I'd been surprised that Heather Potter even knew my name. But then I remembered my notoriety and politely declined her invitation.

A few days later, the pretty volleyball player Tina, with her multicolored bands on her braces, found me in the quad at break.

She looked at me with commiseration, thumbing the end of her long braid. "I know about your brother, Even," she said. "About what's going on. It must be awful for you. Let me know if I can help."

"You can," I said.

That was how Mike, Tina, Karen, and I found ourselves at Karen's bay-front three-story home on Linda Isle on a Friday night; her parents were out of town for a quick escape to Santa Barbara, and her younger brother was spending the night at his friend's.

We'd planned the get-together for three days, each of us coming up with excuses and explanations for our parents (in my case, Mike's parents), so that we could spend the night with each other.

Mike pushed the doorbell next to the large mahogany door which was decorated with a heron standing on one leg, beak up, with a leafy plant behind it. A slow, solemn, church-like gonging sounded, and Mike said, "Shit. Fancy."

Tina opened the door, wearing a tight T-shirt and faded jeans, looking sweet and kind, and she beckoned us inside.

Karen's affectionate golden retriever followed me around the enormous marble entryway, nosing my crotch as if I'd stuffed the area with kibble.

"Honeybun, stop!" said Karen, pulling her dog by the collar. "Leave Even alone!" She looked at Tina and then at me with a sly smile, while she crouched to keep her dog in place. "Honeybun likes you," she said.

"I like Honeybun, too," I said, my heart thumping in both embarrassment and excitement.

Mike laughed, but when Karen and Tina weren't looking, he sent me a look, letting me know that Karen and her multimillion-dollar home intimidated him.

Mike had an attraction to athletic, rich girls such as Karen, girls with a particular confidence born of competition and wealth and a comfort with the physicality of their bodies. But for these same reasons, these girls puzzled and frightened him.

That night, we sat in Karen's living room near a cavernous fire-place fit for a castle, talking and laughing and passing around a bottle of Irish whiskey that Karen had pulled out from the bar.

Mike and I drank the most to ease our discomfort. Honeybun lay near my feet, now and then glancing up at me with a half-lidded stare. She really did like me.

At Mike's request, Karen played a DVD from one of their volleyball games, pausing the screen to show us what a "perfect spike" looked like and replaying it in slow motion.

As the bottle of whiskey diminished, our voices got louder, until Tina seemed to notice all at once, and she put a finger to her lips and said, "Shhhh," and then we all burst out laughing.

Karen pulled out a plastic baggie of cocaine from her pocket, telling us that she'd found a stash in her mother's bathroom, hidden in a box of tampons, and had been saving it for tonight.

"It wasn't easy," she said of the sacrifice, as she cut the cocaine with her dad's American Express card, which he'd left for her on the kitchen counter. She made fat lines for each of us on her mom's face mirror, saying, "But that's how much I care about you guys."

Finished preparing the drug, she looked up and gave each of us a flash of her traveling-love-beam stare.

Then she bent over the mirror, a cut straw in one nostril and her index and middle fingers pressing the other nostril shut, and sucked up half her line.

She flipped her head and hair back with a wide, dazzled smile. A repeat with the other nostril, clearing her line.

Neither Mike nor I had tried cocaine before—and neither had Tina—but we followed Karen's example.

As I sucked up my line, I thought of Sara telling me, "It's an awful drug, don't ever do it, not worth the pain."

Immediately, my head rang and buzzed with pleasure, my tonsils numbing as the excess drained down the back of my throat.

It felt as if someone had taken the angst-ridden brain from my scalp and replaced it with the zinging, animated brain of a cartoon-like, happy, carefree, loving, and very talkative Even.

But this new Even also thought he could drink and talk more openly. He had no hang-ups or reservations, and the rest of the night became a manic blur.

I remember using an elliptical trainer in Karen's parents' basement gym, stripped to my boxers, the music pulsing in my veins, and watching myself at every angle, surrounded by mirrors, as Karen and the others worked out on various machines in their underwear.

A silvery coiled snake named Anderson Cooper in a glass case in Karen's brother's bedroom fascinated me. Karen had told us about her younger brother's homosexuality, and this was well before Anderson Cooper, the news anchor, came out. But looking back, maybe her brother sensed something in the intrepid reporter.

I hate snakes. Hate them. Yet that night, I wrapped Anderson Cooper around my neck and ran around the house yelling, redundantly, "I'm not afraid of snakes!"

I came to in the morning in the master bedroom, naked underneath the sheets and the nose-clogging down comforter of a king-size bed, a shaft of sunlight beaming down from the skylight above me.

My stomach churned and my head throbbed. A leg twitched next to mine, a foot at my calf—toes tickling me like feelers.

I moved to the side and saw Tina's long, dark, disheveled hair, loosened and freed from her braid.

Terror went through me. Had we had sex? Was she okay? And—terror deepening into my bowels—a memory—a faint whiff of a memory—a confession. What had I told her? Did she know about the video camera?

Her bare shoulders and back moved with her breathing, outside the comforter and sheets.

A yelping noise alerted me to Honeybun, ever loyal at the side of the bed. I rolled to my side, and when I looked over the edge, I saw her tail-thumping wag. I shifted to my back for comfort. Not looking at Honeybun, I gave the top of her head a few-fingers scratch. She licked my wrist in appreciation.

I tried to go over what I remembered about what I might have said. What came back to me: a long, earnest conversation outside on the dock—all four of us—a boat creaking in its berth, sitting cross-legged in a circle on the wood planks, staring up at the endless black and star-studded night, Honeybun at my side.

I couldn't remember what had been said, only the expressions on their faces, flashes of intense compassion and identification.

Someone crying. Me.

I sat on the bed, breathing deeply, and Honeybun lifted herself to greet me.

Tina stirred, moving to sit up. "Oh," she said, clutching the sheet around her, "I feel awful."

"I know," I said, looking over my shoulder at her. "Me, too."

"I don't think I'm going to try that again. "

The blood pounded in my temples. "Hey, Tina," I said, adjusting my back against the bed frame to face her, "did I say anything weird last night?"

"We all did," she said, her expression giving away nothing.

"Like what?" I said.

She gave me a shy smile, and pulled the sheet to her chin. "Don't you remember?"

"Sort of," I said, and a sense-memory did rise, of my tongue swishing in her mouth and grazing the bumps of the braces on her teeth.

We heard a knock at the door, and then Karen and Mike came into the bedroom, fully dressed.

They appeared refreshed, as if they'd already showered and had breakfast. But they also seemed awkward, as if playacting at being adults.

"Sleepyheads," Karen said, tugging playfully on Tina's toes beneath the covers. She thumped around on the bed with her other hand, looking for my foot.

My stomach lurched, and before she yanked my toes, I moved my leg and groaned.

I lay back on the bed, explaining, "I don't feel so good," envisioning Karen or Tina calling R. Sam Michaels to give him a great story. But maybe they'd keep my secret? Maybe they wouldn't tell anyone?

Mike came to the side of the bed. He stood beside Honeybun. My heart shot through my throat, thinking he was about to tell me that I'd blown it and confessed to the girls.

But he said, "My cocaine career is over."

I nodded.

"And to think it had only just begun," he said.

"There's always heroin," I said.

A slight smile, and then he turned his attention to Karen and Tina and said, "We've got to go. I promised my parents we'd be there for my sister's soccer game."

DURING THE CAR ride back to Mike's (there was no soccer game), I gathered from him that we'd had a deep and long, coke-addled conversation on the dock, where we'd each confessed a dark secret.

Mike: He didn't like football. Never had. And now, for the first time in his life, he was doubting the existence of God.

Karen: She struggled with depression, and once, after a bad breakup (she wouldn't say with whom), she even thought—very briefly—about killing herself.

Tina: An eating disorder in the eighth grade had left her hospitalized for two weeks.

I'd told the group about my responsibility for my brother's legal woes. "If he goes to jail," I'd said, "it's my fault."

The girls had protested, saying that I felt a false sense of guilt. I was adamant to the point of tears. But before I could back up my claim, Mike pulled me into an embrace and let me weep onto his shoulder, and then he whispered into my ear, "Now's the exact right time for you to shut the fuck up."

30.

THE TRIAL—WHICH lasted over a month—was a bizarre, disjointed time for me. I helped myself to a generous portion of Gabe's Xanax, as well as Dad's Percocet and Demerol. It began in mid-June and lasted till the end of July—over a year elapsed between the rape and the verdict.

Those first weeks, Dad insisted I come over for dinners to show my support. I didn't want to, but I did sometimes, and we ordered in: Mexican food, Chinese, Thai, and, one night, sushi, which Gabe hated.

After Dad went to sleep, Gabe and I spent much of our time zoned out on the couch and on Dad's recliner in front of the TV, smoking Dad's cigarettes and drinking six-packs of beer, often falling asleep.

One night, near the beginning of the trial, I noticed Gabe was wearing Dad's watch, which dangled loose at his wrist.

In the last nine months or so, he'd grown at an alarming speed. He still wasn't as tall or big as the Ks, but, nearing five feet nine inches, he was closing in on me.

"Why're you wearing Dad's Rolex?"

"He gave it to me," he said. "I didn't want it, but I can't tell him that."

"It's big on you."

"I know. I don't like it."

"Do you have to wear it?"

"Yeah. At least sometimes. He said it'd give me strength."

"You don't look so good."

He touched his palm to his forehead. "I need another Xanax."

"Are you out?"

"Yeah. You took some and I took more. But I know someone."

"What about your Klonopin?"

"Yeah. I've got those. Also Effexor."

"What's that?"

"Antidepressant. Doctor says that I have 'substantial maladaptive personality traits, compounded by my substance abuse and depression.' Probably has to do with me telling him that I'm hopeless, helpless, useless, and worthless." The back of his hair had flipped up like a mushroom-cloud explosion.

"The first night of the trial," he said, "I woke Dad up. I'd had a nightmare. I told him that I wanted to go to the judge. Told him that I wanted to man up and end this thing for everyone." He paused. "But he won't let me."

"The point of the game," I said, adopting Dad's voice, "is to win."

But Gabe didn't respond, looking away from me.

"You don't need his permission," I said. "You can go to the judge without Dad."

"He'd kill me," Gabe said, looking at the wall. "Do you know how much money he's spent?"

"I don't want to know," I said.

The media coverage had intensified and shifted somewhat against our dad, portraying him as an absentee father, disconnected by his money, prone to spoiling Gabe. "What do they know," Dad said, "about love?"

They were simplistic, undemanding news accounts, blaming Gabe's behavior on the rap music he liked or his substance abuse problems, but not digging deeper.

"Gabe could use your support in the courtroom," Dad said. "I'd like you to make an appearance, Even."

Both Sara and Mike offered to go with me, but I sensed their relief when I told them that it wouldn't be necessary.

At about the midpoint, I went to one day of the trial (that was all that I could take), and during a break, I saw Ben Kagan in the bathroom, and we had our awkward conversation about paper towels.

When I got back to the courtroom, Cavari was looking over his notes, preparing to grill Tove on the witness stand. Dad had paid for a full-time audiovisual specialist, a bald man with a pointy mouse face, who pushed aside the prosecutor's twenty-seven-inch television for his own setup: four high-tech television monitors in the jury box and a fifty-inch Hitachi plasma screen, reminding me of our TV at Dad's house.

The courtroom itself seemed to be from an episode of *CSI*, swinging doors leading to the blond-wood-paneled room, and opposing sides for the prosecution and defense, with tables and lawyers and clients before the judge's bench. Jam-packed and with a body odor smell. A court reporter, plenty of officers in uniforms with their clunky gun-holstered belts, and the spectators' area filled with family members, friends, reporters, and what our dad called "looky-loos."

Gabe and the Ks wore suits and ties, and they sat solemnly with hands folded on the table. Sometimes Gabe pressed his forehead against his hands, elbows on the table, as if in fierce concentration or prayer.

Not only was he taller, but the bones in Gabe's face and body seemed to have spread—he looked swollen—and his eyes had become darker and more wary.

Tove wore a blouse and skirt, demure and ladylike, and sat with her parents, but she had a strong determination in her expression that I recognized from our childhood. Her eyes grazed past me—ignoring me as she had that afternoon at Dad's house—but then I caught her looking right at me and my whole body went hot. When she saw me notice, she quickly glanced away, and I watched her face go red.

Ben and Luanne avoided looking at me as well, though once Luanne sent me a look that pierced right through me, as if I'd been the one in the video, not Gabe.

I sat next to Dad—his labored breathing somehow a comfort to me—and in the row behind us, Mom murmured with three of her friends from her walking group.

Dad turned in his seat, gesturing for me to do the same, and then he pointed to a man four or five rows behind us.

He said in his gruff, angry voice, "See that nerd right there with the beard and the blue shirt"—staring the man down—"I'm pretty sure that that's R. Sam Michaels."

The man looked back at Dad, and then Dad raised his hand in a makeshift pistol, shot the man, and turned back around.

The man shifted his gaze to me, and his expression seemed to say, Your dad just shot me with his hand!

I know, I said with my eyes, I just saw it happen. What did you expect? and then I turned back around.

Judge Bissell had a thick black beard sprinkled with gray and a natural confidence and authority, but with a tinge of swaggering charm. With an eye-patch, he could have been a pirate.

The jury—mostly white men—seemed openly bored, and they were yawning, though they perked when Cavari approached them.

Cavari nodded to the jurors, as if they were old friends, cleared his throat, jingled the keys in his pocket, and stared at Tove, now seated in the witness box.

He approached her, promising that he didn't want to shame her.

But then he asked if she'd had sex with all three of the defendants the night before the alleged rape.

Tove said that no, she hadn't. She'd had sex with two of the boys the night before. Gabe Hyde and Kent Nixon.

Cavari asked if it was true that her favorite rap song was "Put It in Your Mouth," and whether she liked anal sex, giving blow jobs, or doggy-style sex the best.

"Objection!" shouted the prosecutor.

Halfhearted groans came from the spectators.

Cavari asked Tove about the video of her having consensual sex with Kent Nixon a week before the alleged gang rape. "Why didn't you mind being filmed?" he asked.

She said that she did mind. She told Kent to stop filming as soon as she saw the camera.

"Hmm," Cavari said, nodding. "I'd like to show that film, to prove that at no time did Tove Kagan ask Kent Nixon to stop filming."

Another objection.

Cavari convinced the judge that watching the film would prove that Tove had lied, because she never said a word to Kent during the sex.

The bailiff dimmed the courtroom lights, the videotape started, and—even though we were supposed to listen for Tove telling Kent to stop filming—Cavari repeatedly paused the huge plasma screen monitor, so that Tove's naked image froze for us and, more important, for her to see.

"Were you on top?" he asked.

"Yes," she said.

Seconds passed, and then he paused the tape again, pointed to the screen, and asked Tove to identify herself.

He started the video, only to pause it again seconds later, asking, head tilted, as if we were all just connoisseurs, whether she noticed that the intercourse had been filmed from a slightly different angle.

Kent had set the camera on a tripod and used a remote control by the bed to direct his shots.

Cavari rewound the tape at least twelve times, asking her questions, each getting a loud objection, including "Who is that on all fours on the bed?"

"Did you notice the penis fell out of the vagina?"

"Is that your hand that puts the penis back in your vagina?"

"What did you think about when you rode on top of a man?"

"Did the sex feel good?"

"Have you demanded anal sex?"

"Have you ever orally copulated with a guy after intercourse?"

After a close-up of Kent's penis entering Tove's vagina, Cavari asked the audiovisual specialist, "Is there any way you can show this in slow motion?" Then he asked Tove, "Can you see his testicles?"

Tove began to cry. The bailiff turned on the courtroom lights, and Cavari gripped the podium. "Did you hear yourself talking to Kent Nixon? Did you hear yourself tell him to stop?"

"No," said Tove, wiping her tears with the palm of her hand. The judge reached beneath his bench and handed her some tissues. She thanked him and blew her nose. I noticed that the Ks looked at her in triumph, and Gabe's head was down. But then she said in a steely voice, "That comes later. You only showed the very beginning."

Cavari brushed aside her explanation and set up another screening.

He insisted that Tove leave the witness stand, walk across the room to Dad's plasma screen, and look at another image. This one showed Tove at the beginning of the gang rape video, a tape that she hadn't seen yet.

"Is that you?" Cavari asked.

Tears streamed down her face. "I'm not saying that it isn't," she said.

The judge called for a recess so that Tove could collect herself. I left the courtroom and never returned.

31.

I REMEMBER WHEN GABE and I were preteens, flying home from a family trip to Washington, DC. Our parents sat in the seats in front of us, and Dad let us each take a sip of his Jack and Coke when Mom left for the bathroom.

Toward the end of the flight, Gabe and I watched a movie. We had a choice of five films, and we chose *The Iron Giant*, since it was animated, and we wanted a kids' cartoon.

With our headsets on, we tilted our seats back and watched the little screens embedded in the backs of our parents' seats.

Before long, we glanced at each other, understanding that we'd accidentally picked a weighty movie, even if it was a cartoon, but we continued to watch.

Something about being on an airplane—the condensed, recycled air and the actuality of being in a container zipping through the sky—can heighten feelings. That must have been what happened, because I've subsequently watched the movie, and it doesn't strike me as that emotional.

But by the end of the plane flight, we were both in tears. A giant sorrow unloosened inside of us, having to do with the impending dissolution of our family and its history, and a sense that now, with the sanction and excuse of a movie, we could release our feelings. But once we did, it became a problem: We couldn't stop.

I looked at Gabe and he looked at me, and then we were laughing through our tears, embarrassed and confused and a bit shocked. I made a gasping noise, trying to catch my breath.

Dad turned from his seat and saw us. He shook his head and said, "What the hell's wrong with you two? Pull it together."

We tried. We really did. But we couldn't.

For the entire car ride from the airport to our home, we avoided looking at each other, knowing that it might make us cry again.

It felt like that during the trial, after the day that I went to court for Gabe. Gabe couldn't look at me, and I wouldn't look at him, as if there might be an explosion of emotions if we did.

Days passed, weeks, and, surprisingly, I was able to disconnect from the trial in a self-imposed exile, ignoring the media coverage and any discussion of it. Though somehow I knew it was turning in Gabe's favor—a flow in the air, a wave of intuition, and simply by the way our dad said hello to me on the phone, his voice less hollow.

But Gabe and I continued to avoid each other, until the second day of the jury's deliberations, when Gabe called me in the afternoon on my cell phone and said, "Even, I'm dying."

"What's the matter?" I asked, waving at Mike to be quiet. We'd been throwing a Nerf football around in his backyard, and Mike held the football with a one-handed grip and waited.

"Listen to me," Gabe said, his voice frightened. "I think it's a brain aneurysm or something. Maybe a heart attack. I can't feel the left side of my body."

"Do you want me to call 911?" I asked, thinking that he might have overdosed.

"Just come over."

He lay on the couch in Dad's living room, a wet paper towel across his forehead.

"I feel really bad," he said when he saw me, sitting up and holding the paper towel in place. "The left side of my body is all numb and I can't breathe right." He gave a few raspy breaths as proof.

"Take it easy," I said.

"I'm trying," he said, tossing the paper towel to the floor. He wore long board shorts and nothing else. His hair had fanned in the back and his eyes were red and shiny.

"My pulse," he said, "it's beating in my head: boom. Boom. Boom."

I put my hand on his shoulder; his skin was warm.

"Take deep breaths," I said.

He looked at me. In a mournful voice, he asked: "What the fuck's wrong with me?"

"I don't know," I said.

"Should we go to the hospital?"

"Where's Dad?"

"Don't call him," he said, putting his face in his hands, Dad's Rolex sliding down his arm.

"Gabe," I said. "Where's Dad? He needs to know."

"Please, Even," he said into his hands. "I can't take it. Don't call Dad. He's with Krone. Don't tell him."

"What pills did you take?"

A silence, and then he said, "Maybe too much Xanax."

"All right," I said. "How many is too many? Did you take anything else?"

He looked at me with a sudden belligerence. "What do you
think?" he said. "Of course I did."

So I decided to take him to the hospital.

He put the car seat all the way back while I drove him to the ER
at Hoag. In the distance, I saw a fleet of sailboats with tilted masts
and sails to the side, and the sky was a pale blue.

I watched with a sideways glance as he lit up a joint and took
small, neglectful tokes, a thin whiff of smoke drifting out the
cracked passenger-side window.

"It helps," he said.

I said nothing.

He shut his eyes and rested his spliff-knuckled hand on his
stomach.

By the time I parked in the garage, he didn't want to go into the
hospital. "I'm better," he said, lifting his seat to the regular position. But he looked bad, sweating and pale.

We listened to the echoing beep of a car alarm until it stopped.
He pinched the butt of the joint dead and flicked it out the car window. Glancing at the large watch face on the inside of his wrist and
pretending to be concerned about the time, he said, "We should get
back. Really, I'm okay now."

So we drove home, the sky purplish and the sailboats gone.

When we got inside, Dad still wasn't home. In a burst of energy,
Gabe did push-ups and sit-ups, and then he did chin-ups, pulling
himself up on a steel pole mounted in the doorway. Dad had had it
installed to "help with stress."

"Remember," Gabe said between pulls, "as kids, the way that we used to skateboard all over the place in Cucamonga? How we talked Mom into letting us skateboard to school?"

"Sure," I said.

He let himself down, and then he spread out on the floor. "I loved that," he said, gazing up at the ceiling. Then he closed his eyes. "Up past the Klingers' house," he said, "turn left at that cracked sidewalk."

It was like he was talking to himself, mapping out his favorite route. His words came slow. "Keep going northwest," he said, "then left, then right, past the Starbucks and the McDonald's; keep going, got the earbuds in, listening to music; that's right, that's right; over there, a heron? No, man, that's not a heron; it's too small, probably a blue jay; that right there is the blue bird of happiness. The blue bird of peace. It's a bird, but I don't know what kind. Turn up the volume, ride past that flower shop, over the manhole near the gas station. Look at the leaves and the way the sunlight shines on them. So beautiful, so beautiful."

By the time Krone and Dad arrived home later that afternoon, Gabe was sleeping on the couch while I watched the news on TV.

Krone, in a Hawaiian-print shirt, had a bottle of aged Scotch, and he poured me some in a Dixie cup, using real glasses for himself and Dad.

He and Dad spoke in a dark corner near the Jacuzzi for a few minutes, Krone's hands on Dad's shoulders, both their heads lowered. He left soon after.

Dad set a blanket over Gabe and then gazed down at him, watching him sleep. He ran his fingers through Gabe's hair and said, "This'll be over, soon, Son," as if Gabe were listening.

My cell phone vibrated and buzzed in my pocket, and I took it out and flipped it open, not recognizing the phone number.

"That's okay," Dad said, "take it," and he turned to go to the kitchen.

"Even?" a male voice said when I answered. "This is R. Sam Michaels."

"How'd you get my number?" I asked. My heart banged so hard I felt it in my earlobes.

"A source," he said.

"What do you want?"

He said that he needed to meet with me ASAP, and that he had crucial information about my brother's case. "I'm not sure," he said cryptically, "whether or not I'm going to use it."

He gave me the address of an apartment in Costa Mesa. "Hurry," he said.

"Why do you need me?"

"It all depends," he said, "on what you have to say."

32.

I FOUND THE APARTMENT and parked, noticing the faint outline of a ghostly moon, the day's light draining from the sky. When I got out of my car, I heard the *whish-whish* of the sprinklers whipping across a lawn.

Michaels answered the door before I knocked. I followed him inside—a clean place, nothing out of the ordinary, and I got a better look at him. Cropped brown beard, thin lips, and a receptive and brooding gaze. I remembered Dad shooting him with his hand in the courtroom and the look he'd given me.

Sitting across from me in a chair in the living room, he said, "Even, I know you turned over the video camera."

I had believed this might be coming (why else would he want to see me?), nevertheless, terror sliced through me.

He smiled at me, as if savoring the dramatic pause, allowing my astonishment to bloom.

"I don't know what you're talking about," I tried.

"Oh, okay," he said, looking at his hands folded in his lap and nodding, still smiling.

A long horrible silence, the initial shock over, as I squirmed and shifted and worried about Sara, about the story that he'd write, and then I said, "How'd you find out?"

He shrugged. Another smile, and he reached for a file on the coffee table, opening it and handing me a photograph of me under Sara's towel: a still from the police surveillance video, and not a very good one.

I stared at it, recognizing my foot and the lower part of my leg. The shape of my head and shoulders.

"I know about Sara's involvement," he said.

"What do you want?"

He cupped his chin with the fingers of one hand, as if in thought. "It's probably gonna be a mistrial," he said. "Just so you know. One holdout, thankfully. A female juror. But I'm sure your daddy already told you all this."

He straightened his posture and brightened. "You know what would make me feel better?" he said, as if he were just coming up with the idea. "To write a story about how Gabe's own brother turned over the camera, because he's guilty, and Daddy couldn't pay enough money to make it go away."

"Can I have a glass of water?" I asked.

He left for the kitchen and I heard him moving around, opening and closing cupboards, as if he didn't know where he kept the glasses, and then I heard the sound of the faucet. Maybe it wasn't his apartment. It looked generic. No photographs and rudimentary decorations, like an apartment in a TV commercial.

He came back with a glass of water and set it on the coffee table. But I didn't drink it.

Then I said, "So write it."

He glanced at me sideways. "I'd be stupid not to," he said.

I didn't say anything, recognizing a coldness in his tone and manner. In that moment, he reminded me of Dad, a comparison that would no doubt have bothered both Michaels and my dad a great deal.

"It's a juicy story," he said.

I had no desire to argue, which is what he seemed to want from me.

"I need to go," I said, lifting myself from the couch.

"Hold on," he said, raising a hand.

I let my backside fall back onto the couch.

"Relax," he said. "I'm not going to write about it."

"Why?"

He gave me a pained look. "Because," he said angrily, "I promised my source that I wouldn't."

I digested this information in silence.

"I want to know why," he said.

"Why what?"

"Why you did it."

My vision blacked out for a second and a buzzing noise reverberated in my head. "I need to go," I said, and this time I stood and walked to the door.

He followed close behind me. "Your dad's gonna find out," he said, "that is, if he hasn't already. He's probably getting the phone call right about now."

I opened the door, but before I got outside he said, "The Kagans."

I glanced back; the expression on his face was impossible to read.

"You should know the source," he said. "They're protecting you. God knows why. I just want to understand, figure some shit out, hear you say it. But I can't write about it. I promised Tove. I'm her reporter, so that's how it goes."

The Kagan's PI, he went on to explain, had found out that I'd gone to AA meetings for Gabe, met Sara, and probably heard Tom L. speak at the church.

"Tove doesn't want to hurt you," he said, "and her parents agree. But they disagree about letting your dad know."

Before I could respond, he shut the door between us.

That was the last time I saw him. Though he kept his word and never wrote about me or Sara, I still avoid reading his articles.

33.

I DROVE BACK TO Dad's for dinner as I'd promised, and the sky was darker now, with a bright, lopsided moon. As I walked up the front walkway, I smelled honeysuckle.

I would tell Dad and Gabe, I decided, before the Kagans' PI or someone else did. I felt an urgency to get it over with, and a desire to capitalize on that urgency.

I didn't trust Michaels or necessarily believe him about the Kagans at first. But it didn't take much longer for me to understand that the Kagans had indeed hired a private investigator to counteract my family, and that he'd been a good one.

I now believe that Tove was the one who didn't want to tell my dad, but that her parents wanted to hurt my family by letting them know.

I saw our neighbor mowing the lawn, and he nodded and raised a hand to me, so I waved back.

As soon as I stepped inside, I knew something bad was happening—the air had a static, menacing feel—just like I'd known on July 5 when I'd come home to Gabe and Kevin in the living room.

But this time I found Dad and Gabe.

Gabe was sitting in Dad's recliner and Dad stood in front of him with his hands outstretched. I wouldn't have been able to see them too well in the dark, except that a flickering light came from the muted TV.

"What's going on?" I asked, coming toward them, a panic fluttering in my chest, and then I saw Dad's pistol in Gabe's lap, a Glock 19 purchased legally with a weapons permit, another benefit of his relationship to Krone. I'd known Dad owned the gun but hadn't known where he kept it. It made sense that Gabe had found the gun before me, just as he'd found Dad's pharmaceuticals stash.

Gabe glanced at me for a second. "Goway, goway, goway," he slurred. "Allufyougoway." He sounded very drunk. I saw that he had the gun gripped in his hand, his finger on the trigger.

"Even," Dad said, remarkably composed, or at least faking it. He had a cigarette fingered in one of his outstretched hands, and though he was talking to me, his gaze didn't leave Gabe. "Perhaps you can help. I'm trying to explain to Gabe why he should hand me back my gun."

Gabe continued to shake his head, mumbling to himself. I noticed Dad's Rolex on the coffee table next to an ashtray.

I took a few steps toward Gabe. Dad said, "Easy, Gabe. Easy now," reaching his hand out.

But before he could take the pistol, Gabe jerked in his chair, bringing the muzzle toward his temple, and he shouted, "Goway!"

We both stepped back, Dad's hands in the air. "Okay, Gabe," he said. He leaned forward and ground his cigarette into the ashtray, saying equably: "Gabe, I understand that you think we'll be better off without you; I understand that's the way you *feel*. But it doesn't work like that."

"No," Gabe said, his tear-streaked face clenched in anguish. He wiped the hair from his forehead with his forearm, the gun unsteady.

"It's almost certain," Dad said, "to be a mistrial. No jail, Gabe."

Gabe shook his head.

"Gabe," Dad said, "this is *good news*."

"You hate me?" Gabe asked.

I waited for Dad to console him, and then I realized with an earth-swaying shock that he had been speaking to me.

"No," I said, the gun and Gabe and everything blurring in my tear-blocked vision, "no, Gabe. I love you."

"You're my little brother," he said, his eyes shining. A small, appeased, shy smile.

"Yes," I said. "I'm your little brother"—the tears coming hot—"I love you, Gabe. Everything's going to be okay."

He shook his head, his face anguished again. "No," he said. "No, it's not," and he raised his gun hand.

Dad and I closed in on him.

Everything happened so fast. I remember glancing at the TV and the feel of the metal on the side of my hand as the gun fired, and a Budweiser commercial, a close-up of the water-beaded bottle swirling in an icy blue light.

The smell of smoke and metal and flesh—somehow I knew that the flesh belonged to me even before I acknowledged that I'd been shot—conscious of a burning in my left foot and leg, and I turned to see Dad holding Gabe's arm and hand in the air, and the gun pointed upward.

Dad wrenched the gun free while Gabe stared at me in horror, and then they were both staring at me.

I couldn't understand what had happened, and then I looked down to where it felt like fire on me and I saw both the blood pooling up from my sock and a brown-edged burn streak on my jeans, the blood beginning to darken around it. "Oh, shit," I said. "I think I've been shot."

Dad, holding the gun by the handle like a soiled piece of toilet paper, walked to the kitchen and set it down somewhere, flipping on the living room light on his way back.

My forearm went to my eyes to shield the burst of light that made my wounds hurt more and brought an undeniable attention and reality to our situation.

I crouched to the floor. With my back against the couch, I peeked through the space beneath my elbow.

Gabe's head went back against the recliner, his eyes horrified. Blood had speckled his shoe, and he looked as pale as I'd ever seen him.

Dad came and knelt beside me.

I let my arm down and squinted against the light.

He took off his glasses and rubbed them on his shirt. "Even," he said, "listen. We don't have a lot of time. The neighbors might have heard the gun go off."

"I've been shot," I said.

"I know," he said, his head bowing for a second. "I know, Son."

"I feel like I might faint," I said.

"Hold on," he said, putting his glasses back on. "Don't do that."

Gabe looked at me in terror. "Did I do that?" he asked. "Did I shoot you?"

Dad stood and said, "No, Gabe. We all went for the gun and it shot off a round. It was an accident."

I put my forearm to my eyes again. Despite the pain, a sense of calmness came over me, and I heard myself say: "You need to leave now. Give me the gun and leave."

I heard nothing, so I moved my arm. Gabe had his head in his hands and Dad stared at me. An acknowledgment passed between us, and he said, "Okay, Even."

I placed my forearm back over my eyes and kept them covered, listening to Dad moving into the kitchen and Gabe crying. Then I felt a weight on my lap, and I set my hand on the warm metal of the gun.

"Are you sure about this?" Dad asked.

I nodded, my eyes covered.

Before they left, I asked our dad to turn off the light.

I pulled out my cell phone and dialed 911. "I accidentally shot myself," I told the female dispatcher, and as soon as the words came from my mouth, I understood that it had to be true.

I'd shot myself while fiddling with the gun. A stupid accident.

The dispatcher wanted to stay on the line with me while we waited for help, but I hung up.

In my head, I went over what I would say to the paramedics and officers when they arrived, and I covered the gun with my fingerprints to hide any others.

Something like relief blossomed inside me, interspersed with my physical pain. A sensation not entirely unpleasant, like a heightened, aching hurt and an equilibrium and acceptance.

I lay on the floor in the blessed dark with the gun at my side and waited for the sirens.

34.

T HE BULLET HAD skimmed my shin, burning my jeans and leaving a shallow wound. It pierced through my left foot: The
entrance wound was at the top and the exit wound was at the bottom near my ankle.

I underwent an open irrigation and debridement to remove any
retained bullet fragments.

Fortunately the bullet had made a clean exit, the residue lodg-
ing within my soft tissue, missing the metatarsal bones.

I have two circular scars. Both turn pink in extreme weather.

Within a week of the gunshot, I could walk without the aid of
a crutch with a wary heel-to-toe gait in my bare feet.

Although there's no neurovascular impairment, whenever I use
my foot for an occasion requiring physical endurance, such as a
long walk or more than a half hour of heavy lifting, or if I'm under
physical stress, I experience hot, shooting pains: ghost memories of
the actual gunshot.

But I'm told this is purely psychological.

Dad brought me the newspaper clipping from the *Orange
County Register* in the late morning following the shooting. I lay
in the hospital bed with my left foot wrapped and read:

An unidentified Newport Beach teen accidentally shot himself in the foot Monday night while trying to unload a Glock 19.

The teen also suffered a minor injury to his shin when the weapon unintentionally discharged, deputies said in a press release.

The teen was taken to Hoag Hospital and is expected to make a full recovery.

No one was present during the accidental shooting. The sheriff's department declined to provide the teenager's name or any other identifying information, beyond what was detailed in the press release.

Dad pulled a foldout chair close to my bed, opened it, and sat. He looked like he didn't know what to do with his hands, like he needed a cigarette. Gabe, he let me know, had been admitted to a Laguna Beach hospital for depression and chemical dependency. No verdict yet, but any moment now.

The usual hospital noises rang out—beeps and clanks and buzzers going off—and it smelled like lonely, antiseptic death.

I set the article aside and used the remote to prop up my hospital bed into a more upright position. Dad picked up the article, folded it, and then placed it in the front pocket of his shirt.

His cheeks were sunken, he looked sullen and depressed, and the hair on the top of his head had molded into a frizzy wave.

"I need to tell you something," I said.

"I know," he said.

There followed a long, unpleasant silence.

"How do you know?" I asked, feeling curiously empty and light-headed.

He took off his glasses and rubbed his eyes with his thumb and forefinger. Without looking at me he said, "All right. Tell me."

"How do you know?"

"I want you to tell me," he said.

A buzzing noise echoed in my head, but still I managed to say, "I did it, Dad. I'm the one who turned in Gabe's camera."

There was an awful silence. This, I decided, is when he rejects me, disowns me, discards me from his life.

But he just stared at his hands.

Unable to stand it, I said, "Dad. Dad, say something."

"There's nothing to say," he said.

He put his glasses on and gave me a frank, defeated look, forcing me to say, "I'm sorry, Dad."

He scratched the sparse tangle of hair on his head, coughed, and said, "Me, too. Me, too. I'm sorry, too."

He half lifted from his chair and pulled out a folded piece of paper from his pants pocket. "Here," he said.

Dad, a believer in lists, had brainstormed options for my future on the yellow-ruled paper that he used for business, while adding what he couldn't say to me directly.

This is what I read:

1. Finish your senior year of high school elsewhere. Your aunt Sheila's in Oregon or your uncle Ted's in Washington.

2. This is a long shot. Take a year off and travel to Paris. Isn't that where the artists go, and you've always said that's important?

The point is: Get out of town. Leave. You can finish high school early or later with tests. Gabe did it. It's not that difficult.

3. Finish high school in Newport but continue to live with the Woods family.

I don't want you to be around the house if there's another trial.

I love you and always will, just like I told Gabe I'll always love him. You're my son.

This doesn't change my love for you. But I don't want you at home. It doesn't feel right.

"How long have you known?" I asked. "Did you get a phone call?"

"It doesn't matter," he said.

"Does Mom know? Is that why she's not here?"

He shook his head but he said, "Probably." A pause and then, "It's not something that we'll discuss."

"That's why Gabe had the gun," I said. "You found out before I came home."

No answer.

"I don't want Gabe to hate me," I said.

"You underestimate him," he said, in a calm, quiet voice.

I began to cry.

"Before I forget," he said, fumbling to pull his Rolex from his pocket, "Gabe wants me to give this to you."

I didn't take it, so he set it on my hospital tray.

"I'm afraid," he said, looking at me with a heavy sadness, "that this is good-bye." Then he lifted himself from his chair and left.

But not before bending over me and whispering, "I do love you, my second-born son," and his lips pressed wet on my face in an open-mouthed, anguished kiss.

His back was hunched as he walked through the door, leaving it ajar.

I stared in despair at the slice of hospital hallway beyond my room. I felt a jolt as Dad crossed the area a moment later. Slump-shouldered, hands deep in his pockets, and head down—tears streaming down his face and steaming his glasses, gasping for breath in air-gulping sobs—hurrying past without turning to see me.

He must've gone the wrong way in his grief and confusion, since he crossed my doorway once more.

That was the last time I saw my dad, and only the second time I'd seen him cry.

The first, of course, had been when he'd held Gabe, and then me, close to his shoulder, promising both of us that he'd take care of everything.

35.

I'D LIKE TO tell you that I'm free of Dad's influence and money. But I'm not. I've been wandering and traveling and trying to find my way ever since that summer.

I've attended four colleges and had multiple menial jobs, and I've lived in five different states, all along the East Coast, far from California, finally settling, at least for now, in New York City. In these last ten years, I've managed to get a BA in English literature, and I'm a thesis short ("The Reality of Suffering: A Socio-Psychological Exploration of Fyodor Dostoyevsky's Characters") of my master's degree. My every step and breath has been subsidized by a trust fund.

Ron Inouye, Dad's accountant and a financial wizard, who was a prisoner in his youth at the Manzanar Japanese internment camp in California, is my only connection to my family. He knows more about us than anyone.

When we speak, it's about financial matters, though he has let me know more than once that my dad would welcome a phone call. But I have no idea what I would say.

If I hint at wanting information about my family, Inouye plays dumb. I have the impression that though he's a man of few words, Inouye reports back to my dad about me.

After the mistrial, Tove refused to settle, and the Hyde Three were tried again the following year, in 2005. I was on a rattling bus deep in Morocco close to the time the second verdict came in. I remember because I had a bout of severe diarrhea, and barely made it to the hole of a toilet in the ground, the sympathetic bus driver stopping the bus with a gear-shifting, dust-breaking jolt and waiting for me, despite the angry protests of my fellow passengers.

They were found guilty on two felony counts of sexual penetration by intoxication (one count with a foreign object). The judge ignored the Ks' and Gabe's late apologies and appeals for probation. He could've sentenced them to more than nine years but chose milder punishments, considering that they were minors at the time of the crime. All had three-year sentences, but none served longer than fifteen months.

After our gun incident, Gabe made one last thwarted suicide attempt, trying to hang himself with a sheet in his jail cell. But the guards stopped him.

Sometimes I look at his sexual offender photograph on the Internet. It's Gabe, but it's a different Gabe. With a faint mustache and stubble along his chin, he looks like a broken man, and I see the old Gabe—sensitive and sad and wounded—and something else now. A surprised vulnerability in his eyes, and I might as well say it, whether you believe me or not: a visible kindness.

For a few years, the side of his body and face appeared in a picture on a website for a quaint cottage-style restaurant in Laguna Beach, owned and operated by a husband-and-wife team. Smiling, in his traditional server garb of black pants and white shirt with black bow tie and vest, hip apron, and a towel draped across his forearm, he is leaning forward to serve what looks to be a plate of Cornish game hen to an elderly lady with a gray bun.

But on the same website, an anonymous source revealed his identity—which is how I found it on the Internet—and hundreds of commenters both local and not pitched in with their disgust, calling for, among other punishments besides his job termination, his castration. The husband and wife held out for a good long while, expressing their belief in Gabe, even with their knowledge of his past, but then one night his photograph disappeared.

SARA KEPT ME posted through emails and letters during the second trial, which she attended, no longer intimidated by her role in the case. The media never did find out about our involvement, and R. Sam Michaels kept his word.

Joe came back and Sara married him. She's a nurse in the ICU at Hoag. Joe had an organic produce business, but it went bust and I'm not sure what he does now. They have one kid (Samuel) and another on the way.

I'm Sam's godfather.

THE KS, AS far as I know, now work for Kent's uncle's flooring company in Palm Desert, and they no longer have contact with Gabe, blaming their downfall and conviction on our dad's aggressive defense campaign. Had they settled, they would've gotten shorter sentences in juvenile hall and parole, rather than years fighting the criminal system detailed in the media, only to land in prison as adults. There've been a couple of DUIs for both Ks, but otherwise they've stayed out of trouble, or, just as likely, they haven't been caught.

Kevin Stewart lost an appeal in 2008 to overturn his conviction and the requirement that he register as a lifelong sex offender. At the time, Sara wrote me in an email:

> I've learned something. We love it when people express huge public displays of remorse. But it's bullshit. We don't know what's going on inside a person. At the sentencing, Kevin cried and seemed earnest when apologizing to Tove and her parents, more so than Gabe and Kent. Everyone in that courtroom choked up. My money was on Kevin for sincerity.
>
> But here we are, and now he's doing an interview, saying that he shouldn't have to register as a sex offender because it's "emasculating." He's wearing those mirrored sunglasses—someone should've at least told him that he looks like a douche with those on—talking about how he went from being written up in the papers for being a varsity football star to being in a rape case. Poor Kevin! He says he resents having to wear a GPS device until he gets off parole. It messes with his surfing! "Have you ever tried to go in the ocean with one of those on?" he says.
>
> Then, I swear, he's asked whether or not he feels that what he did that night was wrong, and he says, "Had it been any other girl, maybe." What an asshole! To think that he was the one at the sentencing that seemed the most sorry. He hasn't changed at all. That same old arrogance and entitlement and stupidity.

AT AGES TWENTY-SIX and twenty-seven respectively, Melissa Stroh and Crystal Douglas are both on their second marriages, still living and working in Cucamonga, and Melissa has a toddler daughter, and Crystal has a newborn son. Old MySpace pages and current Facebook profiles provide the ubiquitous midparty photos, tongues extended and hands wagging in "peace" or "hang loose" or hard-rock devil-horn signs, alcohol and drug paraphernalia visible in the background.

But one can hope that now that they have offspring of their own, they're settling down to become the good girls that they portrayed themselves to be during both trials while at the same time so viciously attacking and betraying Tove.

DAD, CAUGHT WRITING off Gabe's defense as a fraudulent tax deduction, agreed to cooperate in a federal probe of Krone in order to avoid jail time. Three times, a body wire was taped to his chest, and in the candlelit atmosphere of Banditos Steakhouse, Dad recorded Krone discussing his various schemes and cover-ups.

You name it: Krone did it. Money laundering, bribing, selling badges and gun permits for financial favors, participation in prostitution, infidelities, interfering in criminal investigations, and illegal deals with crooked lawyers and bail bondsmen, including Jonathan Cavari.

Cavari was convicted of illegally paying bail-bond agents to steer clients to his firm, but like a cockroach, he's back practicing his version of the law and making loads of money.

According to the government, Assistant Sheriff Scott Jimenez "schemed to defraud the public of honest services," as well as filed a false tax return, and he served seventeen months in prison.

Krone is still serving a sixty-six-month federal prison sentence in Colorado. He'll be out next year.

The only one who didn't go to jail, if you haven't already noticed, was my dad.

MIKE GRADUATED FROM USC (football scholarship) and is now married with two young sons, living in Irvine, California. He's a pastor, and his church, Daybreak Christian Fellowship, just moved to a high school cafeteria to accommodate the weekly influx of parishioners, while they search for a more suitable home.

Last year, his book, *Learn to Listen*, won the Christian Book Award. In it, he encourages Christians to spend as much time and energy listening to God as they do praying and talking to Him.

His chapter "Listening Is Patience" begins like this:

> In high school my best friend underwent a crisis of enormous proportions. My family took him in. I felt challenged and burdened by his predicament, as if the moral implications rubbed off on me. This time in my life, with all my fears and worries, taught me to listen to God. I learned to quiet my ego and open myself to The Source.

MIKE'S PARENTS AND I exchange emails (theirs are chatty and upbeat), and they send me birthday, Christmas, and Valentine cards each year. I still address them as Mom and Dad and they call me their son.

TINA—COLOR-BANDED braces long gone and still just as sweet and kind—flew to Spain to travel with me for three weeks after her high school graduation. We fell in love. She moved to Massachusetts and we lived together in an apartment while we both attended Boston University.

I dropped out of college, but we stayed together.

There was marriage talk. But then she broke up with me, telling me, "For you, love is linked with disappointment."

"I'll do better," I said.

"I don't mean to imply," she said, "that you can ever be at peace knowing what happened to Tove, and the role that your father played in protecting Gabe and attacking her and her family. But I do think—or would hope—that you'd find peace, because you did the brave thing, even if you couldn't see it at the time. You do know that, don't you? You do see it that way, don't you?"

She talks to me on the phone now. I plan to pursue her again.

ABOUT THREE YEARS ago, I got a letter from Tove via her lawyer. Here it is:

Dear Even,

I wish I could say that this isn't a difficult letter for me to write. I wish I could say that I'm okay and that everything's in the past now and that we can all move on.

But here's the thing. Although we can't be friends again, you'll always be in my heart and I'm hoping I'm in yours. So that's something.

I know that you were the one who turned in Gabe's video camera and set everything in motion. I think about it all the time, and how that must have been for you. How it must still be for you. Not a day goes by that I don't think about you.

I'm doing much better. You probably know about the Oxycontin bust, and how I got into opiates. I couldn't take it. I needed an escape. It got really bad. I was dying.

But I'm clean and sober now, and I'm volunteering at a women's shelter. I work at a doctor's office, and I'm back in college, taking classes, working toward a degree. I want to become a counselor. I want to help other women.

No boyfriend. Trust issues, says my therapist. Oh well. The doctors say I won't be able to have children because of residual scarring. I try not to think about it.

But I've got a little brown and black mutt from the shelter, Monkey, and Monkey and I are good. We live three blocks from my parents.

Things were bad with my mom and dad, then they got worse, and now they're better.

Please don't write back or try to get in touch. We're sort of always connected anyway. Does that make sense to you? I'm sure it must. I hope it does.

One last thing. I don't want you to go through life questioning what I think. So in case you wonder whether or not I'm glad that you turned the video camera in, I want you to know for certain that I am, and that you did the right thing.

Love,
Tove

EPILOGUE

ABOUT TWO WEEKS ago, eating healthier, exercising, and three weeks without a cigarette after a close-to-three-pack-a-day habit, Dad suffered a severe heart attack while on a treadmill and died almost instantaneously.

I found out from a late-night news program. (Ron Inouye called me the following morning with the details.)

While in bed flipping the channels, I saw Dad's face, and I turned the channel back just in time. A terror plunged through me as I listened and watched.

"Daniel Hyde," the far-too-cheerful, hair-slicked, and tanned newscaster relayed, "a self-made multimillionaire who became a central figure in a case against the sheriff he once supported, died this morning in Newport Beach, California. He was sixty-one. Hyde died unexpectedly of natural causes.

"Hyde's relationship with Sheriff Krone, as many may remember, began to sour after Hyde's son was convicted and sentenced to three years in prison for a 2003 sexual assault in which an unconscious sixteen-year-old girl was attacked in the elder Hyde's Newport Beach home." At this point a photograph of Gabe in an orange jumpsuit, hands handcuffed in front of him, appeared. "Gabriel Hyde was released in 2007."

The photograph switched to one of Dad, Jimenez, and Krone in golf gear, arms on each other's shoulders, laughing and holding cigars. "At one time affectionately nicknamed 'The Three Amigos,' the sheriff, assistant sheriff, and their most well-known contributor had an alliance that seemed unbreakable. But everything unraveled, and Hyde reemerged as a star prosecution witness when Krone was tried on corruption-related charges."

Another photograph of Dad sitting on a bench, sparse golden-orange hair flapping in the wind and a thoughtful expression on his face.

"Friends say that Hyde was heartbroken and devastated by his son's arrest. Hyde has been described as generous and down-to-earth." A quick cutaway to Nancy, older, sadder, pressing a tissue to her eye. "His wealth was not noticeable," she said, "and he was devoted to his family," a meaningful pause and gaze into the camera, "to his ultimate detriment." Back to the smiling newscaster: "A private service will be held for family and close friends. And in other news"—I turned the television off.

Soon after, Inouye gave me Nancy's phone number because she wanted to speak with me. "He loved you so much," she told me, her voice breaking. She wanted me to know that a few weeks before he passed, he'd told her: "Slow learners like me should have two lives, one for trial-and-error experimentation and one for real, serious living."

I SUPPOSE THERE'S nothing left for me to tell you, except what it felt like to come back to SoCal for Dad's funeral.

Dad finally found his resting place on Sunshine Terrace in Rose Hills with our relatives. His funeral was on a hazy, gorgeous afternoon, slight breeze, lean clouds swimming across the sky, matching gravestones spread along the hill, row after row, reminding me of the tract homes in Cucamonga.

A blue canopy had been set up to protect us from the sun, with twenty or so of us sitting in plastic foldout chairs beneath it.

I sat in the front next to Gabe, and Mom was seated next to him. At one point, she reached her hand across Gabe's lap and pressed it into mine. But we haven't pursued this possibility of reconciliation further—at least not yet.

Though we didn't speak except for pleasantries, Gabe's presence comforted me. He looked like his sex-offender photograph come to life, except that now he wore a suit and had shaved his mustache and stubble.

Dad's casket had been propped on a stilt-like apparatus, next to an easel holding a photograph of him in a business suit with an opal background—hair combed to the side, sideburns, thick glasses—probably taken in the '70s.

A lawnmower rumbled in the distance, and it smelled of gasoline, grass, and dirt, from the fresh mound next to the dark pit into which Dad's coffin would soon be lowered.

The pastor, a droopy-lipped and sad-looking man, droned on about Jesus and the Bible, and for a long time I occupied myself by watching a cluster of ants in a bald dirt spot in the grass between my shoe and Gabe's.

"If the deceased were here today," the pastor said, pressing the Bible to his chest, "he would tell you to place your trust in Jesus Christ, for he knows more today than ever that Christ is the way, truth, and light, and that no one gets to the Father but by him."

If Dad were here today, I couldn't help but think, he would tell the pastor to get his lecture done with, so that we could all move on.

Everyone but Gabe and I left before a baseball cap–wearing Latino lowered Dad's coffin into the earth with a crane.

We stayed and observed, and then we both threw in fistfuls of dirt and watched them splat in dirt bombs against the casket's wood.

But it wasn't until my flight home from John Wayne Airport that I thought about how after we threw the dirt, Gabe held my hand for a moment.

On the flight back to New York, I had the inside seat. Mercifully, the middle seat was vacant, so that I had some privacy.

I leaned to tilt my forehead against the window, watching as the plane ascended, the homes and buildings turning into dots and the lights twinkling below. The toylike cars with their headlights twisted and snaked on the winding roads.

Twilight was spreading and clouds drifted; the ocean deepened, expanding in all directions. Everything flimsy, an echo of a dream, including Gabe's hand reaching to hold mine as if we were kids again, and not alone.